A

a COSMIC COLLISION with FAITH

ANNICE CONWAY IRVIN

A COSMIC COLLISION WITH FATIH

Copyright @ 2025 by Annice Conway Irvin

DEDICATION

For my girls, Teeya and Tyra—
Thank you for being my biggest fans.
You are my greatest gifts.
You remind me that with a sincere trust in God.
All things are possible.
His Grace, His Mercy, and His Favor
Makes the impossible, possible

For my sisters, Pam and Wanda—
Thank you for being my compass.
You grounded me when I wanted to fly higher and faster than life
allows.

"I genuinely wanted to give all the glory to God—that was my heart's desire. I knew that without His Grace and Mercy, none of it would have been possible. But somewhere, tucked quietly beneath my gratitude, was a small voice whispering for recognition. Not from others, but God Himself. I had poured myself out—trying to stay within His will. Yet, though I wanted, desired to lay it all at His feet—trust Him, a part of me still hoped He saw how hard I had tried. It wasn't pride exactly, but a yearning to know that the efforts mattered—I mattered!"

Clarice Taylor

Table of Contents

Introduction

The small group of soldiers tied their tents together and nestled them between the trees. The intense humidity had given way to treacherous rains in the region. Paul had been on other missions, but this would be the first one of this type. It was simple, standby to secure the drones, for both preflight and recovery. The squadron was under his command, and he recognized what that meant.

"It is going to be a long night, no denying that." Paul began speaking, trying to find the words that would instill confidence, as if he really was in control. "Do not forget, your job at this moment is to wait. Actively wait. We are always ready, regardless of the circumstances. We are the best at what we do! So, lets tighten up, and stay dry. Get a couple of hours of sleep in while we can."

As the rain continued, each soldier blended into the backdrop of the jungle, retreating within to their own mental thoughts.

Separating the sounds of thunder from the explosions caused by the drone attack was unsettling. Late into the night, they could still hear the drones as they took flight toward their intended targets. The distant horizon's dull flashes of light from the rockets hitting their targets cascaded across the cover of darkness. The night was endless.

Then, just before daybreak, the rain stopped. The quietness of the jungle set in. The sound of impacts slowed. And after several hours, though each one felt like an endless day, the brutal signs of destruction ceased.

"Let's go!" Paul said as he gathered his gear.

The unit moved with resentment. Not towards Paul or the mission. But the call of the jungle was not a very forgiving one. The terrain, along with the hidden dangers of the relentless predators—snakes, spiders, giant mosquitoes, and other creatures made the brave soldiers want to go screaming through the dense vegetation.

The air was thick with the scent of wetness. Foliage mingled with the smoke from the blast extended for miles. They had been walking for most of the day, engaging in small talk, joking around while still being on alert. There was always someone watching, ahead and behind as they etched their way closer to their target.

The sun had begun to set when they came upon a small village. Instinctively, everyone stopped. Laid out in front of them with the setting sun casting shadows over the horrific landscape, they saw bodies. They were scattered everywhere. Spread along the dirt roads that connected the small stone houses, were lines of people that had been shot in their backs, falling in their tracks as they tried to get away.

There was nothing else out of place. There were no signs of conflict, no apparent signs of struggle. Just dead bodies…which made the bloody bodies even more evident. The smell of the jungle was no match for this. The aroma of death overtook them.

"I don't understand. I thought it was supposed to be empty." One of the soldiers said not recognizing how much his voice carried through the still air.

Paul responded in a subdued tone, "This is not the results of the drone strike. We are too far south. The village is still a few more miles ahead. Pair up, start looking for survivors."

"Survivors? Not likely."

Even with the latest technology, the search for any survivors seemed to be hopeless. But that didn't stop Paul. He knew what it felt like to be hurt and alone. The team continued to walk every inch of the small village. The more area they explored, the more they realized the attack had occurred only hours beforehand.

There could still be survivors.

Paul suddenly started to move with a sense of urgency. His heart pounding in his chest, mind occupied with the words of a small prayer. This eerie inner silence grew within him.

He then made this glaring observation. 'Where are the men?'

"Keep your eyes open." Speaking to the unit, with a cautionary tone. "We don't know what to expect." Paul was trying to alert them of something more. The only bodies visible were women and children.

That's when he heard it, a faint, muffled cry. Paul's heart seemed to echo outside his body into the air. Listening intensely, he followed the faint sound. There, a few feet away, peeking from beneath a lifeless body, he spotted a small foot. He quickly fell to his knees and rolled the figure off.

Paul froze. There was the most beautiful child he had ever seen. She couldn't have been more than two years old, still crying when Paul freed her. She must have felt the weight of the body lifted, cause amid her cries, she turned her little head towards him. Looking directly into his eyes, she suddenly stopped crying, smiled, barely moving her dried out lips. But the smile was undeniable, at least to Paul. The unexplainable connection had been sealed. He fell in love with her and would risk it all to secure her passage. Regardless of the dangers of the mission, Paul was not willing to let her go. She was a reminder for him of all that was good in the world.

His heart smiled!

Breathe In-Breathe Out

Visions of destruction bombarded his inner sight as he stared out the window, guided by knowledge he knew he was not privy to.

'*I gotta get out of here.*' Paul quickly grabbed his bag, took a few other things off his desk, including the watch, threw them in the bag and turned off the lights. Leaving midday like this was quite uncommon for him. Paul was typically the first person at the office and the last one to leave.

As he rushed down the hallway heading to the elevator, several people tried to stop him. Some with pending questions, while others were just being friendly.

Paul kept repeating to himself, '*I don't have time for this.*'

"Hi Mr. Martin, leaving?"

Paul never slowed down. He couldn't. The only response he could muster was just a faint smile, accompanied by a slight nod. He wanted, no needed to get out of there. He needed a place where he could wrestle with the information he had just learned. How could he come to grips with it?

How was he supposed to live with this? He couldn't even see how to begin comprehending any of it.

Paul reached the elevator. He began pushing the button like it was a lifeline. It seemed like it was taking forever. The world had to be playing a cruel joke on him. He began to think even the elevator was in on it. The floor numbers were at a crawl. The elevator was stopping at every floor. It was an obvious attempt to mock him in his hour of desperation. He knew it was insane to think that way, but he didn't know what else to do.

Finally, the doors opened, and he stepped in. That's when he heard someone yell.

"Hold the elevator!" The voice echoing from down the hall.

'They're too far away…I don't have time for this.'

Paul started erratically pushing the button to close the door. They finally began to inch closer together.

Just as he began to settle back, Paul saw this oversized hand shoot through the narrowing gap, preventing the door from closing. The elevator doors jerked back open. Standing before him was one of his employees.

"Sorry about that—I almost missed it," the employee said as he slipped into the elevator, barely glancing at the person already inside.

"Yes you did—almost miss it!" Paul said in a dry, borderline sarcastic tone.

The employee stiffened. Finding Paul in the elevator was unexpected, and a bit awkward. It wasn't exactly proper protocol to ask someone of Paul's rank to hold the door, and now he was on the elevator with his boss.

Flustered, "Good afternoon Sir, uh…I—I have some things I need to go over with you," the young man came across as someone trying too hard to appear as an important asset to his superior.

Paul as well was trying to maintain a level of professionalism, responded, "No problem. Schedule a meeting for early next week." He didn't trust himself to say anything else. He didn't want to get into anything for fear of a total mental breakdown, right there on the elevator.

Paul's eyes kept drifting up, watching the floor numbers. People got on and off. All seemed to want to make small talk. On any other day, Paul was the one everyone wanted to be associated with. He was typically a well-liked individual. Everyone wanted to be a part of his team. But today, he had been less than sociable. He just wanted to unravel in peace, away from everyone and everything.

When they finally made it to the ground level, the elevator dinged, and the elevator opened. Paul rushed out without saying another word. He was on autopilot. As he made his way across the lobby, his legs started to buckle. The very air that he was breathing felt like increased pressure on his chest. His muscles were being deprived of oxygen, legs gave out causing him to stumble.

"Just a little farther," he muttered, startled by how loud the words were as they slipped out. He made his way to his car, fumbling to steady his hands as he reached out for the door reader.

"Press button, open door," repeating—"press button, open door." He was calling out the steps as if they were part of a complicated task. He had learned the ritual as a coping mechanism. It gave him the illusion of control, a way to defend himself against the chaos hammering in his chest.

Something had rattled him.

By the time Paul opened the car door and slipped into the driver's seat, every nerve in his body felt like they were being snapped from their weave. He gripped the steering wheel, then released it, then gripped it again—his fingers drained of blood from the repetition trying to steady himself—to drown out the frustration from what he had discovered. It was too overwhelming—too unbelievable.

"This can't be happening, no, no, no." he kept repeating, still barely aware of the volume the words were escaping from the pit of his soul. With no outlet for the enormous pressure building within, he started to pound the steering wheel with his fist, hitting it continuously. That's when he noticed someone from security walking towards him.

"Are you okay, Mr. Martin?"

Quickly gaining his composure and defusing the outburst, Paul lied.

"Yes, sorry. I'm mad at myself. It's my anniversary, and I forgot to pick up a surprise for my wife," he said with a forced smile.

"Better take care of that! We know how they can be." Both laughed as Paul waved and drove away.

Paul was barely out of the parking lot before the events resurfaced. Confusion of a lunatic quickly replaced the illusion of a sane man. He tried to calm himself as he merged onto the interstate corridor. Calmness found no place to land. Once on the road, he weaved through traffic with a reckless edge, barely registering the honks and flashing lights all around him. His world had narrowed itself into a tunnel of anxiety and disbelief.

His eyes glanced upward. *Hwy 17.* Without hesitation, he veered off the interstate, the tires screeching as he took the exit ramp too fast. Paul let out a dry, breathless chuckle, muttering to himself as he gripped the wheel tighter.

"Probably safer for everyone if I'm not out there with the rest of them," he said, talking aloud to the imaginary passenger riding with him. He heard a response coming from inside the car.

"Where are we going today?"

It scared him. In his current state, he had forgotten he was part of a team working on how to include AI as a driving companion. The idea was to increase safety in the driver's seat of cars. Because of how expensive traveling had become, drivers were traveling long distances alone; isolated, falling asleep or distracted driving.

Paul laughed.

But the humor quickly faded. His mind messed up with the weight of what he had just uncovered. Information he was never meant to see. Files that had been hidden, locked away, with the highest level of security. And now, *he* had seen them.

But why him? And more pressing—what was he supposed to do with the revelation?

The truth sat solid on his chest, pressing down like a storm cloud ready to burst. Whatever this was, it was not something he could ignore.

This wasn't something he could tuck away and pretend it never happened.

It had found him. Chosen him. It never mattered by who had chosen him. In his heart he knew the moment he opened those files, life as he had known it was over. There was no going back.

Everything had become a blur. Nothing made sense.

JADE.

Another vague acronym for another vague initiative. Thinking back to all the times he had been in meetings and the name *JADE* would come up, but nothing ever seemed connected. The conversations had to have been in code. Nothing had made him think the information he was hearing would be of any value to him—or to the survival of mankind. It had always seemed like a science fiction movie, or at best some hypothetical situation created as a training exercise.

And yet…Could everything that he had overheard in the past few years been a real possibility?

Paul needed to take a neutral stance on everything. His thoughts were betraying him. He was being guided by himself, through his own internal emotional turmoil. Since he had been working with the bot for the past couple of weeks, it seemed like now would be the perfect situation to try it out.

He had named the bot after his childhood friend, Roy. Talking to the bot reminded Paul of times long gone. His friend had been killed his first year in the US Marines. But the bot had made great strides in learning his personality, and preferences in such a short amount of time.

Even in the state of things, Paul desire to explore technology had not waivered. So, he decided have a conversation to test the bot's capabilities.

"Roy, I am having difficulty with a problem. I can't see a solution." The Paul gave Roy some parameters to go on without revealing too many details.

The bot responded with a pep talk more than anything else. But that was exactly what Paul needed at the time.

"You are better than this. You have been in different types of situations where there was immediate danger. This is no different. Steady yourself. Look at it logically, make a plan to deal with it, find a solution." The bot repeating itself. "Review logically, identify the true problem, devise a solution, make a plan."

It was sound advice. Paul could hear himself saying it. He smirked at the idea of the bot altogether. But for now, Paul just needed to follow his own instructions. He started with his breathing to lower his heart rate. Next, music to control the stress. Before long, he was tapping the steering wheel to the beat of the songs.

Paul's mind began to rewind, replaying conversations like fragments of a puzzle he never knew he would have to assemble. One by one they resurfaced—incidents that had occurred and then filed away. Now, he needed to recall them all. They were returning with an eerie clarity of thought, overlooking details that suddenly fit into the big picture—piece by piece, ushering in. It had been at least two years when he first heard anything pertaining to *JADE*.

"The laser will be in a remote area off the coast of Egypt."

Yet another conversation came to focus. "There is an underground bunker left from World War II in Germany. This could be the site for the rebuild."

A wave of regret was swelling up in his chest.

Why didn't I question what was happening? Why didn't I pay more attention to what was being said? His breathing patterns returned, erratic, interrupted. He could feel the stress—panic returning. But he wouldn't allow it. There was an obligation to his family—their survival was on the table.

With that, he kept interrogating himself, talking to Roy, searching for the last time he heard the word—*jade*.

It had been about six months earlier. The Director was conducting a high-level briefing with a committee working on cybersecurity. At the end of the meeting, Paul's manager walked past him with a level of urgency over to the Director.

"We just got a message about '*JADE*.' It doesn't look good. The collateral damage will be huge."

Without saying another word, the two of them exited the briefing room, quickening their pace as they huddled in urgent whispers. Paul had paid little attention to it. There was always some—blown out of perspective—emerging threat, some crisis requiring immediate attention.

Filling in the blanks, analyzing every word from remembered conversations, Paul spiraled into despair again. It all just left him creating even more empty lines between fragments of broken conversations.

Trying to stitch together strings of words that may or may not have been said. Paul's frustration returned, raw and unrelenting—and so did the banging of his hands against the steering wheel.

He was grateful for the long drive. He could feel his blood slowing to a more calming flow, his heartbeat stabilizing. Driving home along this stretch of coastline, at this time of the year, was tranquil. The world seemed smaller. He loved it. The weather was changing. Late fall had brought about the crisp air, winter hinting at its arrival. The trees along the roadside had started to thin out. Most of them were no longer able to keep a grip on their leaves. In their various hues of color, the leaves simply refused to hold on, tumbling out in the middle of traffic as they gave up providing their warm covering for the tree limbs. It was peaceful, far removed from the noise and chaos of the city.

Paul's thoughts drifted away from the chaotic day that had bombarded his mind, to a more pleasant time—his personal life, capturing the things that still tethered him to himself.

He had always resented being an only child. As a boy, he'd often imagined what it would be like to be part of a big family—siblings laughing, and fighting, staying up way too late, the chatter around the tables at crowded dinners… the mess and warmth of it all. He'd longed for that kind of belonging, in addition to the unconditional love his parents had given him. And now with his blended family, he had found just that.

He thought of them, missing them terribly. He recalled the day he had received the message. His world cracked from the core.

He'd been out on maneuvers. The moment the call came, and Paul saw the digital image of the admiral, his stomach dropped before a single word had been spoken. Standing in the field, he knew there had been a tragedy. That kind of call only came for one reason: communicating someone in the immediate family was deceased.

He remembered it vividly at that moment, driving in the car, as though it was happening all over again. The memory still had an intense emotion attached to the very thought of it, still hitting him like cold steel piercing his body, sharp and deep.

"Captain Martin, we have a call for you, Sir."

The young soldier's voice was steady, but he would not look Paul in the eye. He was trying to maintain formality to mask the untrained emotion that he felt for his captain.

The admiral stood before him, not physically but as a projection in his official full gear, as he read an official script.

"Captain Martin, I regret to inform you, your parents, John Martin and his wife, Dorothy Martin were killed in a car accident. Sir, I am deeply sorry for your loss." The admiral said—reciting duty, voice flat, coated with no emotions.

The projection flickered once and was gone, leaving Paul standing there—alone. The words had landed like a punch in the gut. Before he could absorb the news, the young soldier made an intentional step towards him.

"Sir," he said quietly, "I thought you'd want you to know—your daughter, Zuri, uh…sir, she wasn't in the car. She's safe. She's with friends of your parents. She's okay."

Paul turned his head towards the soldier and looked him in the eyes with a grateful acknowledgement.

"I thought you would want to know." The soldier added softly as he removed the projector.

Paul's world shattered that day…His parents were his true north. He was always travelling with the Navy on some type of mission. He loved it. But when things got heavy, he would always call home, just to hear his mom's voice or the approval from his dad. His dad had often told him how proud he was of him, serving his country in a way he never could. Paul was not only grateful for everything they had done for him to make his life full, but after rescuing her from the village in Africa, Zuri's home of record had been with his parents.

Paul lingered on the day of their funeral. It had been a perfect spring day—almost cruel in its beauty. The winter that particular year had been brutal, lasting longer than usual. He remembered thinking at the time how the weather must have confused the trees. Some of their leaves had dared to peek their heads out of the protection of their tiny buds to welcome spring, while others had refused to even dip a toe into the new season. The fluctuations in the temperature that spring had been unbearable and unpredictable. Just one week before that *day*, there was a winter storm that dumped nearly six inches of snow in just a matter of hours.

And yet, on the day his parents were buried, the Eastern Redbud trees were everywhere and in full bloom. They lined the cemetery path, branches draped in pink and purple blossoms. It was as if they came out to say goodbye to two of the best people God had created.

Paul found himself quietly sobbing as he drove. Remembering things from long ago was not very productive. This was not the time.

A loud noise quickly snapped Paul's attention back into his current situation. He had veered out of his lane and into the oncoming traffic. The noise he heard was the echo of loud horns, blaring from every direction. Paul jumped back into reality, quickly wrestling with the wheel to regain control.

Paul could hear Roy's words, "In…out. In…out."

Paul began to speak the words. "Breath in—breath out" repeating, "breath in—breath out."

His breathing normalized.

"Why didn't you warn me?" Paul said to the bot.

Responding, "I am only voice activated or in the case of an emergency. Your heart rate increased out of range."

Paul continued his breathing exercises. He gained a sense of calmness and could feel the sun piercing through the windshield. His skin warmed as it manifested itself like glistening speckles tickling his arm as he was driving. He smiled to himself, thinking *this must be what Jazzette feels when she is trying to get me to take one of her famous baths.* He had to admit, it felt comforting. There were bigger things to worry about. He just wanted to get home to talk to her.

Almost there.

It was the middle of the week; Jazzette would have suspected something was wrong when he called. She would have known. She always knew.

Redeemed Time

Clarice sat up abruptly in a state of confusion, with the cloudy remnants from what apparently had been a bad dream. Shaken and drenched in sweat, her heart was racing, having been overtaken with obvious fear. The kind of fear radiating from an unknown source hovering over you, brushing against your skin like water droplets in a dense fog. Eerie sounds linger from the distant, blurred rings of light penetrating the darkness. She couldn't remember the dream but sensed there were some threatening implications hidden. Glancing around the room, searching for a safety thread, trying to settle the disruption within herself, Clarice looked upward. Her eyes were drawn to the moon and stars scattered like ornaments across the night sky. Their warm glow pierced through the glass roof. The curve of the cascading roof blended seamlessly into the bedroom windows. The architectural design was intentional. It offered not only a spectacular view within the estate, but also one beyond the mountainous walls that surrounded the compound. The view from their bedroom was the best view from any spot anywhere on the land.

"Time?" A small bot responded, "Hello Clarice, the time is 3:33 am."

"Lights." Clarice said, still wrestling with the fog of her dream.

"Would you like illumination at 25%?"

"Yes."

Stephen was not in bed. Still feeling uneasy, Clarice made her way into the kitchen, stumbling as her bare feet connected with the cold floor—immediately regretting leaving her slippers. The lights triggered as she crossed the kitchen threshold. Looking around, still no sign of him.

Just as she passed the tall glass doors leading out to the courtyard, there sitting perfectly still was Stephen. If it had not been such a familiar sight, she would have freaked out, thinking he had frozen to death. Yet again, there he was, staring out as if he could actually see the wind blowing the remaining leaves off the trees. Clarice chuckled. The sight really had caught her off guard.

He has to stop hanging out with Jack, she thought, shaking her head with a light humorous smile.

The season's first snow had shown its head; a few flurries had fallen, but not yet cold enough to stick.

Clarice grabbed shoes and a blanket.

"Sweetheart," calling out to him as she walked across the patio. "Take this blanket…why are you sitting out here in the cold?"

Stephen looked up, eyes widening with the pleasant surprise— smiling as he motioned for her to sit next to him.

"Join me, the heater's on…" pausing for a moment to help her sit next to him. "Couldn't sleep, thought I would come out to get some fresh air…we won't have many more nights like this before winter sets in."

"Like this? Before winter?" Sarcastically smiling, letting him know it already felt like winter had set in.

Clarice positioned herself next to Stephen, and as they snuggled together underneath the blanket, Stephen noticed small flickers of movement.

"What's wrong? You're trembling."

Clarice sighed, straining to recall any of the details of her dream. But to no avail. She was only left with fragments that danced at the edge of consciousness, trying to reveal themselves. Clinging for awareness past the outer edges of the morning fog left over from her dream, had unnerved her. She knew there was no need to worry him. After all, what good would it have done? She couldn't remember any of it.

"I'm fine. I woke up and didn't feel you next to me." Her voice trembling as she struggled to hide the sense of urgency brewing just beneath the cracks of the haunting fragments in her mind. However, the smile she directed towards him was genuine.

Clarice adored Stephen.

Stephen held her close, his voice a steady whisper of reassurance against the quiet rhythm of the night. They spoke in low tones, weaving words of comfort and memories as the last hours before sunrise slipped by.

Clarice eventually drifted off in his arms. Her breathing became soft and even—comforting, heartbeats in sync with one another other. There was a kind of stillness—peacefulness in the moment. The safety of her body curled—weaved into his own. It was the type of peace that only comes when you are completely known and deeply loved.

Stephen glanced down at her face. Each new line etched represented their life. He had memorized each one, reminding himself of their moments together, the way a song stirs emotions of years long past. Even now, after all they had been through, he still couldn't believe he had found her, and in such an unlikely place, a conference room filled with strangers.

Sitting there holding Clarice, Stephen's heart began to warm, and he found himself smiling, reminiscing.

Clarice had been a guest speaker at the international agricultural summit in Las Vegas that year. Her lecture focused on sustainable agricultural practices. How emerging technologies could revolutionize vertical farming. It would make it viable not only for residential outputs but also large-scale outputs. Her passion was helping corporations—

regardless of their industry—maximize their output while contributing and preserving the environment.

So, at first, for Stephen, Clarice's topic had drawn him to the lecture. But once he was there, it wasn't the hook that drew him in. There was another pull. From the moment Clarice stepped onto the podium, he felt a shift within himself, an inexplicable tug. It was an intriguing topic, yes—but Stephen was captivated by *her*, and it was before she had even spoken a word.

He saw *her*.

There was something about the way she walked onto the stage. She leaned slightly against the podium, scanning the room. Slowly, she then walked to the center. And as everything stood still for her, she began.

She was brilliant, wrapped in grace. She spoke with such tenacity, commanding the stage as she discussed a topic dear to Stephen's heart. There was a shyness in her, lurking behind a thin veil of confidence.

He was lost in her. Thoughts of the probabilities anchored him— too vast to comprehend.

This encounter had to be by design.

So, it was only natural after the lecture ended, Stephen would make his way through the lingering crowd for an introduction.

Clarice and Stephen often teased each other about that day. The kids loved the stories. Whenever either of them was feeling out of sorts, they would always come back to that *chance meeting*. Each time the story was told, no matter who told it, it always ended up with the same ending; her giving him *that look* during the lecture.

"It was subtle—yet, an intentional moment that was undeniable," he would always say, using different hand gestures each time he told the story. And she would always do the same schoolgirl giggle.

From that moment on, facing each other in a crowded room, her entire presentation had been just for him. Their connection was real. Their story was one that could make one believe that in the fullness of time, love will find you.

Stephen lingered behind after the lecture. Pretending to be making notes about some important fact he didn't want to forget. In truth—and obvious, he was stalling, trying to muster up enough courage to approach her. With a mild panic attack held at bay, Stephen gathered his thoughts and started the final approach towards her. He reached his hand out to shake hers. Although he reached a little too soon, leaving it hanging in the air, Clarice noticed. She smiled and took a couple of steps to meet him, lessening the awkwardness that was quickly revealing itself. Stephen in turn gave her a slight nod in respect and admiration.

In reality, he was quite nervous and thought shaking her hand would buy him time as he gained his composure. He had practiced his first words to her in his head while pretending to take notes, secretly writing out his script. His plan was to say something thoughtful, maybe even clever, and charming. Unfortunately, when the time came, what came out was a mesh of words, incoherent even to him. He wasn't entirely sure if he'd asked her a question or blurted out how captivating he thought she was.

She smiled yet again, letting him off the hook. She extended her hand in acceptance—gracious and composed in the moment, as he pointed toward the two seats on the front row.

It was at that moment he felt—no, he knew he was complete.

Stephen's interest had not been one-sided. Clarice had been intrigued as well. Once their eyes locked, everything else had taken a backseat. They had become unaware of the other people in the room. Sitting there in that conference room, they talked about everything.

Clarice found herself telling this stranger how she grew up on the streets in the South—following her cousins as they committed all sorts of criminal activities. She never really did fit in though. She would always help plan, but when it came to the actual activity, she couldn't go because of her mom—you know curfew and all. She traded the hood in for college.

She told him how she ended up at the University of Nebraska as an Environmental Science professor. It had seemed like the logical thing to do once her daughter had moved away. She found herself retired and lost, with little purpose. So, when the opportunity presented itself, she saw it as a sign. God was giving her a new beginning.

They lost track of time, engrossed in each other. And when she noticed the time, she stood, apologized, and walked away.

In the weeks that followed, Stephen took long walks across his family's land. His nephew, Logan, would often join him. Although the business required them to spend a great deal of time together, it was after his chance meeting with Clarice, that regardless of the subject, somehow it always led back to her. Those brief moments he had shared with her changed his life forever.

While on the other hand, Clarice, hundreds of miles away, was having her own resolve. Even though Stephen had given her his personal contact information, she didn't use it. She wouldn't take the chance of being disappointed. She had seen enough of that in her life. Romance and from a distance, at her age, would be ludicrous—like signing up for unnecessary heartbreak.

This way, finding that one love, and believing God would redeem time for her was still in her realm of possibilities—hope at its finest. There was no need to test it. So, for her, all was well. She would not take their chance encounter and reduce it to yet another sad love story. She was enjoying her fantasy.

But as for Stephen, he didn't see it that way. His nephew had helped convince him it didn't have to be just a passing moment. At this stage in his life, it was worth exploring. It wouldn't take long for them to devise a plan.

This was no fantasy.

It had been a few months since that *chance encounter*. The best part of Clarice's life, so she thought, was over, and she didn't want to be distracted by something that might end in disappointment. So, after

Sarah volunteered her for an assignment to conduct an international seminar, she accepted. She had a week to put things in order, after that she would be out of the country for a few months. It was a welcome distraction.

She was crossing campus, making a checklist in her head when she suddenly stopped in mid-stride. In disbelief, she felt a rush of joy. There, leaning casually against a pillar, looking out into the courtyard, was Stephen. He seemed to be distracted by a group of students' laughter.

At first, she just stood there, barely breathing, soaking in the moment, too afraid to look away. Not quite sure it wasn't an illusion.

He hadn't noticed her when she left the building. She stood there, wanting to retreat back into the building, and with a quiet prayer she mumbled.

"Lord, please don't let me obey my legs. They so desperately want to turn around, and run before he sees me…" Just as she uttered "Amen," Stephen slowly turned towards her, smiled as he caught a glimpse of her.

His smile.

The speckled glow of sunlight encased him. He belonged to God, undeniable. A quiet warmth radiated from him—it was elusive. But she could see it. Clarice felt her heart smile. The joy overwhelmed her, with tears in her eyes she knew there was no turning back. She saw every meaningless relationship she had ever had, and now in the fullness of time, at that very moment, Clarice fell in love with Stephen.

She had been a part of him, and he a part of her, anchored in a divine belonging that was impossible to deny.

Clarice shifted her position in Stephen's arms, interrupting his dreamlike state, jolting him back to the present. He made a slight adjustment, ensuring she was warm and then settled back into his own deep thoughts.

Clarice stirred again, ever so slightly, only this time it was enough to wake him fully. As the sun broke the mountain's horizon, the sunlight warmed Clarice's face. "Why didn't you wake me?"

"You looked so peaceful. I didn't want to lose the moment." Clarice smiled, and after lifting his hands to kiss them, she stood and went inside.

***

Waiting for the coffee to finish brewing, Clarice leaned back against the counter, arms loosely crossed over her chest, allowing her mind to drift. Lost in the escape of her subconscious, plagued by the restlessness of her thoughts, she suddenly felt a warm sensation travelling throughout her body. She could feel the heat searching for an exit. What seemed to have started within her feet, quickly moved upward, suffocating her as it got closer to her chest.

In a desire to grasp for air, she unfolded her arms with such force until she hit the cup on the counter. It went crashing onto the floor. The entire sensation overtook her. She tried to wrestle with the effects of the episode, grabbing her head, eyes wide, terror settling in behind them.

"Clarice!" Stephen yelled as he ran to the kitchen.

She barely heard him. He placed his hand on her shoulder as if to bring her in closer. It steadied her. It was at that moment she saw the look on his face, panic was quickly setting in.

"What was that? I heard a crash…are you okay?"

The instinctive desire to ease his mind, Clarice casually dismissed what had happened. Just as Stephen was about to press the issue, they heard the notification from the communication system.

"Jazzette is calling." As the bot announced the call.

"Answer." Stephen said in response.

"Hi Jazzette, glad to hear from you. How's the family?" Stephen said picking up the handheld communication device.

Jazzette responded, "Everyone is great. Zoe just completed her first year of college, and Lizzie is officially a high school junior, with honors.

"That's my girl."

Everyone loved Zoe, but everyone agreed, there was something strange about her. She appeared to be lost in her own story most of the time. Lizzie, on the other hand, was that fresh drink of water you didn't know you needed. She was the closest one to her grandmother—could it have been they were both cut from the same cloth? Either way, they enjoyed each other's company. It was not unusual for them to spend hours together talking just about anything, and yet—nothing.

Lizzie loved Clarice, and Clarice adored her.

"Paul and I were thinking about coming to visit for a couple of weeks during the Christmas holidays. The boys are so excited they are trying to come early."

"Your mother will be thrilled." Stephen said while looking at Clarice.

"It's all set then. I will text mom and give her the exact dates, let's say in a couple of weeks."

Jazzette hung up.

Clarice overheard most of the conversation, and by the time they hung up, she was already deep in thought about the preparations. She was ecstatic. Barely containing herself with all the excitement, the earlier events had already been captured far in their own boxed corners of her mind. Stephen lingered in the doorway, shaking his head as he watched her.

"Love, they are not coming tomorrow; it will be a few weeks yet." chuckling as he continued to watch her.

"You are just as excited as I am. It's been so long since we've seen them." Clarice said, as if to tease him.

He knew better than to interfere with her unstoppable enthusiasm. His lips mimicked a kiss, not quite understanding how one person could captivate another with such intensity. He was just thankful it was he who got to love her.

Stephen turned and left out the back door heading towards the warehouse. As he took his first steps into the brightness of the new day, tiny pricks of coldness tickled his face. The slight crunching sounds made by his boots while walking on the thawing grass flashed thoughts of the farm. It took him back to his own family. In those few minutes, he could have easily been back on the farm, walking out towards the barn to work on some new invention.

He found comfort in his thoughts.

Stephen had come from four generations of proud farmers, each one leaving its mark on the land. His family had a legacy of more than just tilling soil; they thrived on it. And their success in the farming community proved it. Each generation committed to adding its footprint for technical innovation to propel the next generation. The family was part of a long line of innovators, both in science and agriculture. Stephen was no exception.

The latest family venture had been something different, something that felt almost like a calling. Stephen and his nephew had created ways of helping provide personal natural food sources for residential neighborhoods. They would create lush backyard gardens where owners could grow their own fresh fruits and vegetables. The gardens were woven seamlessly into any landscape, from sprawling lawns to the tiniest inner-city windowsills. It was a way of tackling the global malnutrition pandemic. The food industry had succumbed to a national security threat. Each year, the food sources provided to individual families were either chemically engineered or genetically altered. Profit over quality.

People would learn to grow their own crops, even if it had to be on their community's land. It had become the backbone of many households' daily living.

As Stephen approached the warehouse door, he considered how long it had been since Jazzette, and the kids had visited. More than that, after all these years, this would be the first time they would celebrate the holidays together on the compound. He loved them as if they were his own. Stephen especially wanted everything to be magical for the twins. He had already begun making quiet whispers to himself about all the things they would do.

Shortly after he married Clarice, Jazzette had the twins. Stephen had taken his role as a grandfather quite seriously—from the very start. In the early stages of renewing the land, he had an area on the outskirts of the mountain cleared of all overgrown vegetation. This was a place designed specifically for the twins. It was perfect for snowboarding in the winter or chasing butterflies in the summer. His face would light up thinking about how much they would love it, igniting that spark of excitement within himself—a familiarity of a lost boy from long ago

.

Breathtaking

Dreams—or visions, she wasn't quite sure what to call them, but Clarice hadn't experienced one in weeks. To call them dreams seemed to do them an injustice, far too small and ordinary. As strange as they had been, it felt like they were meant to be—deliberate, however cautiously the fragments may have been revealed—allowed for discovery.

On the other hand, to her, calling them visions felt wrong. Visions were prophetic and given to chosen people, those who carried a divine purpose, steadfast in an unshakable faith. She knew there were plenty of others that could do a much better job. Whatever was going to be needed to fulfill the requirements of a vision, she knew she was not it. God certainly would have chosen better.

Clarice didn't know what they were called, but they had been a constant presence in her life for the past few months. Fleeting images that faded with each break of dawn—yet always leaving her standing at the edge of clarity. Frustrated with the knowing of something that had happened—but unlike the edge of dawn where truth emerges with the light, Clarice was always left with nothing revealed.

But for now, they had been absent, and she began to wonder if it had all just been the stress of the semester coming to an end. She was seriously thinking about retiring from the university, staying at the compound full-time. Teaching class two days a week over the past couple of years had become taxing. She had been promising Stephen she would quit for several years now. But once they bought the land, time just slipped away.

Clarice would often stay in the city with Sarah to avoid late-night drives back home. Then there were other times, the unpredictable weather would cause her to become stranded. She would win debates with Stephen every semester, claiming it would be her last. But the truth was she still found enjoyment in mentoring and doing research. This time, however, it had been a little different. She had recognized how hard it was to leave him and the life they had built in their own private sanctuary.

The weeks flew by for the couple. Christmas Eve had finally arrived. Clarice and Stephen were putting the finishing touches on all the decorations—soft, intimate music filled the air. Music they had discovered together during the early years of their marriage.

Nostalgia quickly set in for both. Playfully teasing one another, laughter spilling over between them as they danced, savoring every moment as if reclaiming lost time. Love remaining as complete and unwavering as the day they were married.

Though life had shaped them individually, their love had never demanded their individuality be lost. Instead, they grew stronger together, each enhancing the other. Stephen understood her need to continue at the university for as long as she could. He knew that in time, age would bring its own set of issues. Some accompanied by aches and pains—yes, but he knew age in itself would never diminish their love or weaken their commitment. They were, in every sense, perfectly matched.

Clarice had always felt the constant presence of God's favor, and now with Stephen beside her, she was simply happy—grateful.

As Stephen twirled Clarice around while dancing, they both saw Zoe at the same time, leaning in the doorway watching. She was smiling, admiring the connection they had.

"You guys are exactly what I want."

Stephen and Clarice looked at each other as if they knew a secret. "To get us to this stage did not come overnight. We as individuals, before we met, were slow to surrender. But in the fullness of time, when we both were ready, God ordained it. It had indeed taken us a lifetime to understand the wisdom behind love—simply to remember *who says you have to always be right?*" That was the key.

Just then, a dim glow of light came from the path. Without hesitation, bursting with excitement, Clarice and Stephen rushed outside, while Zoe lingered in the background shaking her head.

Clarice, giddy with anticipation, looked at her husband, saying, "It's showtime." Standing on the porch, at the top of the steps, they frantically waited. Everything had been beautifully decorated.

It had all been for their family. This moment was of greater value, and more spectacular to Stephen and Clarice than the days when there would be a Christmas tree lighting ceremony in Times Square.

Christmas lights bordered both sides of the entrance leading into the compound. As soon as they entered the mountain path, motion sensor lights illuminating the road gave way to a personal invitation to the main house. It was all part of a grand design for that initial kick-off of the holiday season. They wanted the family to experience every emotion centered around the holidays, starting at the very beginning.

During their honeymoon, Stephen and Clarice spent their time wandering the countryside in search of a place in the region to call their own. They wanted something special. Something large enough to grow crops, as well as provide comfortable living arrangements to host large gatherings of family and friends for generations to come. But it couldn't be just any property. Stephen wanted to create something that was as perfect and breathtaking as Clarice was to him. The design effortlessly integrated the main house with its natural surroundings, rugged stone, cascading elements of color in the backdrop. Every detail had been meticulously considered. After all, the house and its primary purpose in design were done as part of a commitment each had made, *honor Jack,* his passion for his ancestors, his generosity, and the land's bounty. They wanted the commitment to be known, even with the choice of trees lining the driveway to the compound. Everything had been chosen intentionally.

As the car rolled down the driveway, Jazzette could see Stephen and Clarice standing at the top of the porch stairs.

"Mom looks like she is about to take off running." Jazzette said, laughing.

Clarice was standing next to one of the large porch posts. If not for Stephen holding her hand she would have leaped off the porch.

As Paul and Jazzette emerged from the tunnel's opening, the SUV headlights became visible to the Taylors for a few seconds before fading into the setting glow of the evening sun behind them. As Paul and Jazzette approached the house, all conversations they previously had with Clarice or Stephen suddenly gave clarity as to just how truly unique this place was. No one could have given it justice in describing the obviously inspired designs, reflecting their love for the environment and each other.

"We arrived at the perfect time. Look at how the lights are twinkling." Echoing from the back seat."

"Paul, this is everything for them. I am thrilled for them to be able to experience life in a place like this, priceless." Jazzette said as she looked toward the back seat, "boys look at all the trees."

The essence of the place was even more apparent as you got closer to the house. It blended into the rock terrain—large windows trimmed in natural stone and wood.

"Where's the house?" asked one of the twins, quickly being interrupted by the other. "Right in front of you, dummy, can't you see?"

"You're the dummy."

Both together, "wow!"

It truly was breathtaking.

As Jazzette continued to gaze out the window. She could feel her heartbeat rising with a warmth that made her feel secure. She was home, even if she didn't grow up there. It was her mom she saw, hands waving widely. Jazzette was reminiscing about her childhood, being in a field of flowers, running, singing, playing. She put her hands out of the window, feeling the cold air rushing over her fingertips. All the emotions previously conceived of what it must be like to feel God's love, Jazzette knew she could be at peace here. She now truly understood why her mom had chosen to come here at such an age.

As the car pulled to a rolling stop, Jazzette and the boys quickly opened the doors—half-way opened before Paul could come to a complete stop.

"You made it!" as Clarice broke loose and hurried to the car.

Zuri stood at her bedroom window, gazing, waiting on the family's arrival. She had been away at the Naval Academy and was excited to see everyone, but especially Paul and the twins.

It had been nearly twenty years since Paul had found Zuri in that remote village in East Africa. Even now, that same fire he saw, still burned in her eyes. From that very moment, they had been inseparable.

Once his parents died, Paul traded in operational missions for a desk job at the State Department. Zuri's lifeline had always been Paul and the bond between them was not one of obligations nor circumstance, but one of choice, of love freely given, protection under any circumstance.

To Zuri, Paul wasn't just the man who had given her a new life. He was the steady hand that guided her, the unwavering presence that had reassured her she was never alone. Paul encouraged her spiritually. Although they both felt the presence of something greater, Paul didn't feel the spiritual connection Zuri had when she was sixteen during and after her baptism in Africa. Yet, he was her refuge in every other way that mattered.

To Paul, she wasn't just the girl he had found, she was home, a piece of his heart, as much a part of him as if she had been born of his own blood. Zuri had been both a daughter and a son—everything he could have hoped for in a child. Their bond was so natural, so easy, that people often forgot she wasn't his biological child. Only when they stood side by side—Zuri's dark skin in contrast to Paul's blond hair, blue eyes. It hardly seemed to matter between them or anyone who knew them. The chemistry of a father and *his* child was undeniable.

Zuri had always carried herself as if she felt smaller than she was, shrinking into the background, trying to disappear. In any situation—crowded or intimate—she would retreat behind a quiet wall, offering little more than a polite acknowledgement. Even the thought of being drawn into conversation tightened the muscles in her chest. Yet beneath that guarded exterior, she ached to belong—to laugh freely, to connect, to be seen.

However, whenever she did let herself step into the light, it was magnetic. She was sharp, articulate, and like the meaning of her name, she was strikingly beautiful. She was fearless in ways that often surprised people. Within her, was a willingness to try almost anything, at least once. After all, Paul was the one who had trained her in all types of warfare and weaponry.

There were times when he was so hard on her, she would say, "Dad, remember I am a girl—not an operative!" It was an inside joke for them.

As soon as the twins saw her standing in the window, they ran past everyone, teasing, laughing, shoving each other as they competed for who would reach her first. By the time Zuri stepped away from the window and made it to the top of the stairs, about to descend them, she saw Paul Jr push past Cody. Both boys were already halfway up the stairs, the laughter of their voices echoing through the house as they called out her name.

"Zuri!"

Zuri had always felt a special attachment to the girls—Zoe and Lizzie, but when Jazzette told everyone she was pregnant with twin boys, everyone thought, finally, a boy, and twins no less! It was a celebration for everyone in the family.

Zuri encouraged the twin's fearless spirit, their boundless curiosity. They encouraged her in turn. She understood them in ways few others did. She knew what it felt like to crave adventure, to seek freedom in movement and discovery. Perhaps that's why they clung to her, why they saw her as more than just an older sister. She was their friend, their partner in crime.

Above Your Clearance

As everyone stepped into the house, the layered whispers of joy filled the air, the kind of joy only children could create. The twins' movements emitted laughter of unfiltered innocence. There was simply no replacement for that kind of energy.

Zoe and Zuri had arrived the day before. As they made their way towards the entryway to greet the others, Clarice felt it immediately. Something was off.

Not tonight. Tomorrow was Christmas. She dared not mention it. She wanted to enjoy the evening. So, she told herself.

"Not tonight, there'll be plenty of time after the celebration they had planned."

Long ago, Clarice made a promise to herself—never to push the girls, not even Jazzette, to share before they were ready. She had learned a valuable lesson over the years when she had done otherwise. So instead, she simply was—the calm, steady presence, a place where they knew they could land if the time ever came.

And for now, that would be enough. With her family gathered under one roof, laughter was music ringing throughout the house. Clarice felt a quiet contentment settle over her. In that moment, she had everything her heart desired.

The evening was indeed a happy one, full of laughter, old and new stories. The kids got to open the traditional one present, and then off to bed as commanded by *Naval Academy Cadet Martin*.

"Aye, aye!" giggled the twins as they ran past Zuri.

"Let's give the ladies a chance to talk. I've got a new piece of equipment I would love to show off!" Stephen said as he stood and motion to Paul to follow him.

Clarice said playfully, "Please, I have heard so much about that stuff, it's nice to have someone else around for him to talk about it with."

Where laughter had been moments ago filling the room, as Paul and Stephen grabbed their coats, and stepped out through the sliding glass doors, the mood shifted. They walked toward the warehouse in silence. The crisp evening air made them shiver as they cross the yard. Stephen had sensed something off with Paul, just as Clarice had with Jazzette. He waited until they were far enough away from the main house before speaking.

"Paul, is something wrong?" Stephen asked, his voice calm but probing. "I couldn't help but notice you seem uneasy—distant."

Paul hesitated, his hands fidgeting, his movements restless. Stephen stopped walking, turning to face him fully. "Paul, you know you can talk to me—trust me. Whatever it is, I'm here."

Paul exhaled sharply, his shoulders tense. "I know I should wait to tell you this," he admitted, his voice barely above a whisper. "But I can't. Every minute feels crucial, and if I don't talk to someone about this now," pausing, "I'm afraid I'll fall apart."

Stephen shifted his focus. This was obviously something major.

"About nine months ago," Paul began, his voice solid—deliberate as if giving a briefing at a strategy meeting, "I was sitting in my office working late when I came across an acquisition that needed immediate approval to release funds. My commander was on vacation at the time, and I didn't see any reason to bother him.

"I am given temporary clearance to cover most types of emergencies when he is gone, so I reviewed it myself. Initially, nothing seemed unusual. Then I noticed something at the bottom of the requisition. There was a set of letters, all caps, *JADE.*

"I'd heard the name mentioned once or twice during briefings, but just in passing. To be honest, I never thought much of it. It's quite common for different projects in the State Department to have coded names. It's just an easy way to identify a project…a committee, or whatever…not important." Paul said it as if he was checking himself. He then paused, the slightest flicker of unease passing over his face, as if he was silently questioning his last thought and preparing for the heart of the conversation.

Taking a deep breath, he continued. "I was about to approve the requisition automatically without giving it a second thought. Instead, I decided to dig a little deeper into the project, at the least figure out what it was. I ran a query through every database I had access to, but nothing came up. Not a single reference."

Paul's tone shifted from confusion to suspicion mid-thought as he went on.

"It threw me. I must admit, I was a little baffled. It didn't make sense. Even if I didn't have clearance, there should have been a trace—the name of the file—something, somewhere. But there was nothing. The project didn't exist.

"It really shouldn't have been a big deal," Paul admitted, even now second guessing his own thoughts, "but for some reason, I was drawn. I wasn't giving up and found myself determined. Not really sure why it mattered so much to me…maybe a little bored with work of late. I have missed the days of being out on a mission."

Paul fell silent, hesitating, toying with the reasoning behind his lingering curiosity. In that moment, he was actually still trying to figure out why it had mattered so much.

Stephen leaned forward, impatiently listening, wondering to himself *why he was trying to figure that out now*, but said nothing.

"Anyway," Paul continued, his military tone returned as if giving the daily briefing. "We have a restricted file room. There are certain files that can only be opened on-site. This would be the only place I could search for the file without special authorization or clearance—if, I could gain access to the room. It was after working hours, and I knew it would be the next day before I could try the room, so I dismissed it.

"Well…I walked away. But the truth was…" as he let out a heavy sigh, "I couldn't stop thinking about it throughout the night."

Stephen continued to listen, focusing on every word, looking for something that would bring clarity to the story he was hearing. He tried not to interrupt. He could sense Paul needed to tell the story in his own way. So, he remained silent. Secretly wishing he would get to the point.

"The next morning, I got to the office earlier than usual, determined to find out whatever this *JADE* project was. I wanted to access the file room before anyone else arrived. But just as I was heading there, a message came through. There was a briefing with the Defense Secretary. I wanted to dismiss it, but when the Defense Secretary calls a briefing, you don't hesitate. I had no choice but to set *JADE* aside for the moment and head to the briefing room."

Paul was busy talking and hadn't noticed Stephen had gone to a refrigerator and got a couple of drinks. The drinks were a welcome diversion. It gave Paul an opportunity to gather his thoughts and Stephen a chance to divert the anxiety creeping up inside him. This was beginning to sound like some conspiracy by the government.

Paul took a deep breath and exhaled slowly, continued. "The meeting stretched on longer than usual, though maybe it only felt that way because my mind was elsewhere. I sat through the reports, updates, and discussions, only half-listening, my thoughts circling back to *JADE*.

"When the briefing finally ended, I saw my opportunity. As the room emptied, I approached the Defense Secretary directly. I introduced myself, steadying my voice, trying to sound casual. Then I asked if he could tell me a little about Project JADE.

"For just a brief moment, he didn't react. His face still—no emotions attached—or just unreadable. Behind his eyes—disgust, sharp, and cold. Then, the secretary responded in a slightly annoyed tone, as if *how dare I approach him about this.*

"'Above your clearance,' looking past me, as if I was being dismissed or irrelevant as he walked away.

"I don't know how long I stood there, staring after him, my pulse pounding in my ears. It wasn't the words that got me—I'd heard worse, been in similar positions before. Not that it was bureaucratic garbage, it was the way he said it. Like I'd stepped somewhere I didn't belong. I'd been in this game long enough to recognize the difference. This was something else.

"I hadn't made it back to my office before I received a phone call from my superior. His voice was low and urgent.

"'I don't have time to explain,' he said, barely above a whisper. 'But listen to me carefully, shut down any and all questions you might have about *JADE*. Forget you ever saw it. Do you understand me?'

"Before I could say anything, the call disconnected. I had ventured into an area that whatever *JADE* was, it wasn't just above my clearance. It was something I wasn't supposed even to know about. I knew to drop it without hesitation. And so, I did.

"At least until about six weeks ago, when everything changed."

Stephen could tell this was serious.

Paul went on to say, "I went to lunch, and when I returned, just as I got off the elevator, I heard someone call my name, telling me I had a package.

"I simply remembered saying '*thanks*' or at least something like that as I grabbed it. I noticed it had been opened, thinking security must have intercepted.

"Once inside my office I removed the item. It was a small well-crafted box. Inside was a wristwatch." Paul now telling the story as if he was reliving the moments. "I had never seen anything like it. My first thought was of its uniqueness…it was an antique, no, yes definitely an antique. It had four stones embedded in the traditional quarter-hour positions. The dials and mechanics seemed to have been updated. Old century craftsmanship but with the latest technology. It was magnificent."

Directing his attention to Stephen, as if a justification was warranted. "I didn't think anything strange about it since my birthday was coming up."

Lowering his head again, hands cupped as he sat there, he continued.

"I looked for a note, but instead, only found an invoice, marked paid in full. I smiled out of gratitude and sat the watch aside. Several minutes later, still thinking nothing more of it, assuming Jazzette and the girls had ordered it for my birthday, I received an email.

"It was a confirmation of delivery email. Something about it caught my attention. The body of the email read "*JADE wristwatch with 5 stones*". Jade was written in all caps, just as I had seen previously. It probably would have been flagged by security if anyone had known what *JADE* was when they examined the package.

"This time, I looked at it with a keener eye, taking note of anything strange. But to no prevail. I put it on, still nothing. So, I gave up and pushed it aside again, thinking I was just being paranoid."

Paul started to get agitated. Stephen knew that whatever was going on, stress had its foot on his neck. Stephen interrupted him to give him a break.

"When did all of this happen?"

"Two days before we made plans to come visit for the holidays."

Paul shifted his weight, sitting there for the longest without saying a word. Stephen joined in the silence, allowing him to continue at his own pace.

"It was in the next few moments that I realized this was no mistake. It was a deliberate package. The watch beeped, and the stone at the 12 o'clock mark turned green. Then I heard '*identity confirmed.*'

"There must have been some type of sensor on the back of the watch, it had analyzed and confirmed my DNA as a match when I put it on. I don't know how, but the face of the watch changed color, and a message scrolled across. It hadn't appeared to be a typical smartwatch, but something with early 20th century characteristics, appearing analog-like. The message was simple.

Code Name: JADE; Passcode: Q3_2035GR.

JADE

The fire crackled softly, its gentle rhythm providing the perfect backdrop for Clarice and Jazzette. Its warm glow spilled across the living room, dancing off framed photos, polished wood furniture, and carefully chosen artwork. They had quietly slipped away from the noise of the others, retreating to the comfort of the familiarity of their previous homes. They intentionally decorated the space to represent a timeline of their shared lives. Regardless of when you came into the family, the shared history was revealed, love cascading from above.

Clarice was curled up in the oversized chair by the fireplace, a glass of deep red wine resting in her hand. She swirled it gently, eyes watching the liquid rotate in the glass, unsure whether she should take that first sip. Part of her had longed for the warmth of it all evening. But the other part of her knew she should keep a clear head, just in case Jazzette needed her to be *mom*.

The wine had been a gift from Sarah for her birthday, its label as elegant as the card that came with it, simply written—Bold. Expensive. Complex.

The bottle was rare and meant for just the right occasion. Taking glances between the deep crimson in her glass and Jazzette's troubled demeanor, Clarice thought, *if ever there was a time for a special wine, whatever was going on, tonight might just be that moment.*

Across from her, Jazzette sat quietly on the rug, her head leaning back against the couch, legs stretched comfortably across the soft weave of the carpet, with her second glass of wine nearly empty. She allowed herself to relax in such a way, one she hadn't experienced in quite a while. Not since Paul came home on that life-altering day. Here with her mother, and with the warmth of the fire glowing in front of her, Jazzette exhaled.

For the first time in a long time, she gave herself permission to breathe.

Their conversations had been easy, entwined with laughter, highlighting the special relationship they shared. Clarice felt herself relax, thinking it was safe to start her personal wine journey. Just as she was about to embark, she noticed the shift in Jazz.

The wine had begun to release its power. The more she lifted the rim of the glass to her lips, the more the reins guarding her mind loosened its hold. As Jazzette stared at the fire, Clarice could see the tears building in her eyes. The confinement of the fireplace could not capture her thoughts. Her focus was being held by something beyond the coziness of the room—it was distant.

Clarice watched as Jazz slowly raised her fingers to the corners of her eyes, plugging them in a quiet attempt to prevent the tears from betraying the extreme unsettledness brewing inside.

Clarice looked at her glass with the look of a lost love, unreachable—just bad timing. Her gaze alternating between her daughter and the wineglass nestled between her fingers, a richness under her command, eyes lingering on the delicate residue clinging to the inner curve of the glass. The wine slid slowly, connecting—rejoining the rest of the pool of liquid tunneling at the bottom of the glass. Her mind transported to the sensations one gets from that initial burst of flavors. The way the tannins danced as they separated across the tongue and then recombined right there in your mouth.

She was smiling inside, thinking how much she had come to love wine, thanks to Sarah.

When done right, it was more than a drink. It was an all-star performance. Sarah had been teaching her an appreciation for the finest, determined to make her a connoisseur.

But this was not the night for such a tango. Her child needed her. Sitting across from her, Clarice could feel an incredible pulse of sadness radiating from her child. So, with a quiet longing sigh, she gently set the wine on the table, moved to the edge of her chair—prepared to solve whatever crisis Jazzette had exploited for herself. Their nostalgic conversations had apparently made Jazzette remember why they had come to visit. She knew something was wrong. Why could it never be just—a visit, *for one night?* Feeling bad for thinking such a thing, she was, after all, a mom first.

"Sweetie," Clarice said in a tone to reassure Jazzette she was in a safe place, "something tells me this visit is about more than just Christmas…"

Before she could complete her thought, Jazzette took a breath, exhaled and began to lay out before her mom all the details about *JADE*.

"Paul came home about a couple of months ago with the most bizarre story, too hard to believe. I am still unnerved just thinking about what it could all mean. We came here to tell the two of you about his discovery at work. In a secret file there is evidence about an event that is going to occur. Know that once you hear it, your world will change and everything for all of us will be forever different."

Clarice smiled to herself. *Well, that escalated quickly.*

She knew Jazzette had a flair for the dramatics. She loved her daughter more than life itself, but she knew how to make treacherous storms out of summer showers. Nonetheless, she could tell there was something about this that caused Jazzette's demeanor to shift each time she thought of the next sentence.

Clarice reached for her glass with a new resolve—wine was an absolute necessity.

Jazzette leaned forward, eyes wide with too much knowledge to hold on to, and began to tell her mother everything.

"Paul came across some information at work—classified information. It laid out the destruction of a large percentage of the global population, including here in America!"

Clarice took a sip, trying to mask the burst of laughter about to slip out, choking back the sly comment that hung in her throat. This level of revelation, added to the way Jazzette said it, caught Clarice completely off guard. This was a little far-fetched even with her flair for overreacting. But her unbelievable reaction was written all over her face, including a slight smirk lurking behind the glass.

"Mom, this is no joke."

Clarice regained her composure, apologized, took another sip, and continued to pretend to listen. "Sorry, you have my undivided attention."

Jazzette took a breath, her voice cracking under the weight of it all.

"We came for the holidays so we can make plans. We haven't told anyone, not even the kids," her voice surrendering to defeat.

That's when Clarice saw it—fear, real fear.

"Paul and I wanted to tell you and Stephen together, but I couldn't hold back."

Tears began streaming freely down Jazz's cheeks. Clarice hugged her, holding her tight. And in that moment, whatever skepticism may have existed, she understood that whatever this was—it was more than fear. There was a hurt at the base, devastating to her child.

Jazzette continued to tell her mother the story as they walked out to the warehouse to join the others.

"Paul, Jazzette has been telling me the most unsettling story. I'm not sure I understand. What is this *JADE*? Are you sure this is a threat?"

Jazzette interrupted, "I know we were supposed to tell them together, but I had to tell her. I haven't gotten to the point where I explained what it actually means though."

Clarice and Stephen looked at each other as if in total disbelief.

"It's ok Babe, I couldn't wait either," Paul said to Jazzette. "I was about to tell Stephen about what I did when I got the password for a file."

Turning to Stephen, "The very file I had asked about in the situation room months before."

"I waited until I knew the file room would be empty. There was the Thanksgiving holiday weekend coming up. Normally if there was not a briefing taking place, and a holiday, there would only be a skeleton crew on duty. Most of the time they would work out of some other area's offices. I knew it would be my chance to find the file.

"There was a vast network of computers next to the situation room. This particular room had terminals to access servers that other parts of the government could not. You need a special clearance to get into the room, and even after you do, every file has its own unique identifier.

"I found a small area to log into the computer with the username and password that was given on the watch."

Paul looked at that moment as if his own words had defeated him— a battle he could not win. He looked at them, making eye contact and continued. "Every time I think about it, I am at a loss for words, drowning in the moment. There in black and white was a file that outlined the purpose of *JADE*. But more importantly, was a plan to combat the threat."

"What threat?" Clarice asked, growing impatient. You could tell she too had begun to panic. It was one thing for Jazz to be telling the story but now hearing it from Paul gave it true validity.

Paul continued, "There is an asteroid heading for earth, a cosmic catastrophic event. Our government has joined forces with four other foreign government agencies to stop it before it reaches us."

Stephen chimed in trying to remove some of the fear, "but this doesn't sound like anything unusual. This isn't the first time they have redirected an asteroid that was posing a threat. If anything, it's good to see the nations finally on the same page about something. Which countries are involved?"

Paul, obviously annoyed and irritated by the focus, stood up, and raised his voice in frustration. "That's not the point, you don't understand. It's what they plan on doing to divert the asteroid. *JADE* is not the name of the asteroid; it is the name of the plan."

Stephen, the man who always prided himself on leaning towards the positive side of something, a pillar of wisdom in most situations, interrupted. "Paul, you're starting to cause a little worry for me. Maybe you should tell us exactly what the plan is."

"The five nations around the world are collaborating to construct a high-powered laser system designed to alter the asteroid's trajectory. The way it's supposed to work is to fire a concentrated energy beam directly at the asteroid, forcing it off its current course, causing it to miss Earth entirely.

"A massive camera capable of taking photos in space is currently capturing images to determine the most accurate point of impact. The scientists will use twelve months of data from the camera to predict with certainty the highest chance of successfully deflecting the asteroid.

"For the laser to release that much power, it will have to draw energy comparable to that of the sun. Vast amounts of fuel would be required to generate and sustain that much power—especially—at that distance. The plan involves three separate energy bursts, each burst emitting for at least 45 seconds—each lasting three minutes. This disruption could affect all life on the planet."

"But Paul, that doesn't sound so bad considering the alternatives."

"You're right...on the surface. What if no one really knows? What happens if the process strips the basic elements from the air, leaving the average person unable to breathe? The essence of life will be sucked out.

I don't believe this is the crust of the crisis. There is so much more to the story, I can feel it! I just haven't found it! I know the type of people running things. If this was all to it, it would be public—but this is covert—top secret."

Paul paused, his voice lowered, barely audible. "I haven't told anyone except Jazzette. And now you. The person, Timepiece, who sent me the watch had their reasons. I just don't know why. I don't know what I am supposed to do with this type of information. I have confirmed everything. The files are true.

"So now you see why we are here. The world is about to be destroyed. They are playing games with the life of the entire planet."

"How long do we have?"

"They have known for about two years, and we now have almost 3 years left to prepare."

"Surely, they are still searching for a better solution," Clarice said, her voice edged with judgement and hope. "People will eventually need to be warned!" She continued making a definitive statement.

Paul looked at her, wanting to tell her with certainty that he believed, but he knew better—skepticism was a military's way of life.

"Let's hope they are still considering all possibilities," trying to sound hopeful. Then his tone shifted, heavier.

"Even if we were to speak out…who would listen to us? You're struggling to accept this, and you know me. Imagine the rest of the world. Knowing, but there is nothing you can do about it. Their lives would be lived in a state of chaos and worry. Then there would be others, thinking I have made up some conspiracy theory. The government would discredit us. And those who do believe us—what good it would do them, Clarice? They would live every day haunted by something they couldn't prevent. Helpless.

"Yes! It's an impossible position to be in, and yes, I know I can't carry this alone. I hate I am not only feeling these things, but that I must say them aloud."

Clarice looked up at him, placing a hand on his shoulder. She could see it—the true weight he was carrying, not just the fear of what was happening, but the responsibility that comes with knowing—the unwavering argument settling within them all, truth doesn't always make you free.

"Then let's make a pact." Stephen jumped in to relieve some of the responsibility that had fallen on Paul. "If it turns out that as time gets closer and the plan has not changed, we will blow the whistle. In the meantime, we will continue to find out as much information as possible."

Clarice was always thinking ahead. She was practical and wanted to put a positive spin on things before tomorrow. Even the end of the world would not put a damper on Christmas for her.

"We should use this place as our point of refuge. We will act like survival is a real possibility. Stephen and I have been building the estate to be self-sustaining. We will just have to increase our level of readiness and ensure it's ready in three years."

"Agreed!"

Sanctuary

"Good morning, G-Mom," Lizzie said softly as she entered the kitchen.

Startled, turning towards the innocent voice, "Good morning, Lizzie. Isn't it a little early for you to be awake? Breakfast won't be ready for a few hours." Clarice said with a soft smile.

"I couldn't sleep. I've been waiting for you to get started so I could help."

Smiling even more inside, Clarice was secretly glad Lizzie was awake. The house was quiet—too quiet. She had been working mindlessly, prepping for the upcoming festive meals. Trying to fill the gaps consumed with thoughts of what they had learned, praying it wasn't as terrifying as they made it out to be.

Lizzie relished the time they spent together. No one ever wanted to help in the kitchen, so it gave them a chance to hang out. The time had become special to both of them. To Lizzie, her grandmother was nothing short of extraordinary.

Eyes wide with love, Clarice walked toward her, voice soft, giving a warm embrace as she whispered to her, "I love you."

She was still smiling when she told Lizzie, "You've made my heart smile."

The two of them, with a generation between them, had found common ground. What began as a longing for approval from others had blossomed into something far richer. Through food, they discovered a shared sense of purpose, a quiet satisfaction in serving the family. It was a language of love neither had expected to find—purpose seen and felt.

Now, of course, for Clarice, there was the science of it all—chemistry had long found a home in her heart. She had this innate need to explain the *how*. Lizzie found endless amusement in watching her grandmother carefully measure every ingredient—it was like participating in a real lab experiment.

Although when Clarice wasn't looking, Lizzie would slyly adjust an ingredient—add a dash more here, take away there. She would in secret help her grandmother; after all, it was a family joke—her eyes were not what they used to be.

"You better not let her hear you say she needs to wear her glasses..." someone would always say to start a round of laughter.

Lizzie dared not! She simply made allowances where needed. However, somehow, whatever Clarice had prepared, it always seemed to taste like she was a five-star chef.

They had just begun cleaning up from the meal prep when Lizzie realized the time alone with Clarice was about to come to an end. Everyone would be awake soon, and the day's festivities would take center stage. She wanted to talk to Clarice about something but wasn't quite sure she should, considering all the things planned. She didn't want to be a nuisance.

"G-Mom?" Lizzie said, pushing down the lump of irrational emotions rising in her throat.

Clarice was drying her hands but stopped to acknowledge whatever Lizzie was trying to say.

"I have this paper to write over the holiday break. It's supposed to be about any national treasure we've visited." Lizzie paused, looking at Clarice with nervous eyes, searching for reassurance. "When we were driving up to the house yesterday, I thought maybe...perhaps I could write about this place."

Clarice's face lit up, and with a twinkle in her eyes, she said, "What a wonderful idea. There's so much history here." She loved to talk about the compound and how it all came about.

"Everyone is still asleep, and since we have some time before any of the festivities begin, we should get started now," Clarice said to Lizzie as they both responded with teenage excitement.

"Get your material to take notes," Clarice said as she moved about the kitchen gathering ingredients. "I'll light the fireplace and make us hot chocolate. Meet out on the patio?"

"Yes."

A few minutes later, Clarice flipped the switch on the wall outside, sending warm streams of air into a steady flow. The temperature-controlled system was simple, efficient, and to Clarice, nothing short of a brilliant design.

Christmas morning was turning out to be perfect, and it wasn't even daylight. Smiling as she busied herself setting the perfect patio atmosphere to tell her story.

Lizzie stepped out into the tranquility and ambience of an ideal environment. With a recording device in hand, her expression focused, and a little submissive to her own set of dramatics, Lizzie approached Clarice like she was about to conduct a high-profile live podcast.

Clarice chuckled at the seriousness of her approach. Nonetheless, she was intrigued. So, she decided to play along.

"Where would you like for me to begin?" She asked, her tone inviting, handing her granddaughter complete control—a teaching moment—or just another member of the family with extreme tendencies.

"The first day," Lizzie said, leaning back with a sigh of contentment. She was ready, positioning herself for a movie seen many times beforehand and yet enjoyable each time seen.

"Excellent!" Clarice said as she searched her mental database for the proper first detail.

With a storyteller's flair, she jumped right in…stage right!

"It was early in our marriage. We'd made the decision to live in Nebraska, near the university. I had already resolved to move with Stephen to the farm in his hometown. I didn't want him to give up the familiar roots of his family—his life, their legacy."

She paused briefly; her voice touched with love and respect for her husband.

"But he made it clear about wanting our life to be our own. So, he made all the necessary arrangements, and his son took over the family's business."

"I don't remember him," Lizzie said with a certain level of curiosity.

"You were just a little girl the last time you saw him," Clarice replied, her tone soft, eyes warm.

Returning to her story, Clarice stared across the courtyard, lost in her memories as she revisited the events, taking care not to miss any of the important details. She wanted to share them just as they had unfolded.

"Stephen and I had been searching for days," she began, "driving all over the region, hoping to find that one place. We had envisioned the kind of place we wanted to build as our legacy. But nothing felt—right. So, we gave up. We decided to reassess what we truly wanted—needed in a home."

Clarice stood up, pausing the storytelling for a moment. She casually walked across the patio, taking the small box that housed firewood pebbles off the mantel. The steady glow was as vibrant as ever but the other elements of a perfect setting, sound and smell, had started to fade. She refilled the fireplace cup with fresh pebbles, waiting, unaware of anything outside the welcome awakening of her senses of the scattered pebbles.

She loved using them. The fireplace may have been technically a gas heater, but the pebbles, when heated gave off the smell of warmth, mingled with the crackling and hissing of a well-lit fire. She lingered for a little longer, watching the pebbles as they started to glow.

Anticipation built in Lizzie until she couldn't hold out any longer.

"Then what happened, G-Mom?" Lizzie blurted out, unable to contain herself.

Although she had heard the story many times over the years, this time felt different, it was the way Clarice was telling it. She was a narrator telling her own story, weaving in and out of roles. Not as something that she was a part of, but as a guide acting out the characters in an old manuscript, embodying the voices and tones of the participants. The details spoken and heard over the years had suddenly taken on new meaning.

With the fire crackling, the house still asleep, the twinkling lights from the decorations, and the inclusiveness of the drive up to the estate fresh in her mind, Lizzie was lost in the moment. The memory of yesterday's drive, with the breathtaking reveal added to the way Clarice was telling the story, making it all seem to be legendary.

Listening to her grandmother made the events of the place come alive.

Clarice found her voice again, slipping back into character. This time, narrating the story in third person. "Driving back towards the city, just as Stephen and Clarice broke the top of this small hill, off to the side, below in the distance, I—sorry, Clarice saw it...the restaurant sign, hanging like a beacon in the sky."

"Restaurant sign, G-Mom? Beacon?" Lizzie asked in anticipation.

"Yes, a beacon in the sky." Clarice smiled as she said it. "I believe that's the way Sarah described it." She paused and looked at Lizzie, shifting tone slightly—stalling, as she filled in the gaps time had stolen, trying to recall the next scene.

"Do you remember Sarah?" Lizzie nodded in agreement. "She thought Stephen and I would enjoy it if ever in the area. She was right."

"Ah!" Remembering, Clarice continued to the next sequence of events.

"There it was, this quaint little restaurant, well-known throughout the state. With western charm and amazing cuisine, it was said to anchor the entire tourist area. Buildings lined both sides of this narrow dirt street. The architectural design instantly transported us...sorry, Stephen and Clarice back in time, well over a century to the early days of the American West." Her voice, distant.

Clarice was fully immersed in the memory as she continued.

"The area had been constructed with every detail considered, making it the resemblance of a frontier town in the height of its booming days. Even the material the street was made of was not dirt at all, but some man-made soil that looked and felt like the real thing—but it never turned into mud. It was amazing. Every stone laid, and faux wood used had been engineered to mimic a rustic, century aged community."

Clarice chuckled a little, returning to the present—adding her personal commentary, "Honestly, if it had not been for the buildings being too large for the era, you would have suspected they were the original ones, just well-maintained over the decades."

"G-Mom, can we go when we come back for the summer? I would love to see it."

"Absolutely!" Clarice agreed before she fully considered—all things.

The answer hung in the air. She had momentarily forgotten the world. She had forgotten the looming crisis lurking in space, and the silence of those who knew. It was Christmas. The children were unaware, and it was not her place to say anything.

Instead, Clarice leaned back into the story, this time fully engaged in her role as the third-party narrator—a by-stander to her own past.

"Faith intervened that day for Stephen and Clarice. Their unsuccessful and impossible dream collided with faith. That day they met an unlikely couple that would become family—forever connected."

"You mean Jack and his wife." Lizzie said lovingly.

"Yes…" Clarice said, her voice unfolding gently into the bystander.

"Stephen and Clarice were sitting at a small table, discussing their disappointment in the land search, when a couple seated at a nearby table overheard them. The couple explained that their family had lived in the region for generations, rooted deep in the land. They talked about their heritage, recipients of the land—the actual Indigenous tribe's living heirs, native to the area. They spoke of their ancestors with such reverence, both protective and proud.

"As they continued sharing the history of their land, their voices seemed to relax as if finding its home.

"'This place…' the wife said.

"We had yet to learn their names." Clarice added as a side note before she continued in Alice's voice.

"'This place was once considered sacred. The land they assigned to my people was meant as a hindrance, but it was a chosen gift hidden within a lie. Value not yet realized.'

"Jack at this time was quietly studying Stephen and Clarice. His voice now touched with a level of vindication as he continued the focus of his wife."

Clarice shifted her position, deepening her voice as she slipped into Jack's character. Her imitation of him was surprisingly good. She was actually pretty good at the role-playing.

"'The land that had been *assigned* to my family stretched along the Platte River. At first glance, it seemed unremarkable, even undesirable. But the land was vast, with rolling hills, stretching to the horizon. There was one larger than all the rest. The others surrounded it, as if it was placed as the head. Not large enough to be considered a mountain, but exceptional as it stood alone in comparison. Its terrain was rugged, supported with mountainous stones.'"

Lizzie was staring at the fire. Her mind being transformed while watching this one-woman stage play being performed right in front of her. Lizzie no longer heard Clarice telling the story, she was there, standing on the sidelines, watching every detail. Interpreting each moment vividly, Clarice was an artist painting a picture of the four of them—sitting around the table, having a cup of coffee like old friends.

"Stephen and Clarice had been giving each other slight glances. They were both totally captivated by the conversation. It was at that moment they could see Jack smile, as if he was preparing to reveal a hidden truth."

Stepping back into Jack's voice.

"'When *given*, most didn't understand its value. The land was surrounded by fresh water and coated with fertile soil. The mountainous land, although treacherous—unforgiving during the winter months, but if you respected it, nurtured it…it in turn would provide an abundance.'

"The two couples spent the rest of the day together. Jack and his wife told such intimate stories about their ancestors. Their eyes would light up with such pride and respect for not only their people, but the land itself. Having an audience, I supposed, to listen to them with such excitement was just the catalyst they needed. Genuine friendships were formed that day."

Clarice stopped and waited for Lizzie to say something. But Lizzie was engrossed in the play. There was nothing for her to say. She had blocked out the rest of the world. It was just Clarice and herself.

"Stephen told them about how we—they had been looking for land and that they wanted something special but were having little luck. It started to get late when Jack and Alice stood to leave. But before they walked out the door, Jack turned slightly towards Stephen.

"'If you're looking for something that's off the normal trail, meet me here tomorrow at noon. I want to show you a place. Be sure to wear comfortable shoes.'

"As they walked toward their car, Stephen turned to glance at Clarice. She could see the hesitation creeping in about what Jack had said. Not because he was not interested, but the excitement and possibilities had settled in his chest. The anticipation was etched in every crevice of his face. With a returned playful smile, Clarice winked. It was a silent gesture of encouragement. It was her way of giving her approval to a *dare to believe*. Each of them knew this could be something real."

Returning her gaze to Lizzie, Clarice said, "A little secret— whenever you see me wink at your grandfather, it simply means I agree to whatever he is thinking." They both winked—laughed.

"The next morning, Stephen woke up before sunrise. He was so excited he could hardly sleep.

"'Wonder what kind of place Mr. Jack wants to show us? Do you think any of the stories he was telling us were true?'" Clarice mimicking Stephen's voice.

"Before Clarice could respond, he continued. 'Can you imagine growing up in villages along the Platte River?'"

"'Now Stephen, you know he didn't grow up in a village. I'm sure if anything, he was raised on a reservation.'" Clarice responding in her fake voice.

"'I know, but I bet his great-grandparents did. Imagine what life must have been like back then?'"

Clarice chuckled and fully engaged in her Clarice role said, "'Certainly not two Black people looking for land to purchase from a Native American.'

"'Now that is the truth.'

"Both shaking their heads as they let out a sound of laughter that echoed off the walls of the hotel room."

Clarice became more and more engrossed in the acting out of each scene as she told the story.

Lizzie was thrilled. She was seeing a side of Clarice that she had never seen before. It only made her more human.

Clarice was walking and talking like Stephen, mimicking his every move, laughing at first until she was totally into acting out the scene.

"As Stephen and Clarice walked up to the General Store, they saw Jack.

"'Good afternoon Mr. Jack, where's your wife?' Stephen said extending his hand.

"Jack nodded, saying, 'Just Jack today. She had some things to take care of, and hiking through the hills isn't her favorite thing anymore.'

"As he was opening the door, he motioned for Clarice. 'Let's take my truck.'

"After they had been driving for about half an hour; Jack gently slowed the truck. There up ahead was a narrow dirt road. You could tell the road was less travelled. It seemed to have disappeared into the side of a mountain. Jack parked the truck, turned off the ignition, tossing the keys to Clarice without saying a word. This certainly didn't feel like the same talkative guy they had met the day before. Nevertheless, they followed.

"Looking around, Stephen seemed somewhat annoyed out of disappointment. 'Where are we going? This doesn't seem to lead to anywhere.' He kept saying out of impatience."

Lizzie looked puzzled, making a blanket statement. "Wow, I have never seen Granddad impatient."

"It doesn't happen very often."

Clarice continued with the narration. "This narrow road curved into a semicircle. Its curve flowed into a small park, long forgotten. You could see a few weathered benches decaying in the overgrown grass, and a single rusty trash can, barely hanging on by a single hinge. Fading from history, the park appeared to be out of place."

Turning to Lizzie, Clarice noted, "You know, now that I think about it, it looked like it had been staged. Everything laid out perfectly across this picturesque scene…um."

Returning to the story, Clarice drifted off into a trance, remembering every detail. "Just off to the right, partially hidden by a string of trees, there was something unexpected—a huge opening carved into the side of this mountain. Though I remember thinking at the time, *it really wasn't a mountain.*

"Anyway. Jack was already heading towards it as if he knew exactly where he was going. He entered with Stephen closely behind him. I could still see Stephen. He paused at the edge of the entrance, looking around, taking it all in. By the time I got to where he was, he was standing there disappointed once again. It wasn't very large, maybe twelve feet across, ten feet high, leading to a dead end.

"He later told me he was thinking, 'I can barely fit a truck in here, and then what?'

"Before we could fully register what we were feeling, Jack kept walking—straight toward what appeared to be a solid rock face. But just before reaching it, he veered slightly to the left and slipped through a narrow opening, almost undetectable against the rocky surface.

"We followed. I was fully engaged in the details of the different types of stones. The path had been carved with ancestral hands. I moved even slower, absorbing the weight of the moment. I had fallen a few steps behind. We walked in silence for about eighty feet. The passage was organically widening, until we emerged into a massive clearing."

Clarice lost herself in the memory. She hadn't realized she was telling the story from her point of view. Her emotions tied to the memory of that first encounter were raw.

"Standing there, hand in hand, we both came to a complete halt," she said.

"It was magnificent—breathtaking.

"Enclosed by towering rock formations, the space stretched out like a secret world hidden within the mountain. At least five football fields in size, surrounded by various types of stones, nature's own arena cradling this vast and unexpected sanctuary."

It was then that she told Lizzie about the moment Jack offered to sell them the land.

'This land belongs to me.' He told them. 'There are no more members of my tribe I would entrust the future of the land to, nor do I want to leave it to the state. I would much rather give it to someone that would take care of it, honor its history, and tell the story of its ancestors.'

"We stood in awe. Stephen and I walked the land, quietly exchanging knowing smiles, our own unspoken language. Each, in our own way, was falling in love with every step made. Jack told us he noticed the interaction between us and the land. He knew that no matter what happened in the future, it would be protected. He then said to us."

"'I will sell the land to you if you are interested, under a couple of conditions.'

"Before Jack could finish his words, Stephen interrupted him. 'Tell us your price, and we will try to meet it, whatever it is. We would be honored.'

"Jack made a delightful smile, 'You haven't heard the condition. I will sell the land to you under one condition. I can maintain possession of a small area on the NW corner of the property. When you build your future here, build me a small cabin as well in the space. If something ever happens to us, that too will be yours.'

"'Done!,' both of us shouted at the same time. We all laughed, and Jack told us he would have the papers drawn up. And he did.

"We have spent these last few years building this place—a home embedded in the midst of a hill, high as a mountain."

The interview was interrupted by the running and yelling of the twins making their way to the Christmas tree.

The house came alive!

Timepiece

Timepiece was one of the best-known hackers in the world. No one knew who she was, and most assumed she was male. All anyone knew was about two years ago Timepiece showed up on the radar of every government agency—worldwide. She was brilliant. She could find herself inside any network in such a way that it could be months before anyone would suspect a thing. Her coding was unlike anything most had ever seen. She had created a generative AI as her part of her toolbox. The bot was capable of learning the system she infiltrated and blend into its very fabric. It would create predetermined windows when the system would be at its most vulnerable, ready for her to hack at will—at any time in the future, seamlessly. It would then erase all traces of anyone ever having been there. Her style of coding was artistic.

The most confounding problem with Timepiece's code wasn't just its brilliance; it was its duality. To the agencies trying to unmask her, this style of hacker was an enigma. She wasn't simply a hacker. Instead, she was wrapped in ones and zeros; she was her code. One segment of the code was structured—precise, elegant, almost textbook in its execution. But then, without warning, it would shift abruptly, chaotically, as if written by an entirely different person. It contradicted logic. Every hacker has a unique signature, a style that would leave behind faint traces of their identity. But this? This was something else—different. It was as if somewhere in the code there was a special tag designed to guard her privacy, based on her own self-imposed criteria.

Some believed she was a collective, a coordinated team of operatives working under a single alias. Others theorized she integrated machine learning into her code, disguised behind her own patterns. But to those who understood the art behind the complexity of her style, knew better.

This wasn't two people. This was *one*.

It had been Timepiece who had sent Paul the watch about *JADE*.

On her 13th birthday, Timepiece's father gave her a jade necklace. It wasn't just a piece of jewelry—it was a moment forever etched into her heart. He had made such a big deal out of it, presenting the gift, as if it was some mythical amulet. And maybe it was. It was simple in design. A smooth jade stone was set in the center of a gold tag. But to Timepiece, the true gift had been the speech, and the words engraved on the back:

"Be wise. Be just. Be kind."

The spirit of the speech he gave her that day—steady, heartfelt, eternal—became part of her, a guiding force that would shape everything she would become. Wisdom, justice, and kindness—three virtues bound, yet distinct in their purpose. She made a promise to carry them with her always.

Three days later, her father died.

The choices she made, the lines she drew, and ultimately, the identities she created all stemmed from that promise.

It was not surprising that Timepiece's code reflected her inner world. Unintentionally or perhaps instinctively, it became an extension of herself—two halves of the same whole. One half driven by wisdom and justice. The other, by wisdom and kindness. Wisdom served as the constant anchor. She was still young, yet to realize the value of balance.

Justice required action.

Kindness required restraint.

And sometimes, those two forces stood in direct opposition to one another.

Paul hadn't realized it yet, but the watch wasn't just a tool, it was a message. A deeply personal one. She had chosen to reveal JADE—just as she had chosen *him* to do it with.

By day, Timepiece operated under the alias *The Huntress,* a highly sought-after blue hat hacker. Corporations would hire her to test their security systems, exposing any weaknesses before genuine threats could find their vulnerabilities. Her clients only knew they were working with *The Huntress*—a sharp, meticulous expert with an uncanny ability to detect weaknesses others might have overlooked.

What they didn't know was that *The Huntress* was merely the surface. Behind the screen was someone far more advanced than they could imagine. There were no indications that behind the screen was someone far more capable than they could ever comprehend. They never saw how deeply she understood the systems she touched, how easily she could slip past their defenses if she had chosen. She followed their *rules,* adhered to their protocols, ensuring that only the proper people had access, no one else could infiltrate where they didn't belong—except those chosen.

That was *The Huntress*—but *Timepiece* was something else entirely.

She wasn't motivated by greed like black-hat hackers—nor bound by ethical mandates like white-hats. She was a grey-hat hacker in its truest form. Unlike the criminals she tracked, she did not exploit for greed or destruction, nor was she bound by the rigid obedience of those blindly following the authorities trying to catch her.

Timepiece was most at home when existing in the space between order and chaos—walking that thin, volatile line. Excitement for her was found living between control and freedom, between secrecy and revelation. It was Timepiece herself that decided when to reveal her full capabilities.

But when she did, there was always fallout, silent ripples beneath the surface, unseen until they crashed into someone's world. Sometimes, it was a corporation scrambling to cover its exposed weaknesses. Other times, it was a government agency suddenly aware that its secrets were no longer as secure as it had believed.

The most dangerous fallout wasn't the kind that made headlines. It was the kind lurking behind the scenes, creeping up on those who never saw it coming.

Timepiece hadn't learned that every action, no matter how carefully planned, carried unintended consequences. The level of naivety at such a young age made her reckless and emotionally driven. She channeled her behavior as if the world itself was built on absolutes. Even her purest intentions could fracture into unintended chaos. A single line of code could shift power in ways no one could predict. A single truth revealed could destroy more than any one person.

Barely a week before Paul received the watch, Timepiece had been toying around with a new program. While testing it out, she came across a file called "JADE." With the word jade in it, of course it caught her attention. It caused her to pause. So, just out of curiosity, not expecting anything earth shattering, she took a peek. After all, all things jade were special to her.

Timepiece opened the folder. Once opened, multiple files started filling the screen—schematics, blueprints, charts, calculations. She wasn't sure upon what she had stumbled.

"What is this?"

She was totally caught off guard. She couldn't believe what she had unearthed. There, spread out in all its glory was the entire project. JADE explained in detail. She didn't understand all the implications, but she knew she had to do something. This was the primary goal of her study group, an opportunity to influence positive outcomes. So, she and the other members of her group devised a plan. It was the group that designed the watch. It had been Tim's creation. He joined the group as a way to escape—sitting on a stool in his father's watch repair shop.

It had been six months since the team had sent Paul the watch with the information about *JADE*. They left no trace of their identities on the watch. There was no way for Paul to contact the sender or even where to begin to look for them. It would have been too risky. The group was counting on that.

Risking it all, Timepiece was confident that he was one of the few people at the State Department they could trust. Periodically, she continued to hack into their database for information and updates, looking for various ways to keep Paul updated. They watched the government's system, looking only for data worth the risk. No one ever knew they had been in their system.

Several more months passed, still nothing.

Timepiece had been constantly watching, waiting for signs of movement in any of the files. A project of this scale, with multiple government agencies involved, should have some type of digital fingerprint. Logistical planning, updated calculations, contingency discussions, something should've been happening. She could tell the files were being accessed, but no real entries. No revisions. No chatter on the systems she checked.

The asteroid was less than two years from impact. If the laser was their best shot at diverting it, they should have been deep in execution by now.

So why wasn't anything happening?

The Audacity

Almost a year had passed since Jazzette and Paul had revealed the harrowing truth about the asteroid to her parents. Though life continued, an overshadowing tension loomed over them. There was always a silent reminder in everything they did, of a limited outlook on life.

Paul remained at his post at the State Department, despite receiving multiple offers for more prestigious positions elsewhere. He turned them all down—not out of loyalty to his job, but because he needed to stay close to the team working on *JADE*. If there was any chance of survival, of altering fate, he wanted to be at the center of it.

As the months passed, Paul began to uncover unsettling truths about the so-called contingency plans—on a global scale. At first, he'd hoped that preparations were being made for the good of all, that the government and world leaders were working together to ensure the survival of as many people as possible in case their diversion plan didn't work.

But the reality of it all told a different story. One far less noble. Protect the elite. Was that not what the government had always done? This carefully designed survival plan only accounted for the wealthiest, most influential individuals. The ones they perceived to be the most essential to rebuilding civilization. Scientists, politicians, billionaires, and those with the right connections were given priority, while the rest of humanity faced the consequences from a catastrophe they had no idea was going to happen.

Paul saw behind the mask—beyond the veil they used to manipulate the public. It was directly from their playbook. He had seen it all play out before, but never to this extent. This wasn't about saving the environment or humanity. The very people who had led the world into chaos were now securing their own futures, leaving billions behind.

It was inhumane, but he could see no one capable of stopping them.

For years, Paul was in a position to watch the government retreat further away from the constitution. Year by year, little by little, those that were elected were free to do as they pleased, not understanding— or simply not caring about the lasting results. Greed for power opened the door for a government committed to their own rather than the people as a whole. Now the world was left with global power in the hands of a few self-elected individuals.

Paul found himself livid at the audacity of them all.

As the countdown to impact continued, Paul knew he would have to make an impossible choice—remain silent and ensure his own safety or risk everything to expose the truth.

Every chance he got, Paul would analyze the data. There was something unsettling to him. He couldn't figure out what the uneasiness was about, lurking in the data, but he could feel it in the pit of his gut.

The updates were becoming more cryptic. The files were being coded in ways that didn't seem to make sense—at least on the surface. What used to be clear, organized data sets were now inconsistent, fragmented code. And then, there were others that appeared simply incomplete. Was it intentionally? He knew it was important but couldn't figure out what exactly was off. All he knew for sure; whatever it was, buried beneath the noise was a game changer.

It had been dreary over the past few days in the city. The rain had been relentless, and with everything going on, including the long hours going through secret files, it had taken its toll on Paul, and Jazzette didn't need her medical degree to see it.

So, after careful preparations, she decided to drive to the city and kidnap him. Thrown clothes in an overnight bag and a fresh suit arranged to be delivered to his office the next day. She had thought of everything. Paul needed rest, and this was the only way he was going to get it. A nutritional dinner and twelve hours of sleep were the prescription. It took some convincing, but Jazzette would not take no for an answer.

The next morning, just before sunrise, Jazzette was already awake and quietly tinkering around the room. She had Paul's athletic gear laid out across the chair before she woke him. The hotel she had selected was within jogging distance to the office. Yes. She had thought of everything, including a breakfast delivery waiting on his desk after his jog. This was her way of helping him reset. The weight that he was carrying was more than one person should.

The rain had finally lifted, leaving behind a cool breeze in the air. It was the perfect day for a jog. As he ran through the park, he smiled at his thoughts.

I am really lucky to have found Jazzette—beauty and brains. She was the perfect person for him and Zuri. They found each other at the right time…hearing his dad, 'in the fullness of time.'

Paul was halfway to the office when he noticed someone following him. He stopped, pretending he had to adjust his strings. With his body half turned he tried to get a good look at the person but was noticed. The person turned in another direction at the last minute. Paul was about to dismiss the incident, thinking *spotting a tail a couple times a year was to be expected*, but decided against it. So, he made a mental note, just in case it really did have something to do with JADE and his unsanctioned analyses.

When Paul made it to his office, he felt honored once he saw all the details that his wife had considered in planning his morning. He had been studying mathematical calculations for weeks. Now, after his night with Jazzette, he felt his mind had been reset—it was clearer, able to focus on the abstract as well.

It was later that evening, after digging through tons of files—he found it. Buried in an unlikely section in one of the reports, a place that should have been irrelevant to the trajectory adjustments, was a critical update to the calculations required to divert the asteroid.

The laser's target of impact had been previously calculated on erroneous data. The new angle calculations will only redirect the asteroid by a fraction of the angle needed to miss Earth.

The angle is off.

Paul felt his skin warming, skin changing hues—exposing the heat rising within, his heart rate increasing, pounding through his chest.

This was not the original plan.

Searching…What had changed in the last few weeks?

And then he saw it.

The miscalculations weren't just errors. They were errors that had been concealed, buried beneath layers of data, hidden in unrelated folders. Which meant that someone weeks ago, perhaps even longer, discovered the truth and had deliberately chosen to remain silent.

Paul kept searching…The window to alter the asteroid's path had long since passed. Impact was no longer probable. There was no chance of avoiding impact. It was no longer a question of whether or not there would be an impact, but *when* and *where*.

This error in the calculations not only would cause the asteroid to hit Earth, but with this new revelation—something more cynical seemed to be at play. They're trying to control the narrative. But *why?*

Paul kept digging.

The more he found, the higher the level of anger rose within him. He could feel his blood pressure taking the same path as the heat beneath his skin had only moments before. Each line read, each discovery made, gave way to a bigger medical crisis brewing within his body.

They were trying to deliberately predict a desired angle for the impact. They could then pre-determine the impact target—which region of Earth would absorb the greatest amount of fallout. They didn't want anyone to know that they had found the error in the calculations. But *why?*

They were still using the "space camera" to find their target.

Paul didn't understand. The error was caused by the data returned from the camera. It wasn't dependable.

Why would they depend on it this time?

The discussion shifted.

The miscalculations were caused by the mistaken data sent from the camera. Which was the results of human interference. It was not the technology, as they led the other governments' scientists to believe. A technician sleeping in the conservatory and accidentally knocked the camera offline. He didn't notice a piece of debris had broken the camera's beam.

Okay, why didn't the system account for anomalies?

Paul kept searching…

Anomalies must have been considered in the calculation; they're not that unusual. Ah! It had to be manually corrected in the system. The technician remained quiet, believing those couple of seconds were enough to distort the data. Convinced it wasn't that big of a deal, the technician didn't make the adjustments.

At least, so he thought.

Now that Paul knew *where* to look, he saw a pattern focused on financial and ecological developments. They prioritized the value of each region—rare minerals, energy supply, and agriculture. Not about how they could save humanity, or how they could save the world's resources for the next generation, but about *why* it should be them.

The conversations behind closed doors had become limited to the global rebuild. Regardless of where the asteroid hit, they would be in the most powerful positions, ruling the most valuable regions. All they had to do was analyze the data, make the decision, program the laser.

Who would suffer? Who would be spared? *Could they?*

Paul's mind raced, his thoughts were a chaotic storm of fear, anger, and disbelief. The sickening weight settling deep in his gut as he contemplated the implications of what he had discovered overtook all his senses.

This wasn't a simple oversight. He kept playing everything over and over in his mind. The dread of it all, the betrayal. They're meant to honor the institutions they were chosen to serve. It's part of the very system meant to protect the people.

Paul understood protecting the country he had fought for those liberties—but it was for all the people, rich and poor. He had never considered himself naïve but this. This was something dark.

Paul closed the files and pushed away from his desk, defeated.

The Daily's

The events of the day had overpowered him. It had been one set of very painful discoveries after another. It was late, and he decided just another simple reset was all he needed. So, Paul left for his studio apartment in the city. He left his car in the garage and pinged for an autoshare.

As soon as Paul got into the autoshare, he called Nate. When Nate didn't answer the line, Paul began leaving his message.

"Senior Chief," Paul said in a much too forced tone. He wanted to appear as if he had everything under control. But before long, he settled into his message.

They didn't need to actually talk to each other to feel better. They would leave detailed messages to one another. Never discussing the content of the previous messages when they did talk. They had settled into it as their style of communicating and stayed in touch with each other. They would work out much of their problems talking to an open line, hiding behind the one-way communication.

Paul got out of the autoshare a few blocks later. He needed air—a simple moment to breathe. Instead, he found himself standing outside a little dive bar called *The Daily's*. The sign glowed from the dim LEDs outlining its border. There was something about it that drew him in.

As soon as he opened the door to *The Daily's*, he knew he was in the right place. The smell of old money—deep burgundy leather, high wingback chairs, freshly polished wood. A chandelier long past its time, hanging as its anchor.

Paul allowed himself to smile as he walked towards the bar. This place felt like yesterday when certain things mattered…integrity, honor, country. He could imagine the days of old with judges, lawyers, senators, and CEOs making policies with cigars and whiskeys.

"All long gone." He said, snickering to himself when he realized he'd been talking out loud.

"Yes sir, this is exactly what this captain ordered," taking a seat at the end of the bar.

"Whiskey," he said as he motioned to the bartender."

The bartender gave him a nod of acknowledgement in return. Paul was staring at the reflections in the glasses behind the bar, emphasizing the dimly lit areas, shadowy figures engaged in their own world.

Shaking his head, "Some things never change."

A few minutes later, the bartender returned with a whiskey in hand.

"You can bring me a double next time. I'll be ready for it by the time you get back."

It was obvious Paul didn't want to be bothered. The bartender tried to make as little contact as possible. He had seen many customers come into the bar with the weight of the world on their shoulders. To him, Paul could have been the poster child for all who had sat in that seat before him.

The thoughts of the day were slowly fading into the unbelievable column. He had almost reached the mental level of dismissal when someone slid onto the barstool next to him. Paul became instantly annoyed. *Well, I be…Dang-it!*

"Rough day?"

The voice was firm but soothing, knowing but trusting. It caught Paul off guard. Turning toward the man, he was met with a pair of eyes that was full of empathy layered in authority, or…was that duty he saw?

"I've had better." Paul said as he made a quick scan of the man. He appeared to be in his late fifties, neatly groomed, tailored suit, but *cowboy* boots?

Something in his gut told him this was not a chance meeting. In a low monotone voice, the gentleman began.

"Captain Martin, please don't react to anything I am about to tell you. I called you by your military rank to give us some common ground. It is not important for you to know my name or how I have come to know any of the material I am about to share with you. There are some details, however, I am willing to share with you so that you'll be able to at least consider the possibilities."

Paul sat there frozen—in shock. He was thankful for his military training in the moment; it's what prevented him from blindly reacting. Between the whiskey and everything else going on, he couldn't grasp his current situation. Instinct told him this was not an official visit.

This was something else.

The stranger continued. "I am on the security detail for a powerful person in the government. I know you have accessed a particular project that you do not have clearance for."

Paul was about to say something when the stranger cut him off.

"Irrelevant. There is no need to panic. I am not here in any official capacity." He said, taking a sip of his drink to minimize suspicion.

"I tell you this because I want you to know you can trust what I am saying. We want the same thing. People have loved ones they want to protect too. The information I am about to give you is not complete. But I know you can find out more."

Paul was about to object when the gentleman stopped him.

"Please listen, we don't have a lot of time." His voice never adjusted its tone. "Some of it you already know."

He continued. "Project JADE used a space camera to predict the exact time and location of the beam from the laser for maximum impact. There was an outer space issue with debris. It caused the camera's image to become off balance—out of focus," looking up at Paul as if he knew Paul didn't understand.

"The system is programmed to send a message if it detects something outside its parameters. It sent an acceptance code to the control panel being monitored by a technician. The technician, however, was not at his workstation. And since he did not respond to the acceptance code, the camera's data calculations moved forward with the previous readings, and the new data was not included."

"Thus, the miscalculations, yes, I know this," Paul said, staring into his drink, which now seemed like a bad idea.

"As the asteroid fragments enter the atmosphere, they'll shatter into millions of pieces—most no larger than the size of golf balls, raining down over vast regions. Because of the miscalculations, our government officials are now certain they can manipulate the data to steer most of the rocks to a specific hemisphere as their primary impact.

"The problem.

"They have no intention of warning the countries in its path. Quiet whispers and scattered intelligence suggest they already know which regions are being targeted. They are using this as an unintended weapon for global control."

With that said, the gentleman stood up, took one last gulp of his drink, and walked away without saying another word.

Paul motioned to the bartender for another drink, but this time he asked for black coffee. He needed to clear his head. There was no time for self-pity. He now needed to find out which countries were at the greatest risk.

Fragments of the asteroid will shatter into millions of pieces…each one, even at that size, accelerating in speed, slamming into earth, causing widespread damage as they hit the ground.

Paul's mind raced as he followed the spiraling path of possibilities, each more disturbing than the last. This wasn't just a natural occurrence; this was man playing games with lives being traded for strategic advantages of power. Paul was operating in survival mode, he was human, and his mind began to recognize the other side of the problem...the solution.

It wouldn't be a global catastrophe. We could be safe.

The shame hit him instantly. His jaw tensed, slightly shaking his head in disgust, angry at himself for even entertaining the thought, for allowing the smallest flicker of relief. No, this wasn't his doing. He hadn't chosen this. But the idea lingered like a bitter aftertaste. In the end, his world would likely be saved. His thoughts betrayed him.

He knew—it could be worse.

Paul hadn't realized it, but he had made it back to his office. He had already started looking at other data. Inadvertently, he had uncovered the corruption behind it all. In a cynical kind of way, Paul chuckled to himself, lowered his head in shame for all mankind, including himself. He always thought he was a good man. He had always tried to do what was right. To him, this was just another example of an impossible situation.

Good must be subjective, biased to whom.

Now that he understood the gravity of their situation, he knew the role he must take moving forward. This was greater than just him, the survival of his loved ones depended on what was done next. He could no longer depend on the government to do the right thing, it was being run by a select few with their own agendas.

There was a sense of resolve though. He had felt the same determination when he locked eyes with Zuri. It had been twenty years since he first made the promise to always protect her. The same promise he made to Jazzette on their wedding day. They were his priority. He would not give up on the world, but his primary focus had to be his family's safety.

Paul began gathering intelligence about the governments that had the highest survival rates. If anyone knew about the omitted data, it would be them. The more he dug into the data, the more he found out that their survival plans were much different from the others. Just like the stranger had said, instead of telling the other government officials, they decided to pretend it was not there—bury it. But just in case it was discovered, they could always say the information was not known by them either, for deniability. Paul instinctively wanted to blow the whistle, but he knew this would not benefit his family and would probably destroy everything.

Decision

"Hi Stephen, I am at the airport on my way there. New updates have come in that we must discuss. I will explain when I get there this afternoon." Paul hung up before Stephen had an opportunity to ask questions.

It had been months since the kids had moved to the compound. They missed their dad and would be overjoyed to see him. Life for all of them had quickly changed. No one complained or even pulled anyone else into their own personal dooms' day anxiety. There was, however, a quiet absence that they all felt. In the end, they knew...each would be alone.

Zuri dropped out of the academy to help get things ready on the compound. The timeline of the crisis was quickly approaching. There was a lot left to be done, and she prided herself on her organizational skills. Paul had taught both girls the value of readiness.

While Zuri was handling the flow of things at the compound, Zoe was still on the East Coast managing the finances for the compound. Whenever supplies were needed, Zoe would either order them or provide a means of purchase. She had ensured everyone had been assigned responsibilities and the financial resources to take care of their areas. Once the gates closed, there would be no going back.

Clarice had converted a spare bedroom into a classroom. The twins and Lizzie could continue their studies from anywhere, and she was determined to keep their days structured and the weight of pending disaster shielded as much as they all could.

Stephen and Clarice had tried to think of everything. Busy throughout the day carrying out the plans that had been created the night before. The kids being there helped with how they all were dealing with the crisis. In their effort to minimize the gravity of it all for the kids' sake, they managed to control their own emotions.

Paul arrived later that day.

Clarice had prepared an early dinner and served it out on the patio. Summer had been unusually kind. By the time everyone gathered at the table, the sun had already started its descent behind the peak of the mountainous wall surrounding the compound.

Hiding behind a canvas of vibrant colors—deep oranges bleeding into cascading purples, brushed with faint hints of pink, the fading light was making its exit into the night. Warm breezes from the heat of the day were quickly being overtaken under the cover of darkness. The jagged walls of the mountain caused a constant flow of air throughout the compound. Its natural designed shielded most of the rain and snow. It was unexplainable, even for two science degree professionals—a microclimate on sacred ground.

They had barely picked up their forks before Paul started to explain. He was erratic in his tone and delivery. The man who had been trained to be steadfast, even under interrogation, couldn't find his composure. He was fumbling to find his words.

Once he got started though, Stephen could barely keep up.

"The government agencies made a gross mistake in their assumptions about what would happen once the asteroid entered the atmosphere." Stephen looked even more confused.

"We already knew this. It will break up into millions of pieces."

"Yes, that's true. When the asteroid collides with the atmosphere, the accumulation of gases held in place lining the atmosphere would be quite volatile. This is nothing new. The scientists had accounted for this but was assured that even if the small rocks burst into flames, they would quickly dissipate.

The level of those gases continues to increase because of global warming. Climate change, once an insignificant data point, compensated for, has now become critical. When the asteroid stones break up, and pass through the atmosphere, at that rate of speed they will collide with other gases and cause tiny explosions, breaking the stones up even more into even more pebbles. Once the pebbles hit the ground at that speed and temperature, they will destroy everything they impact."

"Dad," Lizzie asked, "How come the scientist didn't know this?"

Zuri chimed in, whispering, "They knew, they always know."

Stephen agreed with Zuri but seemed to have relaxed somewhat. He had started to see an actual silver lining.

"All of them would not be projectiles by the time they hit the ground. People would just have to take shelter," Stephen said.

But Paul quickly rebuked Stephen's thought before it found voice.

Paul squared his shoulders, and stood up straight, as if he was in the field, commanding his troops. "I have made a decision to do nothing, or rather, not do something."

Everyone looked at each other. Lizzie and Clarice made menacing faces at each other, as if they were waiting for details to a dark secret mission.

"There was other intel I discovered. Before I tell you about it, I want you to know I explored every possibility, and there is nothing we can do that would make a real difference." Paul continued with a certain authority in his voice. It was more out of fear than anything. He was in full survival mode now.

"There is information that our government, in collusion with another government, is going to keep this information from the other three agencies. They can, with reasonable certainty, calculate where the greatest impact will occur. Based on the new calculations, we—the U.S. will have less of an impact from the asteroid fragments. The other continents will be in direct alignment with most of the fragments as they enter the atmosphere. This will basically eradicate those countries. We will have minimal fallout if their calculations are correct.

"Only a select few know of this. The other members of the coalition have no idea. They believe they are still working with each of the government agencies with the same chances of survival. I discovered this by accident. If I let the other governments know, this would end in total chaos, possibly war. My focus is our family and the best chance to keep us safe."

By now, Clarice was pacing back and forth. She couldn't believe what she was hearing. Suddenly she stopped, staring at him in disbelief. *How could he even think this was an option?* Paul was better than this.

Finally, after holding her disapproval back as long as she could, she interrupted Paul.

"This is totally unacceptable," she snapped, her voice sharp, words chosen. "We cannot live in a world where we deliberately withhold this type of information. It could potentially save millions of lives—for what, just to protect our own."

Paul tried to speak, but Clarice would hear none of it.

"Where is your faith? If we allow this to continue, would not God hold us accountable—this is madness. I know you might not believe like I do, but the blood of Jesus is real—for all. This lack of faith in Him to protect us is unnerving. This cannot be what we stand for. He has entrusted you with this knowledge. The responsibility of it all, and not the power to choose. Are we not doing the very same thing the select few in the government are doing."

Not intending to go that far, Clarice softened. "There must be a way to leak the information to the other countries without jeopardizing our security."

Paul didn't acknowledge the softening. He had felt the sting.

"Think about what you are saying. I have considered all the repercussions. There is no workable solution. This is the only one that protects us, our family, from what is coming. I know you do not agree, but the decision has been made. The things I have done have been to minimize the effect this has on us in the end.

"If I leaked the information, countries would go into a panic. The very people we are trying to save will never be saved. Where would that leave us? If I thought for one moment, this information could make a positive difference, I would shout it from the rooftop.

"These government entities have not made one attempt to inform their people about the potential of this threat. They have not allowed them to make one decision for themselves, despite their claims of democracy.

"Millions of people will suffer, yes, including people here in this country. We will all be part of the casualties. There is no reason for us to lessen our chances of survival by trying to save those who cannot be saved."

Paul was sick of people using God as the excuse to do or not do. He turned to Clarice without holding back.

"People are always preaching about trusting God and asking for wisdom, well perhaps wisdom is being used in this decision, and not emotions. Ram in the bush? Well, let them believe Him for the ram in the bush." Paul's frustration had taken *front* row and *center* seat. "The decision is made."

Clarice turned and left the room.

Insert Chip—Check

Paul came to reason with himself, or at least some semblance of reason. The turmoil had quieted. And after months of wrestling with the thought of it all, he had finally settled the issue. Regret and what-ifs no longer had a place. If he believed there was a God, then it was out of his hands now, and up to God to deal with things on a global level. He knew in his heart, it wasn't out of faith he relinquished control, but out of self-preservation. It was the only way he could live with his decision—with a license to move forward. He had found his *just in case disclaimer.*

It had been several months since he had shared any updates with the family. Everyone had found some type of resolution. They each threw themselves into their assigned tasks. Tensions had remained heavy, and Paul didn't want to deal with any of the repercussions from his decision—again. Not because he didn't care, but nothing had changed for him. The military had taught him to be a man of action—decisive, relying on intel—logical and strategic.

The governments were still moving forward with their plans, and so must he. He was not going to allow his family to depend on him while he sat on the sidelines *waiting* on a sign from above. He knew it was his responsibility to make the hard decisions if they wanted to have the best chance of surviving whatever came next.

Funds were being transferred from other government agencies to an account named *JADE 2.0 Rebuild.* He was not sure why or who was behind this new group. He had tried to search the government databases with no luck. Access given to him by Timepiece was limited. He did, however, discover the group was not part of our government.

Only a select few knew what was happening with the *JADE* project. Not even Congress was aware of the severity of the crisis that was quickly approaching, nor the devastation that would be left in its path. The entire project was still being managed in the dark. This new group had collected billions of dollars. But *who* were they, and *why*?

Paul knew that more would eventually come out. *He had done as much as he could.* It was a resounding thought, constantly reminding him. He really just wanted to be with his family, to spend as much time as possible. Depression and frustration living in the same space for him, torn. He felt as if something was missing, something critical. But he could find nothing, he was limited.

Paul looked at the watch, noticing the time. Lost in thought, he reminisced about how the watch was given to him by Timepiece had started this unsolicited involvement in all of it. Staring at the watch, but with no true focus, a slight glow behind the "9" on the face of the watch broke through. Paul removed the watch from his wrist, to examine it more closely. He hadn't remembered seeing the glow before. He rolled his finger over the "9", taking special care, and with a slight touch of pressure he heard a click.

But nothing happened.

Putting the watch back on, Paul said, "Nonsense, I need to get away."

Just as he was about to leave, he got a notification. It was an encrypted email.

Subject Line: JADE 2.0 Rebuild.

There had been a link between the watch, pushing the "9" button, and the transmission of the email. It was a security measure setup by Timepiece. Paul was afraid to open the email at work, so he left the office and went home. He knew it would be safe there. Zoe had previously set up a security system inside their home.

When Paul got home, he went directly to his home office. He closed the door, sat at his computer, and opened the email. As he read through it, his expression wildly shifted. Alternating between shock, disbelief, and dread. Line by line, everything unraveling right before him. Months of updates, buried beneath layers of encryption, and deception. Through all the noise of the last couple of years—the political spin, the internal deflections, global manipulations—there, in front of him, laid out in detail—the truth about *JADE*.

Space expedition…Mars…exploration in space…can't be!

It wasn't a random phenomenon from a runaway asteroid—it was the unintended results of the Mars Space Program.

But how? He kept reading.

The space program crew made the initial discovery of the asteroid. But it was in the direct path of Mars—not Earth. In an attempt to redirect the asteroid, the technical team toyed with unrealized potential of experimental technology. The experimental prototype of the laser system was used to nudge the asteroid off course. It didn't work the way they thought, however, it did influence the direction of the asteroid.

The asteroid's path had been indeed altered…success for Mars, devastation for Earth.

Instead of redirecting it into space, the amount of energy used was only powerful enough to slightly alter the path—sending it directly into Earth's orbit.

Technical plans that had been stalled or altered—based on *erroneous data*. Progress that was impeded—*power grabs and struggles*. Failures that had been noted—*coded in documents as strategic pivots*.

The truth before him, behind *JADE* revealed more than he could have imagined. This cosmic disaster was the result of man's need to play God, refusing to recognize his limited knowledge and capabilities.

This wasn't fate, this was squarely on the back of man's ambition.

Finally, Paul fell on his knees and for the first time, he began to pray, to a God he wasn't sure he trusted enough to believe in. But like most in the time of need, the moment of truth was laid before him, this time he truly accepted there was nothing else that could be done.

Paul woke up still on the floor the next morning, curled up in a fetal position. The rug was wet from the tears he had shed most of the night. The email had left him drained and overwhelmed. He was defeated. But with that defeat came a resolve unlike the last five times.

It was a great deal of information to wrap his head around. Still in a daze, Paul ran his hand over his face, removing the tear stain residue. He went into the kitchen for coffee where he found Jazzette sitting at the table.

"Good morning," Jazzette said, surprised by his presence. "I didn't hear you come in last night. Did you sleep in your office?" She asked as she continued looking at the morning news.

Paul didn't respond.

Jazzette glanced up, looking in his direction. She noticed the look of loss.

"Are you okay?" she asked.

He just walked over, grabbed her by the hand, and pulled her to himself. Standing there, with his wife in his arms, he wept, causing her to freak out.

"What's wrong? You're scaring me."

Paul took a step back, grabbed her hand again, as he led her to his office.

Pulling out the chair, he said, "Read this. I received it yesterday by Timepiece, the same person who sent me the watch." Jazzette sat down and began to read. When she came to a natural break, she calmly asked, "How much time do we have?"

"I am not sure."

They both just sat there quietly, contemplating their next move without consulting the other. Finally, Paul spoke. "The one thing we know is our timeline has decreased. So, for now, we will work as if we have limited time to complete all our transactions and arrive at the compound."

"Agreed. I'll call everyone."

Paul interrupted and told her he needed to stay a few more days just in case Timepiece needed more from him. What Jazzette didn't know, and Paul would later find out, the government had already set a date to fire the laser.

Time had indeed run out.

Paul hadn't given Jazzette all the information that was in the email. He deliberately left out the part where Timepiece had given him instructions on placing a microchip on the State Department's server. This would give them complete access to all information—past and current. There were a million laws they were breaking, but it was too late to debate.

The next morning, Paul arrived at the office like any other day. It was the day before a long weekend, and the atmosphere was noticeably quieter. Most of the senior staff had taken the day off, leaving only a skeleton crew of lower-level employees. That was exactly what he had counted on. It meant fewer eyes, fewer questions.

The only way Timepiece could hack the complete system was if she had direct access to the data. No remote breach, no digital backdoor, just old-fashioned direct in-person spy work. And Paul was the only one who could make it happen.

It was time.

Paul made a deliberate tour around the floor the servers were housed on, eyes scanning the area, taking note of the movement of those working in the vicinity. In the lounge, he lingered by the cold storage unit, pretending to select a drink. A few unsuspecting people came and went, engaging in light conversation—part cover, part penance for him—small talk masked the guilt of the impending disaster gnawing at him.

Finally, he saw his opening. The moment had arrived.

He slipped past the glass security doors. Using the access code supplied by Timepiece, Paul found himself standing in the server room, his breath shallow, his heartbeat, steady but rapid. The room was bathed in a glow, with the only illumination coming from the countless LED indicators flickering on the towering racks of servers. His spine chilled by the constant hum of the cooling systems blowing the constant flow of cold air. The sound focused his thoughts. Sleek, black server towers stretched in endless rows.

He wanted to run. Every instinct screamed at him to turn back. But there was no one else. It had to be him. No one else had the clearance, the knowledge, or frankly, the nerve. He had been on countless missions, each one testing his limits. Yet this one wasn't just another job. This task required an emotional detachment from his country. This felt wrong. He had always worked under the country's banner, but the country's banner could now be the one thing to put him in a dark ops hole.

Pull the server card. Place the microchip. Push the card back in. Simple in theory.

Paul exhaled slowly, steadying himself as he navigated to the exact server rack Timepiece had identified. His gloved fingers worked quickly, locating the correct card. He took one final glance around, then pulled it from its slot.

Instantly, something shifted. A low hiss filled the air.

His stomach tightened, holding his breath instinctively. Beneath him, puffs of white clouds started to ascend from the grates on the floor.

Gas. Security protocol must have been tripped. Timepiece didn't account for this. Now what?

"Damn it!" he whispered to himself.

Panic level increased, take a deep breath…now finish, running is pointless.

He knew if he failed, he wouldn't get another chance. His only choice was to finish what he had started.

Hands moving instinctively, arrow pointing left…insert chip.

Paul learned how to walk himself through any high-risk task. It was his way to complete a task and double check at the same time. It was a technique he learned as a kid, later to be diagnosed with generalized anxiety disorder traits. Repetition had become the only thing that helped to manage his anxieties.

Placing the chip precisely where Timepiece had instructed was extremely high-risk.

Pull the server card out—check…Place the microchip—check…Arrow pointing left—check…Push the card back in—check.

Every second felt like an eternity.

Paul waved his hands over his work as validation. He then managed to quickly leave out of the side door. As he left the server room, he passed several members of the security detail housed in the building.

"What's going on?" as a deflection.

"Go back to your office, Mr. Martin."

Paul was startled. He didn't slow down but turned his head as his eyes search for the familiar face. Almost running into the security guards approaching the server room, he saw him. Paul recognized the security guy he had met several months ago in the bar. He knew at that moment he would be safe.

What Paul didn't know was that each time someone entered the server room, an image and timestamp would be recorded. They would have known the moment he accessed the room. Mr. Head of Security, the name Paul had given him, had been in the security control center for the building. Before the alarm went off, Paul was seen.

Tradition and Grace

Paul continued coming to work every day after he inserted the microchip. It was brutal for him, each day knowing his time, their time was running out. He clung to a hope and a prayer that the government would do something, anything. Hoping there was still time. At the least, give people a clue so they can decide on what preparations they should make, and when they need to be made—even if they can't pinpoint the potential location of the impact. But there was nothing.

Now, his potential last day at the office had arrived. He had put in for family leave and wasn't sure if there would be anything left to come back to.

He had finally convinced himself there was nothing left to do that couldn't be done in Nebraska. No more calculations, no more theories, no more waiting. The outcome was inevitable.

Paul stood glancing out of the same window that he had almost twenty months ago, when he first learned of the impending catastrophic event. He now longed for his first encounter with the potential destruction of the world. A lot had happened since then. Things had gone from bad to worse—using extreme energy to divert an asteroid, to a global siege of power—murder, extortion, betrayal, crime at the highest levels of modern society.

His eyes glided across his desk, lingering on the events of a life once thriving, now replaced with potential death, at best the singularity of destruction for some—most.

His eyes paused, taking intentional notes, putting to memory the personal items he had collected over the years. His fingers hovering, finally settling on two framed photos. One of Jazzette with the entire family, the other of Zuri and him. Staring at the two of them, Zuri in her baptism garments. She was special in more ways than he had known.

His vitals slowed, lost in the memory of the day the image was taken. It was a perfect reminder of their bond—bound by her spiritual awakening and his witnessing of the ritual.

It had been an enlightening trip, parts of which he had never mentioned to Zuri. It was the only lie, even if it was a truth not told, a lie by omission between them. Paul remembered the promise they made on the trip back: to always be honest with each other. And since then, he has tried to keep that promise.

It had taken nearly ten years for Paul to gather enough information about her heritage, and he planned the trip to coincide with her birthday. Sixteen was a special age in their culture, an invitation to step into adulthood, walking with purpose in the same faith of past generations.

Now, with him standing there before the framed reminder of her baptism, Paul rewinding the events in his mind, felt like he was standing on the sidelines as he did over five years ago. Zuri dressed in white standing there before two lines—tradition and grace.

Men dressed in their traditional garments on one side, women in white robes with violet sashes lined on the opposite side—tradition mirrored to grace. The ground covered in a white cloth, made a pathway between them.

Paul remembered feeling too unworthy to be a part of it, even if he was an outsider, standing on the sidelines. He was in awe of the sincerity of holiness etched in every aspect. It wasn't like anything he had ever seen. A devotion, grounded in true belief, evident by the look on their faces.

Zuri walked between tradition and grace—promise and hope. There were little children walking ahead of her, laying rich red flower petals before her on the ground. Paul had never seen flowers like those, assuming they only grew in the region. As her feet stepped on each flower, each petal would release a fluid.

Paul remembered being so caught up in the ceremony, he actually considered the possibility that the flowers were shedding tears, while moments later, shifting his position to perhaps bleeding from the bruises created with each step?

Even standing there he wondered what type of flower it could have been.

The entire ceremony felt like a wedding, and she was the bride. *But I suppose what is a wedding but a commitment.*

Paul took a deep breath staring at the picture, he could almost smell the memory. Jasmine mingled with the scent of the burning incense. The heavy smoke rising from the arbors, carefully positioned around the area.

As Zuri followed behind the line of girls, they made their way down the aisle. Soft and inviting music was being played in the background. Once the children made it to the end, they took their places on the right-hand side of the spring. There was another group of kids, this time all boys. They came in behind Zuri and made their way to the other side as Zuri made her way to the edge of the spring.

A spring that felt almost out of place, but you could tell it had been placed there by design. An oasis carefully placed—carved out from the beginning of time. Surrounded by landscape that was beyond beautiful. Paul recognized the words in his vocabulary were too limited. He had tried many times over the years to describe what he had seen but could never give it full justice.

Flowers framed the rocks around the spring. In some parts, it looked like the flowers were growing straight out of the rocks, no soil necessary—same flower in different variants of reds and blues, its essence blended together in its bud—each unique in design. Flowing water from an eighty-foot waterfall set as the spring's backdrop, filled the spring, bringing the entire area alive.

The Elder was already standing in the water—waiting. He was dressed in a black robe, unlike what one would expect him to be wearing—the traditional white robe. Instead, he wore the opposite. His garment was black, with cords of purple, red, blue, green, and yellow, braided together as one. It made Paul think, pulling from growing up in the church.

Ah, baptism—nothing but a controlled death. Vivid hues of life of a promised made and a promised received.

As Zuri was making her way to the Elder, Paul could tell she was struggling to keep her balance on the slippery stones as she descended deeper into the water. The water must have been cold. He could see her shivering. It was to her breast by the time she stood next to the Elder.

The spoken words seemed to echo off the trees surrounding the clearing. To Paul, it was not an ordinary language, but words spoken in some ancient tongue. Paul couldn't understand any of them, yet the power behind them was undeniable. A power that resonated as the spoken words were heard, revealed by the vibrations rippling from the trees.

Paul smiled again. 'Even they responded.'

The Elder then dumped Zuri backwards into the water. When she came up, the music that was once soft and inviting, became rhythmic and celebratory. One of the women, grabbed Paul by the hand, gave him a wrap, and led him to the spot where Zuri was to walk out of the water. This time, her exit was different—she was strong and confident in her steps.

Paul took her by the hand and wrapped her. The children had traded their flower petals for tambourines. They led them between the lined men and women again. This time the line collapsed behind them. By the time they got to the end, everyone was dancing and celebrating. Another set of women led Zuri to a tent where she changed into the garment on the picture.

While she was changing, Paul had asked the elder what he had said.

"Zuri is a bride to the spirit now. She will be used in the end for the revelation of God's glory. She will lead her assigned to safety before Him." The elder went on, "You have a role to play in that journey. She will need you to help prepare her, and in the fullness of time, you both will be—and others, will be standing as a guiding light before many."

He never told Zuri what the Elder had said. He wasn't sure he believed it or if he should take it literally. So, he hadn't, to this day, said anything. They never discuss what had been said nor what it meant when she was baptized.

Thinking about that time made him smile, but then that smile quickly turned to despair. Paul wondered at that moment if this was the beginning of what the Elder had said. He thought of her village as a whole, knowing there was nothing he could do for them if their region had been chosen for collateral damage.

As quickly as the thought came, it was replaced with the richness of the land and its people, there would be no way our government would not want them as a partner. They would save it, even if they couldn't control it.

Paul went back to the task at hand. He carefully placed the items in his bag, taking one last look of resolve at the office, letting go of what had been his second home since his parents died. Then, without ceremony or fanfare, no pomp and circumstance, he walked out.

The weight of finality pressed down on him with every step. As he moved through the building, walked the corridors for the last time, he exchanged nods and casual goodbyes with coworkers who had no idea what was coming. He smiled, even laughed at a joke someone made in passing. But inside, he felt the crushing sorrow of knowing the truth.

No matter what happened next, he would never see them again. And for many of them, there would be no after.

Paul struggled with the choice, whether to tell them, to warn them. But in the end, he knew it would only be selfish at this point. Panic would spread like wildfire with an even greater number of casualties. Letting them live out these last moments in peace, unaware of what was coming, was the lesser cruelty—yet, lesser determined by whom. He knew he was no better than the others. Nothing was certain for them.

It was a cold truth. A necessary one.

As he stepped outside into the evening air, Paul inhaled deeply, staring at the sky.

Whether it was wisdom or fear—restraint or complicity, he had made his decision. He wasn't sure anymore, the moment he stepped into the light of day, he knew he was not better than the ones who had built the lie in silence.

But for now, he would have to trust that it was the best decision, considering.

Paul walked slowly across a campus, built for his country by unrecognized members of his country. His stride became uneven, constantly turning his head to take a look back for the last time, each time—a snapshot of the glass building being lost in the distant realm of time. The familiar surroundings weighed heavily with the potential finality of what might lie ahead. His movement became a struggle. He felt as if he was standing in quicksand. The more he tried to remove the thoughts of doom, the more they gained control, choking the air out of him.

The dread pressed against his chest like stone. His breath came in shallow gasps. He blinked back the burn of tears, his jaw clenched, his composure hanging by mere threads. And then, unable to carry it any longer, he stopped, in the middle of the oversized walkway—frozen between time.

He felt life move around him.

Soldiers in uniform, young children on field trips, business personnel, even visitors on holiday—talking, laughing, conducting business. The hustle and bustle of life never slowed. No one came to his rescue—he was officially in distress.

A few glanced in his direction, eyes staring at the conflict on his face, and then scanning the box in his arms, taking mental note of the small plant peeking its head out—quickly turning away as if he didn't exist.

He stood frozen, visibly unraveling, the weight of his decision etched deep across his heart. Yet, none stopped—not a single soul paused with a gesture of concern. The rhythm of self-preservation had replaced the days of helping others. In a place built on policy and principles for the betterment of people, compassion had also become a casualty. The Good Samaritan was long gone.

It was then that out of his periphery he saw a shadow in movement, just beyond the garden path. He felt an appeal, drawing him towards it. He could see its long limbs cascading downward like a curtain of green silk—a weeping willow tree. As often as he had passed this way, he had never seen it—before now. Perfectly groomed, with an opening in front it as if to summon you into its warm embrace.

He edged his way to one of the two benches, perfectly positioned beneath the tree. The light bouncing off the bushes cast a reflective background for the cascading tree limbs as they stood guard over all who dared enter.

Paul put his box of personal items on one end of the bench and took a seat on the other end.

A few minutes later, a man dressed as a priest was walking nearby. His cassock was neat but oddly untethered, the white collar startlingly clean, as if it was the first time worn. He slowed when he noticed Paul with his head bowed in his hands, not like he was praying but sad, heartbroken, contemplating life. The heavy stillness of a man whose soul was unraveling.

"Opportunity." The man smiled to himself as if he was a kid about to do something good.

As the priest moved closer, he could see Paul's fingers moving from his forehead, down past his eyes. Each finger moving rhythmically, as if playing the piano, always returning back to the center of his forehead.

"Mind if I sit for a moment?" the priest asked, voice warm yet carrying a faint rasp. "My feet, I tell you, the walk to the building seems to get farther away."

Paul first thought was he sat out of concern for him. Then he realized, as it became obvious the man was making up an excuse to sit, the priest was new at his job—not just the overwhelming scent of incense hoovering over clean, crisp clothes, but his demeanor—an overzealous approach to help.

"I am here to visit my sister," he said, testing the waters for conversation. "Do you work around here?"

"I did," Paul said pausing, and looking up at the priest with tear-stained cheeks, "work here. Today is possibly my last day." Doubt radiating from Paul as he responded—then an unspoken warning in his gut, against talking to this stranger.

"Your choice," the priest asked lightly, "or God's will?"

Paul paused, contemplating the answer, no longer adhering to the quiet warning to shield himself. "I honestly do not know. My choice, so to speak. I had to make a decision." The question had pierced him to his very core. It felt like it had been planted within long ago. And now it had spouted through his dirt.

Paul went on, "One that I thought would be best for my family...but it comes at a cost."

The man tilted his head, the faintest smile curling his lips—not readily interpreted—not kind nor cruel. Something in between—more ego. "Just because you did what you believed was right for your family does not mean it was in or out of God's will."

"I don't understand."

The man leaned in closer—his voice low, words deliberate. His words baiting the trap—deceit wrapped in truth. Paul was on the hook now. The priest's ego had taken over.

"It just means, what you chose was already known. What you were going to do, or what you did or didn't do is known beforehand. God is not caught off guard, in the end, if it is His will, it will be done. If not you, there is no need to worry, He will just have someone else to step in. We all get to choose without judgement."

"Um," Paul said not aware his current state had allowed himself to be influenced. The priest believed what he was saying. But part truth and part ego does not always end up the way it should.

"You did what you thought was the best thing for your family, and you should. If you don't take care of your family, who else is going to do it. You know God expects you to have common sense. He allowed you to find information for you to take care of those you love. You are the head of your family."

The priest stood. Satisfied with himself, he walked away. Paul could feel the air warming the farther the priest moved away. The conversation hadn't made much sense, but Paul felt fate had a hand in it. After all what the priest was saying was not technically wrong, so he must be right. God wanted him to relax and not worry about everyone else—the ram in the bush and all. He has people that are in a much better positions to save the masses. He wanted him to save his family, especially Zuri. After all the Elder had told him as much when they were in Africa.

Long after the man had gone, Paul was still sitting on the bench, staring at the empty space beside him. The words kept circling back, heavy, and deliberate, as though they'd been designed to anchor themselves in his mind.

God's will…God already knew, know…you're not called to save the masses…not necessary…He has others already assigned for that!

Paul never considered the man's words were not meant for him. But no matter how good intention the priest may have been, it only added fertilizer to a seed planted in his time of vulnerability—a mixture of doubt, unwarranted resolve, and quiet surrender to self-preservation.

Diaper Poop

Paul took the same route home he had taken the first time he learned the truth about the asteroid. The original timeline had been changed, but it was just as difficult to accept despite all the preparations made and data collected. Even more so now.

Over the months, he had tried to tell as many people as possible without jeopardizing his identity or source. His family came first, and nothing was going to prevent him from doing whatever it took to save them. Still there was an obligation to humanity—one that could not be denied. With the guilt nagging at them, Paul and Jazzette devised different ways to release enough information to let those closest to them find refuge. They needed to ensure the information they gave was right.

So, they waited.

Country music blared from the car speakers, the bass turned up so high it made the windows rattle. With each beat, the car would shake slightly, the sound bouncing off the interior of the car. The drive home was long, and Paul was grateful for it. Gritty drawls and brokenhearted verses of the country singers made him feel like he wasn't alone. Jazzette preferred the blues, but there was no substitute for heartbreak, like a good country song.

Jazzette and the girls would normally have complete control over the music. Whether they were at home or in any of the cars—R&B, hip-hop, jazz, but never country. The only opportunity to take full advantage of his favorite was when he made the long drive home—best when he took the scenic route along the coast. If he was in his car—and alone, he had autonomy. It was his time.

Now, there was always room for a good prank. Zuri and the twins would often sneak in his car, replace his music for some old school hip-hop and crank the volume up. He would get in his car to pick up where he left off, only to be met with his least favorite. They loved to tease him. And over the years he would expect a prank but never let on. Secretly he loved it just as much. It was their thing.

The scenery was incredible. The weather was perfect!

Paul thought about how weird it was when the priest sat down next to him—just when he desperately needed to talk to someone. Before the oddity of the conversation lingered, Paul thought of his grandfather. One of their conversations came to mind.

It had been a sweltering summer afternoon when he was a little younger than the twins. They were walking in the park, eating a snow cone. It was so hot that day, and Paul could feel the ice melting over his fingers. His memory isolated the heat.

Paul chuckled to himself. Wonder why I always remember the weather?

Paul asked his grandfather, "Are we going to be alive when the world comes to an end?"

His grandfather just smiled at him and said, "There's only one who knows the exact time. But I can tell you one thing with certainty, when it happens, it'll be "in the fullness of time."

"God's time?" Paul had said, not really understanding what it meant.

Paul remembered thinking it was the strangest thing to say to a kid. But then his grandfather had always told them these weird things. He would laugh at the time, but as life continued, Paul would come to understand the wisdom in them. The words would come flooding across decades—only to land at just the right time. It had happened many times over the years.

"Keep living," he would say.

Paul wondered if this was the "fullness of time" for the world. He wondered if this was the beginning of the actual end. But there was an explanation and there was nothing spiritual about it. Everything had a logical reason for how and why it was happening. There was enough going on without him having to complicate things for himself, so he dismissed the thought, and the *priest*.

The next morning, when the alarm went off, Jazzette said "off."

The alarm silenced, and the news for the day came on. She lowered the volume before leaving the room. A few minutes later, she returned carrying a tray with coffee and pastries. She placed the tray on the nightstand, then crawling back into bed, and curled up against him.

Jazzette knew that this would probably be the last time they would spend time in their own home. The last time that she and Paul would make love in their own bed. There had been no real moments for them. As much as they loved each other, the strain of everything had been a constant barrier between their intimacy.

Jazzette knew his heart, and even though he would not say it, he was hurting.

She eased up against him, molding her body to his, whispering, "It's our moment. Let's take advantage of it."

Paul looked into her eyes, leaned forward to kiss her. She gently stopped him, nudging him on his back as she kissed his ear.

"Close your eyes. Allow me!" With her hand softly on his chest, fingers barely touching his skin, she traced the lines of his life, each visibly telling his stories. He had seen so much chaos, so much heartache and loss in the world. She needed him, but he was the one on the verge of a breakdown. This could not—would not be his story.

"You have been through so much," she said, voice tenderly acknowledging each scar as she examined them with the touch of her fingers. She wanted to heal the unspoken brokenness of each wound— the cause forcing him to carry, and with each kiss she willed it.

"You are everything to us, to me." She whispered. "More than that, I want you to know, I am *everything* you need me to be. I am here for you. Always."

Paul laid in their bed—conceivably for the last time, unable to respond. Tears slowly trickling from the corners of his eyes.

Jazzette wiped them away with a kiss. He was hurting, and she could feel the weight. Just for a little while, she wanted him to be first. She wanted him to know someone knew.

His body was perfect. She outlined every detail with an appreciation that he had chosen her. Staying in the moment, she thought how lucky she had been when they met.

Paul tried to keep from moving, but his despair had quickly turned into desire. Every nerve in his body was on fire. He was being over stimulated, and nothing was going to stop him from exploding. Then he heard.

"Diaper poop…"

They both laughed. The tension broke, Paul relaxed, and Jazzette continued.

Whenever they were making love or having an intense disagreement. One just had to say, "diaper poop." It always made them laugh or at the very least, regroup.

When Lizzie was less than a year old, Paul would always wake up early to run. He had the same routine…take a quick peep in to check on her before he left. This one particular morning, when he cracked open her door, the odor hit him like a punch in the face. There was no escape. The entire room was contaminated. He looked for Lizzie. There in the midst of this runny—chunky poop was Lizzie sound asleep. She had taken off her diaper in the middle of the night. Poop was everywhere. The bedding had to be tossed.

It was one of Paul's most impressionable memories. Tracking through the jungle, recovering mangled bodies was nothing compared to *diaper poop*.

Lying there, they were completely lost in each other's orbit. For most of the morning they stayed there, taking in the last moments of just them. They talked about their life together before everything.

Paul and Jazzette laughed, made love, cried…together!

Finally, the time had come, and they both knew it. With nothing left, they looked at each other and said, "let's do this."

They jumped up, showered, and continued gathering their things. With no words spoken, Paul's last official act was grabbing his sword off the wall, just before he walked out of the house.

It was indeed time; Operation Survival had begun. It was now their path to walk. Each time they had gone to Nebraska over the past 2 years, they had taken supplies. Now, all there was left that they needed was packed in the car. Their next home would be their refuge on the compound.

This wasn't the end. Life was just anew.

They hadn't got out of the state before Jazzette leaned back to admire the landscape as they drove farther away from their home—the only home Lizzie and the twins had known. She found herself deep in thought, recalling the events of the past year. They had tried everything to put supplies in place and set up survival bunkers for people if they needed a place to escape. They wanted to make sure they had a chance to make it.

Jazzette felt awful that she couldn't tell her coworkers, friends, or other members of her family. They had played a major role in her life. Even if she took the risk, they would never have believed her. She didn't fit the profile they had boxed her in all her life. But that didn't deter her, she created a mockup disaster plan that practically told everyone what was happening and to prepare. But of course, they all thought she was being extreme. One day, before it's too late, maybe they will remember they have it.

They bought five homes across the country. The houses stood for a place of refuge for those they loved. They were strategically selected for their location and access. If any of them found themselves in the wrong place and too far away from home, they would have a place to go. Each of the houses was gated for security, had a basement, a private water source, and stocked with generators and food. Their plan had been to tell their family and friends across the country the address and entry code to unlock the doors. Only a select few knew about the weapons also in the safe houses.

Just then, the phone rang. It startled Jazzette, yanking her back to consciousness. Zoe's voice came squeaking across the speakers.

"Dad, we were wrong...the timeline is wrong," Zoe was frantically trying to get her stepdad to understand. Her words garbled.

They knew something was terribly wrong. Zoe only called Paul *Dad* when she was sorry about something.

"Zoe, what are you talking about, and how could you know we are wrong?"

Jazzette chimed in, "wrong about what?" Her tone, soft to mitigate the hysteria Zoe was projecting.

"Dad, I'm Timepiece! They fired the laser or some weapon from Germany a couple of hours ago. It won't work—if it hits the target, it will only break off pieces of the asteroid. I'm sorry. Dad, I leaked the information about the miscalculations to the other countries. I had no idea something like this would happen."

Paul didn't say it, but his first thought was *now you are sorry.*

"Paul, what have I done. Germany didn't trust the other governments, so they acted alone. No one knows where the impact will be, or how they calculated the angle."

Paul was flabbergasted. He pulled over on the side of the road. Trying to not seem freaked out for Zoe and Jazzette's sake. Paul finally broke the silence, "Timepiece, Zoe, whoever? How could you not tell me this?"

"I'm sorry, Dad. I knew you would not have listened to me if you had known I was Timepiece."

"You're right about that!"

"See. I knew it…I found out about JADE initially by accident. I will explain everything, but first you must listen to me now. When you put the microdot on the server, I was able to look at all the files in real time. Germany tried to redirect the asteroid with a secret weapon they had developed for military purposes, later abandoned. The weapon was on the dark side of the moon. None of the other countries knew about the weapon or I didn't consider that they might try something like this. They felt like the other governments had double-crossed them, so they put their own plan into action. A couple of hours ago, they fired the weapon."

Repeating herself, "Dad they fired the weapon. It will collide with the meteor in less than 72 hours. Dad, our scientists believe it will break up the meteor, not redirect. It will simply break up into large pieces. Those large pieces will enter the earth's atmosphere, in random locations."

Jazzette looked at Paul, "Can you get in touch with Nate? Maybe he can help confirm."

"Zoe, we will meet you in Nebraska in two days."

Unlimited Credit Line

While growing up, Zoe spent most of her time locked away in her room, lost in quiet rebellion, developing code to conquer the world, one data point at a time. Even now, after being away at school for the last couple of years, not much had changed. The emotional safety net she had woven for herself was fully in place.

After one of the family's discussions and the preliminary plan to move together in Nebraska, Zoe had been quietly accumulating things from her own supply list. She had created several financial accounts. None of them probably legal, but who would know without revealing what *JADE* really was. Besides, there would not be enough people to even investigate the missing funds. The funds were being diverted to a special account from several other government accounts. By the time they figured out what was going on, the threat would be over.

The team needed money. It was just that simple, no need to hold a family meeting to debate right or wrong. It was the reality they were living in. Neither her parents nor her grandparents had that kind of money. With everything necessary to get the compound ready, money could not be an obstacle.

Although Stephen sold his interest in his family business to raise the funds for the construction, it wasn't nearly enough. Little did he know he sold his interest back to himself, via a government account, at an inflated rate. So, all Zoe had to do was transfer the funds to special accounts for each of them. Stephen would have never accepted had he known.

It was important to Zoe, so the one thing she could do was to make sure that when they came out of this, his family's legacy was still intact. Besides, when everything was over no one would be able to depend on the government to help the less fortunate. If they survived, they would step in.

It was obvious, Zoe belonged to a different world, one woven with her own set of rules. She oftentimes drew blurred lines, her ethics often bent, but her version of integrity could never be questioned.

Yes, she failed often, but she would always call herself out for it. No one had to give her a pat on the back when she did something right nor cut her legs from under her when she did something wrong. She always thought she was grounded within herself. But the events of late had caused her to question everything. She wasn't as sure of herself as before. She realized she was not equipped to deal with such tragedy. Zoe was playing with a group of individuals who had been in the game far longer than she'd been alive. She might be *Timepiece*, but behind the mask was a girl who longed for approval—but was validated by the win.

Zoe looked around her dorm room, as though she had forgotten something and couldn't quite pinpoint what it was. With an uneasiness stirring, she made one last stop to the bathroom. Standing at the sink, feeling the warm water on her hands, Zoe's mind drifted to a nothingness. She wasn't quite sure how long she had been there, but as the water cooled over her hands was just enough to pull her back to the reality. But not before she got a glimpse of *herself* in the mirror. She didn't recognize the person staring back. There was a strange look that didn't feel like her own. This wasn't the first time she had felt like someone else was living her life. She knew she didn't belong there—but pretending on a daily basis had become her norm.

She had always thought she was in control of Timepiece. But somewhere along the way, she had lost herself in the code. Little by little she had allowed her narcissistic version of justice to take over through her AI. The code was learning Timepiece in the most destructive way, making adjustments, and manipulating the input data. Zoe's personality had been shattered when her father died. There were now multiple personalities living within one body, wrestling with the code from a broken spirit. Zoe, at her core, was in charge. But when things got overwhelming or complicated, the other wreaked havoc on her life—both good and bad!

Always hidden—even from her.

Observing the faint one-sided snarky smile in the mirror, Zoe turned as if triumphant in her spirit, and sent a simple text 'on the way' to the team. She grabbed her computer bag, a small suitcase, threw her bow and arrow quiver over her shoulder, and walked out of the door, never looking back. As she approached the parking lot, she saw the van and her friends standing next to it. Everyone had a backpack hanging over their shoulders.

"Ready?" one of them asked.

Zoe answered, "Ready." She put her stuff in as one of the other guys held the van door open. They drove off.

After the shock of finally telling her parents she was Timepiece, and giving them the latest update, Zoe needed to breathe. Her group had become each other's sounding board.

There were five of them. Each with their own little quirks, unique abilities, and interests. They had been a close-knit group for several years. Most of whom had gone to high school together. Working alongside one another in the group or telling each other their latest conquest was everything to each of them. They balanced one another—trusted one another.

In them, Zoe had found her voice.

They had all come from different backgrounds—yet there was something exceptional in the way they each saw the world. They had an innate desire to show the world its potential. They lived by their own underlying code: *expose the truth, redistribute the wealth, protect the innocent.*

They wanted to stop the select few that were trying to prevent the world from being its best, believing in climate change, democracy, fairness. As a whole, they had a firm belief that the government was infiltrating every aspect of the average person's life—and not for good, but power manipulation. Even though they wanted the same social interactions that others wanted, for them, everything was built on a foundation riddled with trap doors. The world was not the way people wanted to believe it was.

So, when the opportunity came to prove it, hacking into systems and exposing the hypocrisy that was being fed to people, even globally was a prime directive. They quickly realized no one's native country or heritage was any better than the next. Deception and secrecy were a shared universal language. Sure, some countries were more advanced than others in technology, but man had no borders—corruption was across the globe.

It wasn't strange when the group decided to stay together instead of with their families. They thought together they could somehow help be more effective, even save lives. They were in unique positions to control the information that was being released or rather, not released. So, they told their families everything they knew to protect themselves, then headed to Nebraska with Zoe.

The group had only been on the road for a few hours when the van pulled up at one of the safe houses. Zoe had been shipping equipment there for over a month. They had decided that directing supply deliveries to the safe houses would minimize any financial detection. Zoe created an unlimited credit limit from a group called *JADE 2.0 Rebuild*. Each time she ordered something, she would automatically regenerate a new number. They would joke about how the government was supporting their efforts. This is how she got all the computers, servers, and any other technology that she could think of necessary to provide them with the security they would need, along with any updated information. The problem with *JADE 2.0 Rebuild* was that her stepdad thought it was another government secret team. They were not only working against each other, but Zoe, was also working against the parts of herself she had not confronted.

"Let's stay here tonight. This will give us a chance to see if there has been a new update in the system." Gerard, Zoe's boyfriend, said as he set up the link.

While searching for the latest, he noticed a deleted file. The log was gone. All they knew at this point was the weapon had been fired, with no updates as to what would happen once it made contact. They hadn't had time to dig around for more information. For now, they just had to wait.

They shut everything down for the night.

Gerard walked into one of the bedrooms, only to find Zoe, in tears. Trying to comfort her, he told her everything would be okay. They would find a way to survive.

"Even if everything is lost, the two of us will re-populate the earth." Patting himself on the chest, jokingly said, "Me Adam, you Eve."

Zoe smiled but inside she knew there was very little that could be done. She considered praying but didn't really believe in God. Her parents had been raised in church but over the years, had allowed the world to influence what they once believed. Yes, there was a higher power. There must be, but for there to be Jesus, Son of God—the sacrificial lamb, it was too far out there. Her biological dad, as well as Paul, had a limited view on the subject. All they knew was science could explain most things.

Shadow Stairs

Spread out across the table, the compound's construction plans were a testament to the years of work and preparation. Each section was taking shape beautifully, evolving from mere ideas into a fully realized refugee camp. When Clarice and Stephen first set out to design a self-sustaining space for their family, they had only planned for 50% sustainability in the event they were cut off from the grid. They could live off the land for a short time.

A lot of the construction had been completed, but with the looming asteroid threat, their priorities had shifted. Urgency replaced caution, and their vision expanded. Now, they had no choice but to accelerate their timeline and raise the bar for what their home could withstand.

In the early days, when they first got the land from Jack, they would stay up late, dreaming about all the possibilities. They imagined a place where they could grow and sustain a constant food supply, irrigated by its own water source.

The compound sat in a uniquely orchestrated position. There were fissures running down the inside of the encampment. The water from the rain, melted ice and snow would run along the fissure lines. In early spring, it looked like waterfalls all around the sanctuary. About fifty feet up on all sides of the mountain were openings that lead into the mountain itself. The water would disappear within the walls, only to return on the outside of the mountain, making its own waterfall as it gushed out twenty stories above the adjacent river. Stephen and the architects had found a way to create a freshwater source for the entire compound. It was the perfect place for their family and future generations. It was to be their legacy.

Before implementing any major decision, they always ran their ideas by Jack. He never required it, but they all felt better. To them, Jack and his wife were part of their family now. His wisdom, experience, and quiet approval gave their efforts meaning, grounded in something greater. More than that, they wanted him to feel at home, to know that every change they made honored the gift he had given them.

Just as Stephen and Clarice had invested all of their resources to the vision, they both recognized Jack and his wife had invested everything as well. After all, they had sold them the land at a price far less than it was worth. What they were building wasn't just an investment for themselves; it was an investment in the land, a promise to protect and cherish. Clarice felt a powerful spiritual connection there.

During phase one of the construction, while working on the warehouse section in the back, one of the construction workers lost control of his truck and rammed into the mountain. The impact of the truck caused part of the mountain to collapse, revealing a section no one knew was there.

There, laid out in front of them, rugged terrain had broken away, revealing a small cave. But as they began to clear the debris and explore further, they discovered something far more significant. Behind the bed of rocks was a massive, forty-five hundred square foot chamber.

Stephen was ecstatic. He didn't know exactly what to do with space, but he instinctively knew it would be special. So, it seemed only natural that while the construction crew was building the compound, he would have them reinforce the cave for future use. Never could he have imagined he would find a value of such magnitude.

3:33AM.

Clarice lay there with her heart racing, sweating. Stephen woke her from what appeared to be another horrific nightmare. In a fear-stricken state, Clarice looked at the clock. She realized she must take the dreams more seriously. They had started coming more frequently. *Why 3:33, always 3:33?*

Stephen asked, "What are the dreams about?"

Clarice started to cry, "I don't know. They never make sense. All I have are fragments." Looking directly at Stephen, "What if this is the actual end?"

He responded in his usual calm self. "I don't believe it's the end of time." She looked almost disappointed in his answer.

"But we don't know, what if this is really when Jesus comes back? Stephen, everything was being destroyed. Is it possible?"

"Come, lay here." As he opened his arms for her to lay on his chest. *What am I supposed to do, Lord how do I help her.* "Close your eyes. Be in the moment. Take your time, even if it doesn't make sense, just try to describe what you see."

Clarice laid there, eyes closed, mind drifting…focusing on Stephen's heartbeat, steady—strong. It was aligned with the tick of a clock, soothing.

Clarice began, looking back into the night, ahead to the future. She was reliving the vision and once she had a grip on the fragments, the words started to flow.

"Standing on the edge of the mountain on the northeast corner, is a lion. The lion has a blanket made of gold twine, woven together, thrown across its back. The blanket's border has tassels, draped on each side, long but barely touching the ground, extending out on each side. They look almost like wings, closed but ready for flight, with given command. Sitting on the blanket is this figure. I can't tell exactly what it was or who it was. It appeared to be a man with feet like sheep hooves, and hair made of tiny white clouds that seemed to dance in the wind. He wasn't all there. I mean he was there, but you could see the essence that made up his body. He wasn't a solid entity. More light, than substance."

It was heartbreaking for Stephen, listening to Clarice continue to try to describe what she saw. The more she tried, the crazier the descriptions got.

"There was a glow in the background. I can't tell if it's the sun behind the figure or some other strange light. In one hand there is a sword, and in the other hand a container, umm, a basket. Yes, it's a basket." Straining for clarity.

"In the basket, there are balls of different sizes and various shades of fire—white, red, yellow, blue. The colors appeared to be merging—always in motion, together, with an outer glow."

Clarice lifted herself and looked at Stephen again. This time as if some great revelation had come into focus. "The balls were not burning!"

"That's good, right?"

"As the figure swung the basket back and forth, He yelled, '*The fullness of time is near.*'

"The balls fell out of the basket. Now they are lit—igniting immediately after they left the basket."

Looking at Stephen again, "I have been having these reoccurring dreams for over a year. Bits and pieces coming into more clarity recently. I never told you about it because it has always been so impossible to explain. I didn't want you to worry thinking I was overstressed or losing my mind. That the dreams were the result of what is happening with the asteroid. But Stephen, this time it was different. There was even more."

"How so…"

The more Clarice told Stephen, the more focused everything became. She started telling him as she recalled the vision of a past revelation.

"In the midst of this gray darkness, clouds, signaling the onset of a massive storm in the distance. Thousands of people stood in line, their figures illuminated by a golden glow, with a towering gate centered ahead of them. The line stretched endlessly, winding through existence, yet there was no sound. Only this eerie stillness, as if time itself had stood still.

"At the front of the line in front of the golden gate, radiating a celestial light, its brilliance reflecting off their white robes flowing like water, stood two angels standing guard. Their blue sashes seemed to be used as an anchor holding them in place. They would have floated away without them.

"I stood near a threshold. Close enough to witness, yet too far to grasp the truth of what was unfolding before me."

Stephen noticed an occasional tear make a trail down Clarice's face. But, he said nothing. He just allowed the events to occur naturally.

"I looked to my right, there was this grand staircase, leading upward, a pathway made of woven light in the midst of darkness. Each step glimmered with an ethereal glow, not stone or wood, not anything physical, but light itself. There was a vastness to the scope of what could lay ahead, beyond the clouds.

"Suspended in a cradle of light, veiled in the transparency of mist, the platform revealed itself at the top of the staircase, serene, eternal, as though the stars had parted to make space for it. At the far edge stood a tree, ancient beyond reckoning, its roots woven into the very fabric of time.

"It didn't simply live—it remembered. It was life. Its vast roots disappeared beneath the surface of the platform and beyond, reaching through the folds of time, threading through memories of a world created long ago. Branches, sending and receiving signals across galaxies, leaves dancing, moving, not because of wind, but in rhythm, swaying to the original harmony that must have accompanied the Word as it called the universe into being.

"There was no melody to hear, no notes to follow, only a resonance, deep and immeasurable, that moved through me like the memory of a dream I never had but always knew. The music of creation. I couldn't hear it. I felt it.

"I knew the tree was not planted as a seedling. It did not grow, it just came into existence.

"To my left, another staircase descending. Its steps darker, heavier. Those that were on that staircase were led into shadows that seemed to pulse, swallowed by any trace of light until all that was left were tiny, punctured holes of dim light, fading farther with the descent. Unlike the path above, this one sent a shiver through me. I dared not stare too long. The air around them was thick, suffocating. I didn't want to see where they led. So, I looked away.

"I was drawn back to the angels. Just as I looked towards them, I saw Paul. He was standing in the line directly in front of the angels, talking, but not talking--listening. It was more like he was receiving some sort of instruction. I couldn't hear them. But Paul bowed his head as if in agreement. The angels lowered their swords in unison, stepped aside as Paul entered."

Clarice focus shifted remembering an important fact.

"Wait, Stephen, you were on the staircase, with the twins."

Stephen said out of impulse, "The shadow stairs."

They both chuckled. "No, the one on the right, I could see you there holding the twins' hands. You're looking around as if you were looking for someone else, and then, nothing more."

Clarice just laid there, she was at the end of all she knew to be true about her dreams. Stephen was at a loss for words. He didn't know what to say to Clarice. His head was swirling with what to think. He believed in Jesus, there would be a second coming, and the end was possible. He was just not sure this was that time. There seemed to be so much data, scientific data about what was happening.

The only words Stephen could muster were, "All will be revealed in due season my love, whatever season we are in, we are in it together."

Clarice relaxed now, feel asleep in Stephen's arms. It was her safe place. However, sleep did not come so easy for him. He could not dismiss the dreams. Knowing the Bible, he toyed with the idea of it all.

He eased his arms from under Clarice's head, trying desperately not to wake her, and crawled out of bed. Before he realized it, he was outside, heading towards the warehouse.

He needed to think.

Get In, Get Out

As soon as he broke the plane of the door seal, he heard someone say, "Couldn't sleep either?" Stephen looked around the warehouse, and there was Jack, working on an old piece of equipment.

"Clarice finally told me what had been troubling her. She believes she is having visions of Armageddon, the return of Jesus or something."

Jack looked at Stephen and simply said, "Is she right?"

He didn't respond the way Stephen had expected. Hearing something like that didn't seem like anything out of the ordinary to him. Jack had previously had a strange conversation with Clarice. So, to hear this from Stephen was nothing unforeseen. She hadn't remembered the details when she confided in him, but it had been enough to make her feel unnerved.

The question landed heavier than Jack probably meant it to. Stephen blinked, caught off guard by its bluntness. He paused, then answered truthfully, without flinching.

"I don't know," his voice low but certain. "I really don't know."

Jack began telling Stephen a story.

"When I was a young boy, I lost my parents in a senseless killing. Oh, now, the local sheriff at the time said it was an accident but on the reservation, everyone knew differently. My father was the Chief of our community. They had selected him to be chief as his father was before him. Because of the richness of the land, people wanted to take the land back for themselves. They had been trying for over a century.

Remember, they had no idea how valuable the land was when they gave it to my people.

"My ancestors taught each generation how to protect the land. As time passed, they became more sophisticated in their attempts. The people thought by killing my father, the land would be lost to our people, but my father used their legal system against them to protect both our people and our land. So, when he died, I vowed to take up the mantle. I went to law school, specializing in land law—the west type of land law.

"While in law school, my roommate was a descendant of slavery. He was the protector of his land, also. His ancestors had been given the land as payment when freed. The owners of the land could not afford to pay their wages, so they worked on the land in return for ownership. The land was in the middle of Texas, prime real estate. Over the years, the battle had been fierce from all angles. But Lawrence B. Johnson was determined to keep the land in his family, just as his ancestors had done.

"One year during winter break, I went home with Lawrence. His great grandmother gave each of the young men a scroll. The scroll's paper felt ancient.

"On the scroll was written,"

'In the beginning was the Word,

And the Word was with God, and the Word was God.

He was with God in the beginning.

Through Him, all things were made.

Without Him, nothing was made that has been made.

The light shines in the darkness, and the darkness has not overcome it…John 1:1-3

The Word became Flesh…John 1:14'

"When we finished reading, she handed each of us a pen and asked us to sign our names as an acknowledgement.

"'Whether you believe now—or not,' she said, her voice both gentle and firm, 'you can never say you hadn't heard the truth, at least once.'

"Her philosophy was, if we were to believe everything else that is said for salvation in the Bible. She needed us to first believe He is who He says He is.

"Over the years, I have grown to love the Word. So, to you the question asked becomes a simple one." Focused, looking directly at Stephen with all sincerity, making sure there would be little doubt as to the importance of what he was about to ask.

Jack chose the simplest words. "'What if she is right—or—what if she is wrong? If you truly believe He is who He says He is, then it doesn't really matter.'"

Stephen turned around, looking back at Jack with a true sense of hope. Neither said a word. Jack continued to work on the equipment for the vertical farm, while Stephen quietly exited the warehouse.

Stephen crawled back into bed with Clarice. She had barely moved since he left. He eased in next to her, placed her head on his chest, and welcoming arms drew her closer. He was at peace, and he could now help the love of his life deal with whatever God had in store. *Jack was right, it didn't matter, let God's will be done!*

The next day, Clarice had a late lunch laid out on the patio. It was a beautiful fall day. The leaves on the trees had started to change color. It didn't last long though; the cool nights were causing the leaves to quickly fall to the ground. The sun was still high casting its warmth over the compound. Its high reach from the heavens set the stage for the evening sky.

Clarice would often sit outside or take long walks after lunch. It gave her an opportunity to think about life and what it all meant. She thought of her dreams, feeling as though there was a correlation with what was happening. There was a familiarity about it all. It had been a while since she had the first dream, and that same period since Paul told them about JADE. She eventually pushed the thoughts away, but with the frequency over the past year, and now with new details, the possibility of it all had consumed her. There were so many unanswered questions. All was so very confusing.

For now, Clarice decided not to think of it.

***

"How was your trip? The girls are already here." Clarice said to Jazzette.

Jazzette looked as if there was no hope. Just then Stephen walked in, full of excitement.

"Jack and I got the water system working. The tower for the plants is ready for seeding. We just need to set up its own source of light with the generators, which should be here next week."

"That's wonderful," Jazzette said, turning with a slight quiver in her voice. She moved towards him with a sincere smile, and tear-filled eyes. She hugged him, whispering, "Thank you."

"Where's Paul? I thought he would be with you." Stephen said, reducing the conversation to a more casual one, lighter.

"The boys, of course!"

The boys had been waiting at the entrance for their parents. They knew it was their parents the moment they saw the lights come on as a car passed the outside gate. The twins were running along the driveway as the car quickly caught up to them. They tried to run alongside, but couldn't keep up, especially with all the pushing and shoving of each other, laughing hysterically in only a twin's language. Once Paul stopped the car, he got out, half running himself to meet them. Paul hadn't realized how much he had missed them. It was through their innocence he found the courage to hope. It was a much-needed moment for him.

The lightheartedness of the conversation inside the house quickly returned to the reality that caused the tears. By now, the tears had increased in intensity and flow. Jazzette began with the latest. She explained in detail, emphasizing although they were not sure of the exact date, they had decided everyone would begin their journey to stay, for good.

What Jazzette did not know, and Paul would later find out, Germany had already realized the firing of their weapon would also cause the angle of impact to be off target, and several large size pieces would probably break off, entering the atmosphere.

After dinner, gathered in the living room, interacting with each other, all the adults were of high spirits.

Paul holding a glass of whiskey, twirling it in the glass, watching the small cubes of ice trade places with each other, looked at Sarah, saying, "You always bring the best drinks."

Clarice smiled at her friend, and Sarah responded. "What else do you bring to a couple who has everything? You know me, I try to make it easy, and memorable."

Clarice chimed in, validating the response. "We never forget where we were nor what we were doing? It's all tied to the food, the alcohol, but especially the wine."

"And only the best." They were all laughing.

With everyone having had a little too much to drink, Stephen stood up. "We should all get some sleep," he said, his voice calm but edged with the weight of what lay ahead. "Tomorrow, we start the final stages of preparation."

The room quieted with a distinct shift in the air. It felt like something invisible had clicked into place. The heaviness of responsibility settled on their shoulders.

The night passed with an uneasy stillness—the air, still too quiet. It felt like something unspoken—yet protective, lingered over it. Dreams came and went without rest, never landing in the soft terrain of peace, just fragments, disjointed, and vague. And then the sun rose. Quiet, abrupt, as if the night had been cut short before it could fully exhale. A sunrise that felt too sudden, too soon. Had time skipped a beat?

There was a shared sense realized the night before, unspoken but understood. Things had shifted. Nothing would be the same now. Everyone had their role, their direction, their part to carry forward.

Morning broke clean and cool. The air was sharp with clarity, the sky an uninterrupted sweep of blue, no clouds, no softness. Just sky.

The boys came down the stairs, still half-asleep.

"Boys! Great, you are awake. Get your dad. We're on a mission. No time for breakfast!"

The boys looked at each other, no breakfast. "What's wrong with G-Mom? No breakfast!"

"Dad!" one of them called, with the other one trailing behind. "G-Mom's looking for you! She said you gotta go on a mission!"

Paul stepped out of the bathroom, wiping his hands with a towel. "A mission, huh?" he said, glancing up at the boys. He threw the towel at them before kneeling to tie his boots. "Did she say what kind?"

"Nope, but she looked serious. Like...going on a mission serious."

"Like the time we used all the sheets and blankets off our bed to build the tent outside, serious." the other added.

Paul stood up and smiled halfheartedly, putting on his jacket. "Got it. Apocalypse-level serious."

The boys didn't see their mom before they left. Jazzette walked in afterward and said to Paul, "I overheard. You know Mom, and they say I'm the one over the top."

"Yes, they do, exactly why I love you!" He said as he leaned over to kiss her. "Well, let's see what fresh hell your mother has in store for me." They both laughed as he walked out.

"Good luck, I love you." Toying with Paul.

"I will probably need it. Love you too!"

The boys giggled as they marched ahead, calling out orders like tiny generals. Clarice stood waiting at the edge of the courtyard, arms crossed, eyes focused.

Paul joined her with a half-smile. "No breakfast?"

She looked over at him. "No time. We have a short window. I've packed a morning snack."

Clarice drove the truck through the driveway. In the backseat, the boys were already locked in a playful scuffle, elbows and laughter flying.

"Quiet boys, we have to come up with the plan."

"Plan, what kind of plan?"

"Plan for what."

"We are going to steal a helicopter."

"Oh boy!" they shouted in unison, practically vibrating with excitement. To them, it was finally a real mission. Zuri always created little missions for them. This time it was real.

Paul, sitting in the front passenger seat, didn't share their enthusiasm. He glanced sideways at Clarice, and she returned the look with a sly smile and mischief in her eyes.

"Don't worry," she said with a sarcastic assurance. "I've got everything under control."

Clarice kept her eyes on the road, her voice calm but there was an edge to it, the kind that hinted at a mind already five, ten steps ahead.

"A few months ago, Sarah and I attended a fundraiser at this exclusive resort. You know, one of those places where the air practically hums with pretense. A group of us were having drinks, mingling, when we overheard a man bragging loudly about his son's company. He couldn't stop gushing about their latest project, an aircraft prototype that's completely AI-driven,

"It's not just any aircraft—it's a cross between a helicopter and a plane. Not only that, but it has drones too. Little ones, capable of flying ahead or hovering just above ground?"

Turning to face Paul, and making a side note, "Didn't you notice the guys creating a helopad on the property?" But not waiting for an answer she continued.

A furrow settled into Paul's brow as he tried to conjure the memory, just a vague impression of a slab of concrete tucked away on the far edge of the property. He hadn't thought much of it at the time. Certainly not enough to imagine it was a helipad. If anything, he'd assumed it was just another foundation, laid in advance for one of Stephen and Clarice's ever-evolving projects. With those two, it could've been anything, from a greenhouse to a boat dock. He'd learned not to ask unless he was ready for the full schematic.

"Zoe and I did some digging after that night," Clarice continued, her tone never wavering. "Turns out, the helicopter is being kept at the company's headquarters. They've converted the roof into a hangar, fully equipped, with hanger type doors and everything. It's clever, almost too clever. It's hidden, no one can assess it unless from the elevators, or enter from above. Which puts it in a perfect position for us to..." looking back at the boys, "borrow."

Paul nodded slowly, more out of reflex than agreement. He had long since accepted that when Clarice set her mind to something, the rest of the world had little choice but to keep up. She wasn't reckless, not by a long shot. She planned like a general and executed like a surgeon, each move considered, measured, and tested in her mind long before it ever reached the real world.

"And Zoe?" He asked, though he already had a good idea of where things were going. Asking was just a mere illusion of formality; he was used to keeping his hesitation under wraps.

"Zoe wrote me a program." Clarice said, her eyes narrowing slightly as if the thought of it pleased her. Zoe was brilliant, and Clarice was so proud. "A backdoor into their security system. We'll ride up in the elevators, no questions asked. We just need a few minutes to distract the guards—just long enough to get the access we need. That's where the boys come in."

He glanced at the rearview mirror, watching the boys in the backseat, completely unaware of the weight of the conversation.

"Distraction," Paul said quietly, the plan beginning to take shape in his mind.

Clarice smiled, a flash of something sharp in her eyes. "Exactly. They'll give us the necessary time to get to the elevators. We'll have a small window, and a better chance during shift change."

"Are we really going through with this?" Paul asked, his voice low, more to himself than to her.

Clarice's gaze remained fixed on the road, the weight of his question lingering in the air. "We don't have a choice. The clock's ticking." Clare's voice became competent, assuring. "It might seem as if I hadn't thought this through or I am putting us at some unnecessary risk, but Paul, search your heart. You know me better than that!"

Paul's eyes were still glued to the backseat, smiling at the boys, he allowed them to linger a moment longer. He swallowed the knot forming in his throat. With a sigh, a silence fell between them, but it wasn't uncomfortable. It was the silence of two people who had long ago stopped questioning the other's commitment or capabilities. They just moved forward.

One of the boys leaned forward between the seats, his olive-toned skin catching the filtered sunlight, eyes hazel in color, bright with excitement, still giggling, oblivious to what they were about to do now, nor the crisis ahead.

"So, what's the plan again G-Mom?"

"Yes, what exactly is the plan?" Paul said smiling at the boys.

Clarice's lips curved into a small, knowing smile. It wasn't smug, it was the kind of expression she wore when a plan came together. The puzzle pieces were falling into place in her mind.

"The plan's simple," she said, calm and focused. "We get in. We get out. You two keep the guards distracted. And once we're on the elevator…" she paused, glancing at Paul with only a slight turn of her head, "we don't look back."

Paul's eyes flicked from her to the boys, then down to his hand, which had unconsciously tightened around the door handle. There was tension in his shoulders now, the kind that came not from fear, but from the cost of responsibility.

"I'm in," he said finally, voice quiet but grounded. He knew he couldn't hesitate any longer, he never really had a choice—it wasn't because of the plan or himself.

"Clarice… it's one thing to drag me into this, but the boys?" He looked at her now, eyes steady. "They're just kids. I can't allow this. Not like this."

Before Clarice could respond, one of the boys leaned forward between the front seats.

"Dad, we can do it." he said eagerly. "We want to help."

Paul opened his mouth to protest, but Clarice cut in gently, her voice softening, almost maternal.

"All they have to do is what they always do—go to the security desk, start one of their usual spats, try to outdo each other." She smiled, turning her gaze briefly to the back seat, watching them with a fondness that outweighed everything.

"You'll go in and ask to use the bathroom. Tell the desk guard your dad had to run upstairs for something. Nothing strange. Nothing that sets off alarms."

Clarice gave them a piece of paper with a name on it. "Memorize this name just in case they ask you who is your dad."

"Morgan Dixon, he works in engineering."

She turned back to Paul. "Meanwhile, they'll be stalling. Arguing about who gets to ask, trying to one-up each other, creating just enough noise to keep attention where we want it, off the elevators."

The boys exchanged glances, wide-eyed and practically vibrating with excitement. The seriousness of the mission never quite caught up to them, but the thought of being part of something big, something real was all they cared about.

One of them opened his mouth to speak. They were about to bombard her with questions, but Clarice raised her hand with practiced precision.

"Yes." she said, already anticipating them. "Let them show you to the bathroom. Use it. Stay calm. Don't wander. Once we're on the elevator, it's done. You just wait for us like nothing happened."

"So, Clare," Paul asked, his voice low, guarded, "how are the boys supposed to get back home?"

Clarice didn't answer right away. Her hands rested calmly on the wheel, but her eyes betrayed the calculation behind her silence. Then, with a half-smile that didn't quite reach her eyes, she said, "Oh, how could I have missed that. Change of plan. Just kidding." She turned toward him, her expression sobering. "I'm going in alone."

Paul tensed. "Clarice…"

She cut him off with a glance. "It's already set. I go up, do what needs to be done, and come back down the same way. No theatrics. No one else gets involved."

They both knew it wasn't that simple. There was no such thing as just going in. And especially not with what was at stake.

The truth hovered in the silence between them—this could be a one-way mission. But someone has to stay behind. Someone has to make sure the boys have a way out if it falls apart. It had always been that way—quiet sacrifices tucked beneath the surface of a larger plan. Paul had spent months holding things together, carrying the weight no one else could, or would. He hadn't expected to be part of this. But now, there was no going back.

Clarice turned to face him fully, her voice quiet, but resolute. "Everything's been set up for me. You were never supposed to go in. You've done enough, Paul. This time…allow someone else. We're all in it together."

He looked at her, really looked. He saw the determination carved into her features. He had never admired her more. She had always had his respect, but this was more. He had been on a lot of missions and seen the toll just before the start. But Clarice had a confidence. She knew it would all work out accordingly. The knowledge of what could possibly come was not a part of the plan, just faith. So, she just smiled.

"My plan," she said softly. "I choose."

She stepped closer, resting a hand briefly on his arm.

"If I don't make it out, don't tell Stephen. You haven't seen me. If it works, he'll see the plane soon enough. He'll know what we did."

She laughed. Winked. And before Paul could say another word, "Give me ten minutes," she turned, walked toward the building, and didn't look back.

Clarice slipped through the side door with three minutes to spare. Her heart pounding, but the sight ahead made her grin: the boys were in full distraction mode, effortlessly charming the guard like she had watched them do so many times with Jazzette. Shaking her head, *classic*. She stifled a laugh, they weren't acting, just being their ridiculous selves. A couple of minutes later, the guard strolled off with them toward the bathroom, chatting like they were family.

Perfect.

Clarice scanned the hallway. No alarms. She adjusted her pace, walking like she owned the place. The elevator doors slid open just as she reached them. She stepped inside, pulse steadying. *Halfway there.*

The elevator stopped, and a group of people got on. She had already pushed the floor two floors below the roof. She didn't want to get caught in a situation with no way out. The group hadn't selected a floor. She started to panic, worried they would be getting off on the same floor.

"We almost missed our floor," laughing, one of the individuals rushed to push the button for their floor just before Clarice's.

The group got off, chatting as they went in different directions. Clarice took a deep breath. She truly believed it would all go smoothly, but that didn't stop her from feeling every part of her body tremble with fear. She could hear the words ringing in her ear.

"Where there is fear, there is no faith."

She understood fear and faith could not occupy the same space. So, Clarice started mumbling to herself, repeating, '*where there is fear, there is no faith.*'

She ignored the small quiet voice inside. *But you are stealing a plane...*

She understood fear and faith could not occupy the same space. So, Clarice started mumbling to herself.

"Soo Clare, how big is your faith, how big is the fear…50/50, 60/40, 80/20?"

The quiet voice again...*But you are stealing...*

Just as she was about to get in a full-blown conversation with herself, the elevator opened. Clarice got off on the floor she had selected and quickly found the stairs. Zoe had added her credentials to the company's database. She was an employee with top clearance. If she had gotten caught, she was the new pilot for Mr. Winsky. Clarice went into the pilot's residential area of the hanger floor. Perhaps if the jerk of an owner had not been such a bragger, this would have been much harder. Clarice grabbed a uniform, walked right out of the door and into the hanger. She went to the terminal, plugged into the system using the program exactly the way Zoe had instructed. Keyed in the coordinates, set the timer and walked out. She was back in the truck before she took a breather.

It was a gorgeous night.

Just Gone

Meanwhile, at the safe house, a voice cut through the morning calm. "Zoe. Gerard. Wake up. Something has happened. Turn on the news."

Zoe stirred, groggy, reaching blindly toward the nightstand and tapped a discreet panel. At first, it was hard to tell if anything had changed. The screen blended so seamlessly into the surface, almost invisible when powered off. Suddenly, the wall across from the bed flickered to life, transforming into a full-screen broadcast. The wall had become a live broadcast.

Gerard sat up beside her, rubbing his eyes. "What is it?" he muttered, blinking at the screen as the image sharpened, voices elevated.

Zoe didn't answer. Her breath already with too large of a gap between. She was locked in, eyes narrowing as the headline scrolled across the bottom of the feed.

Something was wrong. And it was already in motion.

Zoe stared at the screen, her pulse quickening as the anchor continued to speak, voice displaying on live air the gravity of the situation.

"There has been a confirmed explosion aboard the International Coalition Space Station. Early reports suggest a collision with unidentified space debris." The newscaster went on to say, "Although the investigations are ongoing, we know that several large fragments from the explosion have broken off and expected to begin entry into Earth's atmosphere within the next couple of hours."

Gerard leaned forward, asking, "Did they just say…?"

"Yes, they did." Zoe responded before he could finish saying the words.

Zoe's eyes remained locked on the screen.

The broadcast continued.

"Officials believe the impact zone will be along the United States East Coast. However, the debris field is expected to disperse as it enters the atmosphere, with larger fragments potentially making landfall across multiple regions."

"Is this because of what Timepiece did? Is it because of the plans sent to Germany?" Gerard asked Zoe. His tone was sympathetic, but he knew the answer.

"You mean what I did." Zoe responding to the undertone.

"It's not your fault. How could you have known what the bot would do? This is not on you. You didn't know Timepiece would be hacked by…" Gerard paused, not knowing how to truly explain what was happening.

"I should have known, or at the least put in some safeguards. I have to find the password to that part of the code. We have to come up with a plan—find a way to bring out that part of me. We have to get the passcode." Zoe's tone was one of desperation.

"Gerard, you can't tell anyone. Promise me you won't say a word. If the others knew, they would never forgive me—trust me. How would they look at me the same once they find out? How do I tell anyone I am having mental gaps, and during one of those gaps, somehow, my code was hijacked by my other code?"

Gerard pulled her in, "You never have to worry about that. We will figure this out. Until we figure it out, it's just you and me. I will watch you closely. No one else needs to know."

Zoe resolved the issue within herself—at least for the moment, as she grabbed the remote to change the news station.

"Authorities are urging residents in potential affected regions to shelter in place. While most of the debris is expected to burn up during entry," the newscaster added, "larger fragments may reach the ground at a high velocity."

The news made it sound like there would be minimal damage. However, Zoe and the rest knew better. This was only the beginning.

"We need to get moving, the roads will be packed with people trying to get out of the east coast area."

The group had a little over an hour before entry. Back on the road, the urgency in their movements sharpened by what they'd just watched on the broadcast. But they hadn't gone far, barely minutes into the drive, when panic revealed itself everywhere.

Cars were jammed in intersections, some idling, others abandoned mid-turn. People shouting, the weight of fear thick in the air. Riding in the van, each trying not to let the other see how much this was shaking them to their core. Each thinking the same thing.

Focus. Stay calm.

But it was impossible not to feel the tremble beneath the surface, like the world was slipping off its axis. With every inch they moved forward, the illusion of progress crumbled. Each gain was followed by another setback.

The team had been watching the news for any updates. Then came the update, the one that takes a bad situation and tells you it's worse than you could have imagined. Pieces of the space station would turn into projectiles—weapons, now predicted to hit near a nuclear plant in Virginia. If the blast hits the reactor, it could flatten at least a ten-mile radius, including a round of radiation that could affect the environment for another fifty miles.

Zoe wanted to scream—her guilt felt deep. She was in direct conflict with another part of herself. She tightened her grip on the wheel. "We won't make it through Virginia. We need to reroute."

Gerard blurted out, "Hardware store, we need to stop at a hardware store."

The others turned to him, puzzled.

Zoe gave a smirk—tone laced with sarcasm. "A hardware store? Seriously, why?"

"Radiation," he said condescendingly without even looking up from the GPS, as if she should have known—the reason was obvious. "If we can't get clear in time, we'll need supplies to minimize the exposure."

The moment he said it, the brilliance of it caused everyone to have a sigh of relief and the mood shifted. Sometimes the team found it hard not to let Gerard get under their skin, especially Zoe. She wasn't sure if it was love, but she knew he was extremely important to her. She respected him in ways she could not explain—fun, and most times quite sweet. When all the barriers are down and your back is against the wall, you want him on your team, no matter what the fight.

It didn't take long for them to shake it off. They had known Gerard long enough to know his directness. He didn't mean to communicate that way, it was innate. Once the sting of his actions had passed, there was always brilliance. Everyone began thinking about what would be needed to shield the van from the radiation.

Zoe eased into the hardware store parking lot, slowly circling to get a lay of the land. She hadn't expected this much chaos, not this soon. It was already a full-blown circus. People were darting in and out of the store, arms full of the most random things imaginable. Judging by the nonsense they were carrying, the useful stuff must have been long gone, or they had no rational conception of what was happening. She kept scanning the area and suddenly, Zoe burst into this hysterical laughter, she was barely coherent.

"Why are they running with ceiling fans and throw pillows?"

To see Zoe let her guard down even for a moment was huge. Somehow, she had managed to lighten the mood. The rest of the gang started making random jokes about what they were seeing, still driving around the parking lot. But it wasn't the Zoe they knew.

"Look, toilet tissue, why is it still always toilet tissue."

"Tell me why, why... is she protecting her new dishwasher, cause a brand-new electric washer will be in high demand...wait, is she waiting on an Uber. Yes, she is...no, really, look. A car just pulled up with an Uber sticker. Are you kidding me?" Laughter eroded.

Laughing still, another one said. "Wait, hold up! I got one. Christmas tree at twelve o'clock. He's really ready for the next apocalypse."

Gerard saw Zoe.

The laughter didn't last long, it stopped as quickly as it had begun. A wave of reality swept over him. He could see her slip away. He touched her softly on her arm, looked her in the eyes, and said, "Let us out here."

Zoe pulled over. Gerard and Tim got out. Zoe pulled away to find a spot away from the chaos.

Gerard and Tim rushed through the shattered glass entrance, the rubber soles on their shoes squealing against the once polished tile floors as they hurried, searching each aisle for anything of use. Tim clutched a wrinkled list in one hand, eyes scanning the signs above each aisle.

To their relief, the shelves they needed hadn't been touched. While others fought over washer and dryers, their targets remained overlooked, yet vital—rolls of lead sheeting, hazmat gloves, radiation meters, duct tape, caulk, gas mask...

They didn't waste time. Gerard shoved gear into a battered duffel bag while Tim stacked boxes in his arms, barely checking labels. Every second inside felt like gambling with time. The noise outside the store intensified the moment they walked over the broken glass and into the sunlight. The broken door had allowed only a small fraction of the chaos to be heard after they entered the store. As soon as they adjusted to the light, they knew inside had not reflected what was happening outside.

One could only imagine what it must have been like earlier in the day. They had found humor before entering, and now the exit was something different.

They quickened their pace, nearly breaking into a run as they carried their supplies toward the van. Between them and the van, stood a man, too calm in the midst of the chaos, a sword strapped to his back, a bow slung over his right shoulder. He didn't move against them—rather watched them with a quiet interest.

As they got closer, "Why?" he asked, nodding toward the odd assortment of supplies in their arms. "Why not go for the same things as everyone else?"

His voice was smooth, distinguished, with an accent that didn't quite belong to any one place. It was English but layered with an ancient mystique.

Tim fumbling for the words, "They're idiots."

The man smiled, not expecting the answer he received.

Tim continued, "If the debris hits where they're projecting, we'll be outside the blast zone—but not outside the radiation zone."

The man stepped forward, reaching out his hands to Tim to introduce himself. "My name is Ralph...Dr. Raphael. Allow me to go with you, I promise to carry my own weight and aid you when needed."

The aura around his voice made what he said sound trustworthy.

Tim, being the shy, scary type, looked at the weapons and immediately agreed.

"Sure."

Gerard looked at Tim. "Are you serious, we don't know him."

It had been done. To put their minds at ease, Dr. Raphael took an electronic ID out of the bag he had over his other shoulder.

"You can never be too careful," he said as he pulled up his credentials. He showed them to Gerard with an understanding. It didn't reassure him though. There was still something off with the doctor.

How many doctors walk around with a sword, and a bow? Gerard kept wondering,

As the team plowed out of the parking lot, they could hear the sirens going off. The screech of the Emergency Broadcast System was constant. The alarms echoed through every device and radio.

"I hacked the feed. They have confirmed one of the targets. Part of the station's wreckage is projected to hit near the nuclear energy facility. The margin of error is small, we can only hope that the debris hits the edge of the facility with little impact on the reactor."

"We need to get farther away."

"We won't outrun the radiation in time." The team realized they weren't going to get far enough away to avoid the radiation fallout.

"There's an abandoned sublevel under the city hospital. It was an old bomb shelter. The entrance is still accessible from the underground garage. It's shielded…if we can get there." Ralph said as if he was trying to give the young group hope.

They decided to adhere to Ralph's suggestions.

"Now, all we have to do is make it through the heart of the city." Gerard said in a low whisper, hoping no one heard him. But Zoe heard him, firing back.

"Then I guess we had better be on guard so we can get through." Her voice cut through Gerard with sarcasm.

As they raced through the inner city, weaving in and out of traffic, parked abandoned cars, and trolley cars had come to a complete stop.

"We need to ditch the van—we can make it if we run. It's less than a mile ahead."

"We can't ditch the van. It's everything we've collected. We need this stuff."

"Make a left," Dr. Raphael blurted. "There's an apartment building up ahead. We can stash the van there. This is where I live. We can use my garage."

The team looked at each other. This can't be some coincidence. They hesitated.

Tim's voice cut through the awkwardness. "We don't have time for this. I will kill him myself if he is leading us astray."

Gerard thought to himself, *yeah right*, but followed Ralph's directions. Moments later, they parked the van in the garage, jumped out, instinctively grabbing their computer bags—the most important thing that could not be left behind.

They ran through the city, helping each other along the way. By the time the hospital came into view, a panicky voice could be overheard. It was the latest announcement.

"Take immediate cover! T-minus eight minutes…"

They had less than eight minutes to reach the underground shelter.

The door, locked.

Gerard gave Dr. Ralph a look of frustration. "No one said anything about a locked door."

Tim stepped forward, calm—moving like someone who'd done this a hundred times before. No panic, no theatrics, just precision. He was in his element, breaking into places. He pulled a compact device from his jacket, flipped open a hidden panel, and clipped two leads to the electronic lock. His voice was low, steady.

"Unlock door."

The lock clicked softly. No alarms. No resistance. Just the clean sound of entry granted.

The lock gave way, and they all surged inside, slamming the door shut behind them.

For a moment, they all stood frozen, the adrenaline catching up to them like a wave crashing over rocks. As the silence settled, so did they, collapsing right where they stood, breathless, hearts pounding.

With the adrenaline fading, they noticed it was dark. The corridor ahead seemed long and empty, lit only by the flicker of emergency lights. Everything felt… off.

"We barely escaped the disaster outside," Tim muttered, his voice low and ragged. "And now we've dropped into... whatever this is."

There was no gratitude in his tone—just the raw, frayed edge of exhaustion. The fact that they were still breathing hadn't sunk in yet. Survival didn't feel like winning, but it would, when the world was falling apart one piece at a time.

Tim wasn't the only one frightened. They naturally started to huddle as they crept down the hallway. They had only gone halfway when they started hearing the muffled sounds of something or someone. With Gerard leading, they picked up speed. As he made it to the corner, he stopped in his tracks, saying nothing.

When the others caught up, they saw why.

Every eye in the room was on them—small, pale faces staring from beds and wheelchairs.

It was a children's hospital. Apparently, not an ordinary one. You could feel it. The stillness. The sadness, the hurt, such pain in the kids' eyes. These were long-term patients, probably terminal, or at the least critical, forgotten in the chaos of the outside world.

A handful of nurses moved quietly through the room, tending to the children with steady, caring hands. They looked like they hadn't slept in days. Maybe they hadn't. It appeared that most of the staff had already abandoned ship. But who could blame them? They probably rushed home the moment the emergency announcement hit. Instinctively, and not without sacrifice. It was their loved ones' survival as well.

It wasn't selfishness.

It was instinct. Survival.

When the world starts coming apart, people will run to help their loved ones just like anyone else. Sometimes you are just all they have. But these nurses stayed. They made a different decision based on their own individual circumstances.

Zoe stood near the doorway, fingers flying over her tablet as lines of data rolled past her screen. Her voice broke the heavy silence.

"I've been tracking updates... Great news! It been confirmed, the debris missed the nuclear facility."

A few in the group exhaled, as a sign of relief, although it was too late to matter.

"But..." she continued, her tone flattening, "it splashed down into the lower Chesapeake Bay. Direct impact. It displaced the water like a mini-tsunami."

The words fell like stones.

Zoe kept going. "Norfolk, Portsmouth, most of the surrounding area, it's all underwater. Thousands of people unaccounted for, presumably dead, thousands more without homes. And we missed it by a sliver. If we'd taken another route or not given Dr. Ralph a ride...we'd be underwater too. It's a miracle this place isn't under."

No one spoke for a moment.

Zoe turned, her gaze scanning the room, dozens of children, some lying motionless in beds, others sitting quietly, wide-eyed, and uncertain of what was happening.

Sick. Scared. Left behind.

They had just outrun one disaster, literally—barely making it with their lives intact. Now, only to walk right into another situation that they had no control over. There was nothing they could do without jeopardizing the family's survival. Thinking about her step-dad, Zoe found herself finally understanding the weight of such decisions he had been carrying alone.

Their heartstrings were being tugged, but the reality of the situation did not lend way to any other outcome but the group leaving, continuing their journey to Nebraska.

"We need to leave...now." Zoe's voice cut through the stillness, calm but urgent. Time was running out, and they all knew it.

She spotted Dr. Ralph standing near a young boy's bed. The boy's face was pale, eyes closed in quiet suffering. The child's chest rose and fell with shallow, exhausted breaths. Each one costing him every ounce of housed energy.

Zoe approached Dr. Ralph quietly, placed a gentle hand on his shoulder and said softly, "Dr. Raphael...Ralph, we're leaving. Come with us."

He turned, appearing startled at first. He took an intentional look around, and with a silent thought, *how?*

The nurses were moving with weary determination, the children too tired to be afraid, the area dimly lit, and the carts had too little food and medicine. He finally looked back at her.

"I can't go—without them. They're suffering." His voice soft and nurturing. "Thank you...for everything. But I belong here. There's still work left for me to do here. But do not dismay. In the fullness of time, God's will, shall be done. I was sent to this place for a reason. This...this is part of *my* purpose. Set for times such as this." Ralph gave a reassuring smile, and said, "They are not forgotten—they are loved!"

He reached into his coat pocket and pulled out a set of keys, pressing them into Zoe's hand.

"Take them. Use them when you go to get your van. You should stay there tonight. Rest, and get a fresh start in the morning. If you see anything you need... take it, I won't be needing it."

There was a pause. A quiet understanding passed between them.

"You have a purpose too, Zoe. Don't let the darkness have you, find your true self." Dr. Ralph added, his voice steady with a kind of knowing. She paused with a thought, *How could he—does he know?*

The team moved in silence, retracing their steps down the dim hallway, lights still flickering. Finally, the hard slam of the exterior door as they stepped out into the open air. Lungs greedy for oxygen not laced with sorrow. The hospital loomed behind them. They were tired, heartbroken, but still standing. The more steps they took moving farther away from the hospital their spirits began to lift.

"Let's spend the night. We can get up at dawn to start the next phase of the journey." Nick seemed to have been the rational one. He understood sorrow. His family had come to America under treacherous conditions. The journey had cost him half of his family. And when his family thought they were safe and part of the American dream, most of them had been deported during the great deportation of 2025. He had been part of a program that helps high school students apply for citizenship during their junior year of high school, and granted after graduation as part of the immigration restructuring program. Through it all, nothing ever truly dissuaded Nick. He was kind, controlled in thought, and intelligent.

"Yes, I could use a shower."

"And food…"

Then.

A deep, gut-punching *boom* split the sky—a fierce lightning bolt. Before they could interpret what was happening, the world behind them was suddenly swallowed by fire and fury. The blast wave hit like a wall, lifting them off their feet and throwing them hard back against the pavement—unconscious.

Dust. Heat. Silence.

Three hours later, they came too, the ringing in their ears fading, they turned slowly, disbelievingly. Trying to figure out what happened.

The hospital was gone.

Not damaged. Not burning.

Gone.

A yawning crater now sat where a nine-story building had stood just moments ago. The earth had caved in, scorched and mangled, as if something had clawed up from beneath and devoured the entire block. Even the garage they had entered through, obliterated.

Concrete. Steel. Lives.

Vanished.

Zoe staggered to her feet—her breath caught in her throat. "No..." She stood frozen, her mouth open but no other words coming out. Gerard dropped to one knee, staring into the crater like he expected to see something...someone, still there, climbing to safety.

But there was nothing.

No sound.

No survivors.

Just residue of smoke...silence—heavy, suffocating. And the awful unbearable knowing of what once was.

"All the children. The nurses who stayed. Dr. Raphael...Ralph...you who chose to remain."

All of them.

Just gone.

In a single blinding instant, everything had been erased.

The wind shifted, but there wasn't a hint of what had been, not even the acrid scent of despair. Their eyes caught the movement of a scrap of paper tumbling across the cracked sidewalk, headed directly for them. It found its destination, and landed against Zoe's shoe. She didn't move.

No one did.

Tim bent down and picked up the charred paper, crumbling, the moment he touched it. After the burnt edges quickly fell away, all that was left were faded letters that looked like they had been written long ago. Against the background of blackened smudges, Tim was able to see a set of letters before it too was gone.

"Isaiah 41:20."

They had escaped with their lives—but their hearts left behind.

And whatever this mission was... it had just become something else entirely.

The team picked up the van and headed toward their next destination. They each searched for their own solitude. No one spoke of what happened. They just retreated into themselves, quietly dealing.

You're in Trouble

It had been a couple of weeks since the helocraft made its dramatic debut at the Taylors.' Zoe had informed everyone she was the hacker known as Timepiece, so all the secrets were out in the open—except the one that would have mattered the most to all of them.

She couldn't tell them the full truth—even though she was the creator of Timepiece, she no longer had control over the code. As far as they knew, it was Zoe who had deliberately sent the leak, but it had all been Timepiece—ruled by another, acting on its own—her own.

Zoe now knew she couldn't directly control that part of herself. The gaps in memory and code she didn't remember writing were undeniable. It wasn't the bot she designed, it was fragments of herself split into two different versions. This part of her code had no boundaries.

Zoe had been the gatekeeper between *The Huntress* and *Timepiece*. She had always assume The Huntress was her safe place, forged out of a need to survive when her dad died. Timepiece was who she hid behind. But recently, after everything that had happened, Zoe and Gerard finally understood the gravity of what her altars were capable of, so they came up with a plan to keep Timepiece in check.

The Huntress, however, was a narcissistic avenger—untethered, standing in the middle of chaos and control—justice regardless of the consequences. But Zoe was unaware it wasn't *Timepiece* whom she needed to keep in check, it was actually *The Huntress* who was pulling the strings in the dark.

The team had managed to maintain communications with different groups around the world. They all knew that it was just a matter of time before their regions and countries would be affected by what was happening.

Chaos had taken over the country. A few large pieces of the asteroid and several pieces of the space station had fallen in different parts of the country. The fallen debris had hit several states. Power grids were offline, riots in the streets, even an entire shipping yard in south Texas had been hit. Supply chains were being disrupted. People had started to break into other people's homes searching for food and water.

But that wasn't the worst of it. The larger pieces of the asteroid that broke off had landed in the northwestern part of the country. It had destroyed ports in Seattle, and hit Yellowstone, creating volcanic unrest. No one knew what the fallout would end up being.

***

Zoe and Clarice were ecstatic. No one could quite understand why they'd gone through with the cookout, considering all the problems and the looming sense of disaster. Yes, the family needed of a break, a moment of normalcy. They'd been carrying the weight of the world for far too long. Just for one night, they deserved to forget everything else. It was one of the few times the entire family would be together.

But for the two of them, it had to be more than just a fleeting distraction. They wanted a memory—something lasting, something they could return to, cling to, and recall the weight of what it meant to survive.

Catastrophic events had been happening all over the globe, and though most people didn't know it, the worst was yet to come. Slowly, family and friends had started to question what they had been telling them. For most a little too late.

They had done everything they could, leaving detailed messages, complete with addresses and directions, for as many people as possible.

The rest was up to them. They would have to find their way, rely on each other, and make it together, just as they had too.

Clarice rose to her feet. With a glass in hand, she tapped the side ever so gently, but loud enough to be heard around the circle. Smiling, she took center stage and began.

"It's an honor to be standing here among such an extraordinary group of people. We come from different corners of the world, brought together by the most unbelievable of circumstances. What are the odds?" She tilted her head slightly, laughed a little, looking towards Stephen and winked.

"I want us to savor every moment we have left," Clarice continued with a soft and reflective tone. "Life is meant to be celebrated—not because of who we are nor what we have done. Not how much we know nor own—but through the seeds we plant along the way."

She continued with the peace of being a part of something of such value. "Wow, look at how incredible the fruit that grows, when individual seeds are germinated together. That's what we have here tonight."

Clarice paused, glancing around this small group of people that had come together. "And I am incredibly thankful—whether it be by fate or faith."

Paul rose from his seat, clapping as the rest joined in. "Let's raise our glasses. I would like to propose a toast."

As everyone lifted their glasses, Paul held his glass out in front of him. "From this night forward, we operate as one." His voice carrying warmth and authority. He spoke as a leader ready to take control of his command.

"We'll plant seeds together along the way. They will be seeds of trust, commitment to survival, hard work, and most importantly to each other. As we raise our glasses to cultivating this bond, we look around at the different groups of people. Like Clarice said, be it fate or faith, we've found ourselves here together—our family, construction crews, and their loved ones alike—friends that have now become family. Let's take this moment to enjoy each other and solidify this bond that has been formed between all of us."

Lifting his glass higher in the air, "It is a glorious night. Here's to survival."

They all shouted, "Hear, hear!"

"Well said!" Clarice stepped in. "Zoe, Paul, and I have something to show you. Oh, and let's not forget, our other little seedlings were a big part of this with us. Boys take a bow." They bowed playfully, of course.

Zoe held a device in her hands, her fingers moving swiftly over the controls. Within seconds, the helopad lit up, glowing softly against the dark backdrop of night sky. The helopad was the stage designed for its debut—its opening act, including the strategically placed seating arrangements. Clarice in youngers years had wanted to be in the arts, so everything to her was a production.

Just when everyone was soaking up the theatrics of the pad, beams of light suddenly appeared from above, converging on a single point in the center of the pad. It was the grand finale featuring the star of the show. It looked like a spacecraft landing on the helopad.

The boys in the background were jumping up and down with excitement. How Clarice described the helocraft when she told them about it didn't come close to what was in front of them. This aircraft, helocraft or whatever it is called was indescribable. No wonder Mr. Winsky was bragging. Anyone would be bragging.

Zoe powered down the craft. As everyone moved in to get a better look, Clarice stayed behind. She had a lot of explaining to do to Stephen. She hadn't told him any of her plans to steal the helocraft.

Clarice began outlining everything she'd prepared. While Stephen had focused on securing the necessities required for survival, she'd taken a different approach, one rooted in minimizing risk, foreseeing anything that could possibly happen. This was an easy choice, aerial surveillance, transport, communications…*he will see the value.*

"We needed our own. We must be able to get an aerial view to survey the surrounding area without jeopardizing our safety. Being surrounded on all side with no way of knowing what was happening was not a level of comfort we were was willing accept."

Clarice left no stone unturned. She was thorough in her planning. She went on trying to explain how Zoe had locked down all communications, and how Paul, with the help of the boys, had handled the diversion.

Stephen listened, not saying a word. He didn't give a nod, not even asked a question—instead, just the stillness he projects when something is out of order—a disappointment. Clarice noticed the lack of expression on his face, she had seen it before, though rarely directed at her. She knew she was in trouble. Babbling—scrambling to fill the space between glances, trying to find the words that would land and minimize the obvious disapproval settling—taking shape behind his eyes.

When Clarice had finished trying to explain her way out of it, Stephen was straightforward.

"Is this who we want to be? If so... we're misguided."

His voice was flat, no room for emotion, no room for misinterpretations. He didn't wait for a response. Without another word, he turned and walked away.

Amid the buzz of celebration, laughter, and curious chatter, Stephen disappeared into the main house, unnoticed by most, but not Sarah.

Sarah, sensing the shift, gently took Clarice's hand and guided her toward the group gathered around the helocraft. They were still riding the high of the moment, laughing, and teasing with playful jabs, comparing her to a secret agent, some kind of James Bond-type operative.

Clarice forced a smile, but Stephen's words lingered heavier than she had anticipated. She knew he would be upset, but this wasn't anger. He was disappointed in her, and the look on his face told it all. She had let him down, never considering that type of reaction.

"'Is this who we want to be, if so, misguided.'" rung in her ears.

As the night drew to a close, everyone quietly retreated to their own spaces. Clarice and Sarah lingered, reluctant to leave. Sarah understood what had happened between Stephen and Clarice, she could tell Clarice needed to talk. As the evening was coming to a close, her energy aura had dampened.

"Let's sit out for a while." Sarah said, settling into the chair beside Clarice. "I leave early tomorrow heading back to the university." Giving Clarice an opportunity if she wanted to talk.

"I hate you have to go back."

Sarah smiled, "Well if Paul's timing is correct, I'll be back for good soon enough." She went on, "You know you're in trouble with Stephen." Making a statement more than asking a question.

"I know. I owe him an apology." Clarice sighed. "And not just any apology, he'd see through anything less than full disclosure. He can always tell when I am not sincere. It's like his super power over me."

They both laughed, easing the tension, somewhat. "Okay, we'd better go in."

Clarice crawled into bed, slithering in with care. She could tell he was asleep. The room was still. The hum of the ventilation system was calming, like waves breaking over rocks—gentle and steady, yet edged with the rough, rhythmic undertone of distant drums. In perfect harmony with Stephen's breath, slow and steady, but carrying a hint of fragility.

Yet, the familiar hum of his deep sleep, was a sound that always calmed her, a quiet rhythm she had come to know like a secret melody only meant for her. With his back to her, she wrapped her arm around him, edged closer, and whispered, "I'm sorry, it wasn't fair, forgive me."

He felt her, heard her, from a place between spirit and flesh. He placed his hand over hers, with a slight squeeze, "Always my love."

***

Paul was fully engaged in the weapon's room, hands steady as he checked the firing mechanism on the sidearms. With a sterile light, the odor of oil and metal, and focused on the task at hand, the weapon's room was his sanctuary. When the world outside felt like it was tilting toward chaos, that's where you would find him. Nothing in the room needed his attention, and yet he was there.

Zuri walked in quietly, but with just the level of tone necessary to break the thickness of the atmosphere.

"Hi, Dad. What are you doing?" She asked, trying not to show the concern she had for him. She had a fairly good idea. But she was actually more interested in his *why* rather than *what* or *how*.

Paul didn't look up at first. "We need to be ready to protect ourselves," he said, tone clipped, almost military. "Things out there are bad. And they're going to get worse before they get better. With the country's new weapon restrictions and the limited supply of ammunition guidelines, we can't afford to waste one bullet. Weapons must be maintained, kept clean. So, I'm just making sure they are dependable. We can't afford unnecessary mistakes because of faulty weapons."

Zuri rarely let him hide behind his military demeanor to avoid confronting the emotions tied to a situation. She saw through the silence, and knew when he was quietly hurting. He needed someone who would prioritize his emotional well-being—and for most of her life, she had taken that role upon herself. They had promised they would always look out for each other. Him when he found her, Zuri when his parents died. Not that he would ever ask or even recognize for himself when he might need it, but she knew. Just like Jazzette knew.

She had a special technique that only she could pull off to distract him so he would lighten up. Whenever he was obsessing about a task, she would have him tell her a story about the days of being in the thick of some jungle or the openness of some desert.

"Dad, how's Uncle Nate? When is he coming?"

She was the only one who got to call him that. It started as a joke years ago, but it stuck. Nate been there the day they found her. Just a little girl, barely a toddler, with eyes that captured the very essence of one's soul. He had always tried to get her to call him Uncle Nate. They would laugh about how she would say it. Secretly, he loved every time he heard her mispronounce it. When she was five years old, she asked him. "Uncle Nate, are you really my uncle?"

Nate had knelt beside her, looked her square in the face, pointed to Paul, and said, "That's my brother, so that makes me your uncle."

She had always known he meant it. He loved her. She was just as much a part of his family, and he was of theirs. The entire team felt a sense of responsibility for Zuri. The first few years of her life, the team had all but raised her. They would just drop by Paul's parents' house to check up on her.

At the sound of her question, Paul's posture shifted, subtle, but real. His spine straightened, the tension in his shoulders eased. He stood upright—head tilted just slightly as if listening to something only he could hear.

"He should've been here by now," Paul said after a pause, voice low and lagging with thought. "He's got everything he needs, the plans, the coordinates."

A bit of silence hung in the room.

"Knowing Uncle Nate," Zuri said to lighten the moment and balance the concern, "he'll probably stroll in just when all the excitement starts."

Paul laughed, the kind that came from a place deep inside, not forced.

Zuri felt the tug on the fishing line—he had taken the bait.

She tilted her head slightly as though she was interested. "Dad, I don't think you ever told me how you and Nate actually became friends. I know he was part of your unit... but not how it actually happened."

Paul leaned back on one of the display tables, the corners of his mouth still set with a smile. "Sure, I have?" He posed his comment as a question, but didn't wait for a response. He took a breath, eyes flickering with excitement to tell one of his favorite stories.

"I'd just been promoted to Lieutenant Commander. First real command. I was assigned to a Special Forces unit, and once the team was selected, we were sent on a training exercise. It was brutal. Well, at the end of the training and before we could be certified, we had to do a survival exercise, and not like the ones we go on." Looking at her with a sly smile.

"Nate was assigned as my Senior Chief. Operational lead from the enlisted side. I'd heard the name—hell, *everyone* had heard of Nate Jenkins, but we'd never actually met."

Paul's tone shifted, like he was slipping into the memory.

"We were out on maneuvers. We had been out there for two weeks. The terrain was horrible. We were sleep-deprived, and with minimal supplies, we had to live off whatever we could find. But I was determined to be a strong leader for my unit. At least, until we lost our navigation gear."

Zuri looked as if she was hearing the story for the first time. "You lost it!"

"Nate told me he dropped the device into a creek. And just like that. We were lost."

Zuri blinked. "He pretended to lose it?"

Paul nodded. "At the time, I didn't know that. He led me to believe they'd assigned me some incompetent burnout with a good reputation long gone. I was furious, letting him have it in front of the whole squad. Nate just stood there. Head lowered, apologizing like a new recruit."

Paul straightened his posture, mimicking the voice: "'*Captain, I'm so sorry, sir. It won't happen again.*' Over and over. To the point, where I started feeling terrible for yelling."

Zuri laughed.

"We kept going, lost, as far as I knew. Trying to make it to the next checkpoint through some awful conditions. The tension in the unit was thick. I needed, no, wanted to be a good leader. So, I took charge of the situation, putting into practice all my earlier training."

He paused—his smile fading into something more thoughtful.

"What none of us knew was… it was all part of the test. The whole scenario. The *'lost'* nav gear, the fake mistake. Nate had been briefed ahead of time. His job was to throw us off-course and then guide us back, just under the wire. And he did. Perfectly."

Zuri blinked. "Wait, so… he acted like an idiot just to test you?"

Paul nodded slowly, a grin returning to his lips. "That man had me convinced he was the weak link. Whole time, he was the anchor."

He shook his head. "Next morning, we walk into the debrief room, the team and me, still recovering, worn out yet proud we made it. Then in walks Senior Chief Nathaniel Jenkins—full uniform, metals covered his chest. Same man, but this time? Whole different energy. Back straight. Eyes sharp. Voice calm, controlled. He wasn't pretending anymore."

Paul let out a soft breath.

"The admiral introduced him with every accolade you could imagine. A respected, decorated Navy SEAL. He then turned to me and said, *That's your Chief, your right hand. He'll either break you or make you into the kind of leader they write about. Your choice.*"

Paul looked at Zuri, smiling warmly now, the corners of his eyes crinkling with genuine affection. There was a softness in his expression that hadn't been there moments ago, "That's when I knew, Nate would be someone I could count on, when we *found* you. Nate stayed by my side in more ways than I can tell you. Ole Nate. He has been my number one ever since."

Paul turned to Zuri as he was walking out. "Finish up in here and lock up."

"What, wait…why? Dad!"

"That's what you get for distracting me." He said with a loving and grateful smile. "Don't take too long."

No one noticed Zoe standing outside the door as she watched their inner actions, listening to their conversation.

Senior Chief

Nate was a Navy SEAL to the core—the kind of soldier who could pull off the impossible without so much as a flinch. He could take the wings off a butterfly from nine hundred yards or defuse a bomb with steady hands while humming your favorite melody. But it wasn't the combat skills that made Nate stand out, at least not to Paul.

It was something quieter. Something steadier.

Nate had a way of reading a room, or battlefield, with little more than a glance. He could take in the chaos and, somehow, by just being there, slow it all down. Ground it. Make it manageable. Make it make sense. His presence was the stability. He grew up on the north side of Shreveport, in a little house that should have been long torn down. His parents died when he was sixteen, leaving him alone. He hid out, and lived undetected by the system. When he graduated from high school, he joined the military.

He drifted across continents with no fixed address, a phantom with a passport. His family had long since passed, and there was nothing tying him to any one place. At least, other than Paul and his family. When the world felt too far away or too big, when the disconnection became too sharp to ignore, Nate would show up at Paul's door—no warning, no expectation—just a quiet knock and a worn-out duffel bag. Paul and his family had become his only anchor. The last piece of home he had left.

When Paul first told Nate about the crisis—the kind that could tilt the world off its axis—Nate didn't take it seriously. Not really. He listened, nodded, stayed in touch, but in his gut, he believed it would all work out. It had to. He was a military man, born and forged in a system built on order and contingency. There was always a plan. Always a response.

For the first couple of years, Nate kept his distance, checking in now and then but never considering what Paul had said. In his heart, he trusted the chain of command. If the threat was real—truly real—then someone higher up would handle it.

The government. The military. Someone.

But then Senior Chief Jenkins started pulling on threads. He could not deny what Paul had found out. He trusted Paul. So, when he called in a panic, after he found out about the countries trying to manipulate the trajectory, Nate knew he could no longer sit on the sidelines—he had to investigate.

He traveled—quietly, carefully—to countries where information still flowed freely, where he thought he might hear whispers of what Paul had warned him about. But there was nothing. Not even a murmur. Nation after nation, same story: no awareness, no preparation, no sign that anyone outside of Paul's circle knew what was coming.

That was when the cracks started to show.

Although, even then, some parts of him clung to the belief that the people in charge knew more than they let on. That the silence was strategic—behind the curtain, someone was steering the ship. He had been hardwired—loyalty, duty, faith in the system. God and country first. That was the oath. That was the code.

But something, deep within, shifted. Doubt crept in—not loud, but steady. And for the first time in his life, Nate wondered if no one was coming. If this time, the plan didn't exist.

Nathaniel made it to Germany. He had contacts in every part of the world and had heard of bunkers being updated to serve as temporary housing for the elite in case of impact. Not only was it true, but there was even more going on.

Germany had a secret weapon on the far side of the moon. They had planned to divert the asteroid off course to avoid their part of the world from impact. This response was to be launched in secret, without warning, as a direct response to what they called betrayal by their allies. The US, his country was the initiators of the deception.

It was hard to process at first. Nathaniel's contact told him about the betrayal Germany spoke of had been whispered about for days in diplomatic backchannels—rumors of withheld intelligence, broken agreements, and covert sabotage. He had to call Paul to let him know. This news—abrupt, surreal, and almost too outrageous to believe. But he knew it was true.

And then came the real nightmare. That's when the order came down. The broadcast was cold, clinical, and absolute.

'All American citizens were to leave Germany within twenty-four hours. No second chances. No diplomatic appeals. Anyone left behind after the deadline would be treated as a hostile combatant. Shot on sight.'

Nate didn't wait.

By the time he reached the military base, there was one flight scheduled to leave for British Columbia. He only had twenty minutes. Nate didn't think. If he missed that flight, there was no guarantee he would make it out. He didn't have time to consider alternate routes, nor time to weigh the risks.

He made a plan—military plan. Once in Canada, he'd go dark—slip across the border, disappear into the backroads, and make the long trip to Nebraska. Paul would know what to do. Paul always did. He would call once he made it to Canada, and tell Paul the latest.

But as the engines of the aircraft roared to life, Nate looked back once—at the country unraveling behind him, at the betrayal echoing across continents—and knew that the world he once loved no longer existed. Something had shifted. Permanently.

And there would be no going back.

It had been three days since Nate learned of Germany's weapon. It had been three disorienting days. The moment they touched down in Victoria, it was clear just how bad everything had escalated. Communications were scattered, unreliable at best. The lines had gone dark, almost immediately after their arrival—no cell signal, no satellite uplink, nothing. Every attempt Nate made to reach Paul ended in silence. Static. Dead air. The silence told Nate more than words ever could. Whatever was coming next, he couldn't afford to wait around. So, he went to the coast, and stole a boat to sail into Seattle. His only hope now was to get to the States. Then hopefully, contact Paul.

Nate had been on the water for nearly two hours, the hum of the engine and the soft slap of waves his only company. The air was eerie, unusually calm, everything felt suspended—waiting, a calm before the storm. Nate had this feeling before most missions. It was an uneasiness. He looked at the navigational equipment. He should be in Seattle soon.

At the edge of a dismissal of thought, he heard it.

A deep, concussive boom cracked through the sky, like thunder in a massive storm. It wasn't natural. It wasn't the weather—but something else—louder, sharper, and closing in.

Nate's head snapped upward, scanning the clouds—and that's when he saw it.

A massive black shape burst through the ceiling of gray clouds, fire and smoke trailing as it fell. It wasn't tumbling; it was dropping fast and clean, like a missile fired and was about to hit its target.

His stomach dropped.

It was heading straight towards him. Whatever it was, it was coming down hard, accelerating fast.

Nate reacted with instinct, gunning the throttle and turning the wheel to increase speed and change direction. But before the boat could gain distance, the object slammed into the water behind him with a deafening roar. The impact sent a towering surge of water hurtling outward, a massive wave racing toward him, faster than he could escape.

It hit.

The force was brutal—lifting the boat like a toy and hurling it toward the harbor. Nate held on as the vessel skidded across the violent surface. Thrown into the side rail, he was barely conscious as the hull cracked beneath his feet. He could hear the sounds of wood splintering, metal tearing. Just then, the broken boat collided with docked boats in a second forceful chain reaction.

His boat completely shattered on impact, fragments scattering across the marina like debris in the aftermath of an explosion. The air was filled with the sound of chaos, muffled in the barely conscious mind of Nathaniel.

The wave reversed, dragging the wreckage back towards open water with a terrifying undertow. Nathaniel felt the current grab hold of him, dragging him with a relentless pull. His lungs screaming for air as he fought to stay above the surface, being battered by water from every direction.

Then—sudden resistance.

The shattered remains of his vessel slammed against a large buoy. The buoy held firm, life-saving, anchoring him in place while the ocean clawed at everything else. It was difficult for Nathaniel to catch his breath between rounds of being covered in a flood of water. He was grateful, though. Had it not been for that brief moment of luck—of fate—he would've been gone, swallowed whole by the retreating surge.

Coughing, bleeding, barely afloat, Nate clung to the buoy. His body felt like it had been substituted for a punching bag. But it meant he was still alive. Holding on, he scanned the water.

Bodies.

Some floated silently. Others thrashing in panic, their cries muffled by waves and debris. Blood bloomed in red clouds across the surface, mixing with oil and salt. The harbor, once calm, had become a graveyard.

Nathaniel spotted a woman struggling, her arms thrashing about as she fought to stay above the surface. Just as the current threatened to sweep her past him, her hand swinging wildly. He blindly reached out, managing to make enough contact to slow her down for her to grab a part of the buoy without him letting go.

The two of them were tossed together in the violent surge, the water pummeling their bodies from all sides. Panic surged through them both. Despite all his Navy SEAL training and countless missions, Nathaniel couldn't suppress the fear tightening in his chest. This was worse than anything he'd seen in combat. The harbor was a scene of devastation—bodies continued to float lifelessly in the water, and crimson streaks bled through the waves, marking where people had been slammed against boats, rocks, and every unforgiving surface in sight.

Every muscle ached—every breath felt borrowed. The woman beside him—her cold, bony grip tight around his hand—was the only thing anchoring him to reality.

After a time, the relentless rhythm of the waves lulled them into a fragile sleep, perhaps more like an unconscious surrender than rest.

The warmth of the morning sun caused Nate to wake. She was gone. In the quake of the day, under the cover of the day's dawn, she must have let go. She was simply gone. He jolted upright, panic spiking through his chest. He spun around, scanning the water, calling out—once, twice, a third time, louder each time.

Nothing. No response. No movement. No voice. No one was left.

The bobbing of the wreckage was quiet now, the storm's rage a fading memory, and she was simply... gone.

Nathaniel let go of his safety net. It had served as his lifeline through the night. His fingers capable of little movement, stiff with cold and exhaustion, while his knuckles were scraped raw. The weight of the ocean clung to him with every stroke. With muscles on fire, and his shoulders screaming in protest, he kept moving—because stopping wasn't an option.

As the shoreline grew closer, the water grew darker. He could see tips of large pieces of wreckage in the water. He had to be careful, weaving through the unseen debris hidden just beneath the surface. What was lying beneath could finish what the storm had taken, and that was almost everything—but survival was still left.

His feet scraped the shallows first, stumbling through sand and stone as the tide fought to pull him back. With the yack of the force pulling from behind him, he fought back, resisting the urge to relax and succumb to it.

He finally made it, collapsed onto the shore, breathless, face buried in cold, gritty earth. For a long time, he laid there, the only sound was his own, ragged breathing and the distant, fading roar of the sea.

When he finally pushed himself up to open his eyes, the sight took the very air he had just learned to appreciate.

Destruction. Everywhere!

The harbor was gone. What had once been his destination, now a broken, twisted landscape. Buildings had been leveled, others with roofs torn clean off, walls missing, windows reduced to shattered glass. Boats were splintered across the shoreline like ceramic models created by a child in grade school. The very ground looked bruised, torn, as if the earth itself had been attacked.

Nathaniel staggered forward, not knowing where he was going, what direction to try, just moving because stillness felt more like surrender than anything. Then, through the chaos, something glinted—a small, round object nestled between chunks of concrete and wood.

A compass.

He knelt down and picked it up. It was scuffed, the glass cracked, but the needle still pointed forward with unwavering certainty. There were no letters on the compass to tell the direction. Just the needle, steady. He turned the compass over in his palm, staring at it from all angles—the time slipped away as he stood there, motionless.

Paul's voice echoed in his memory—the coordinates he had given him to memorize years ago. *'It would always be their north.'* He told him. It was at a celebration Stephen and Clarice had when they moved to the compound. Everyone received a gift with the coordinates engraved. When Paul told him to memorize it, Nate had found him serious and strange, like he'd known something was coming. Nathaniel hadn't understood then. He did now. Family in one spot, their true north.

He nodded to himself. This was a sign. It would be his path. Whatever Paul had meant for him to find—wherever those numbers led, that's where he needed to go.

As he walked off the fractured docks, he searched the ruins, scavenging whatever supplies he could find. Hidden beneath a broken piece of wood—a water canteen, dented but usable. An aluminum pole, bent across the shattered windows of a tailor shop—a tattered leather jacket hanging from its tip. A flare gun, miraculously intact, lying on the side of the debris filled street. It wasn't much, but it was enough to keep him moving.

Nate continued heading inland. The muscles in his legs had begun to twist into unforgiving knots. The pain was quickly setting in. That's when he felt the vibrations in his pocket. His first thought was, *I should have checked the pockets before I put this thing on.*

Patting himself on different areas of his chest, he realized it was the compass he had found. He took it out of his pocket. The needle was erratically spinning, too fast for a clear reading. Its movement slowed for a couple seconds, then suddenly stopped.

Nathaniel slowly raised his head, eyes quickly moving like the compass just seconds ago. As he looked up, afraid of what he would see, his eyes landed, amidst the sea of destruction, more than a hundred yards ahead, sitting several feet above on a small hill, the only seemingly untouched building left standing. Not a single broken window. No damage to the walls. The storm had left everything else in ruins but appeared to have veered around the standing structure as if shielded by an invisible force field.

Surrounded by chaos, it stood—perfectly shielded in silence.

Nathaniel approached it slowly, uneasiness crawling up his spine. The door was what truly stopped him—painted in a dull, teal color that didn't match the rest of the building or anything around it. It was old, but somehow vibrant, too pristine in a world that had crumbled.

It felt wrong. Or maybe it felt right—and that's what unsettled him.

Cautiously, he stepped up and turned the knob. It creaked as it opened, as with a groan, revealing a space that felt suspended in time. The air was dry and quiet, even the minor dust was undisturbed. Furniture positioned exactly where it belonged. Nothing out of place. It was like walking into the life of someone who had simply gone shopping.

"Hello?" he called out, voice low, hesitant.

Silence.

"Anyone here?" he asked again, louder this time. But the house stayed quiet, wrapped in its strange calm.

He let out a slow breath and stepped inside, eyes sweeping the room.

"This will do," he said to no one in particular. Then, softer, almost to himself, "This would be a good place to spend the night."

His voice echoed slightly, swallowed by the walls.

He set the compass on the table and watched the needle settle—still pointing forward, this time toward the door he had entered in. Always toward something, unknown. Something waiting. He sat there, waiting for whomever the home belonged to. He knew it would not happen but took some solace in the wait before he started going through the privacy of the owner's personal belongings.

Nate built a fire, changed into clean clothes, and stocked up on food from a fully supplied storage locker. He packed the essentials into a backpack, then laid down on the floor, pulling a blanket over him. As sleep began to pull him under, a flicker of light caught his eye—something reflective was hanging on the wall.

A sword.

Nate pulled his battered body from the floor for a closer look. He lifted the sword from its hooks on the wall for a better look. He noticed its light weight as he examined the craftsmanship. It was flawless.

Thirteenth-century—by the looks of it. Nate was deep in thought. Polished to a shine, impeccably maintained, it looks like it belonged in a museum, not hanging here.

The shine of the steel gleamed in the firelight as if it had been forged only yesterday, reminding him of a sword given to him by a Japanese dignitary years ago. He had lost it on a mission while in the Middle East.

While holding the sword, Nate started looking around, scanning from all angles, searching for a clue to help him understand.

What kind of place was this? Why would something like this be hanging here—in the only building still standing? Yet recognizing his state, he guided himself to consider it at another time. I don't have the strength to solve it now.

He put the sword back and curled up again underneath the blanket next to the fire. He closed his eyes, turned over the question in his mind as sleep finally took him.

Not Your Call

Zuri woke up early. She moved about, quickly dressing for the day, including boots and survival gear. As she peeked out the oversize window in her bedroom, the sky still painted in soft gray, the break of day just on the horizon. She slung her hiking bag over her shoulder, then rushed down the stairs to meet Zoe. As she reached the bottom, she came to an abrupt halt.

Zoe wasn't alone. Tim and Nick were standing with her, looking ready for whatever the day had in store.

"Good morning, let's get started," echoed from across the room.

Zuri's first instinct was to fake a cough, maybe claim a headache—but the weight of her backpack thrown over her shoulder, her high energy, made that idea a little unbelievable. Besides, she had already agreed to go with Zoe to install the signal boosters.

Before she could stop herself, she blurted, "Four, oh sorry—five makes it an adventure—how exciting." She hadn't seen Gerard sitting at the table.

Nick flashed a half-smile, reached for her bag, and said, "Let me take that."

Zuri faked a reciprocating smile, caught off guard by the gesture. Somewhat hesitating, she allowed him to lift the bag from her shoulder. It felt strange—his being this nice. She hadn't expected it. Nick had always kept his distance, usually with Stephen or absorbed in his own world behind a screen. Gerard and Tim had been more open, perhaps it was because of Zoe. Nick, on the other hand, rarely left his computer screen. One could tell he had a quiet leadership role in their group. However, most people were guarded around him—out of respect perhaps, he was slightly older.

The team began their journey. Zuri with her military mind, thanks to Paul's training over the years, had mapped out the best way to get to the outskirts of the mountain. The terrain would be difficult, but she was prepared.

They moved in silence mostly, boots pressing into uneven earth, eyes scanning ahead for the next step. Zuri stayed focused. At least, at first. She didn't even notice when it happened, but she found herself deep in thought, almost in a dreamlike state. Not about the boosters or even paying attention to her surroundings. She could hear faraway voices, laced with distant laughter in the background of her evolving daydream. Lingering behind just a few feet at first. Then slowly, she had lagged even more, only now with a full view of Nick in front of her. Her mind drifted deeper, fantasizing.

Nick has a perfect form.

Nick moved with quiet focus, Zuri's backpack over his shoulder, while the other hand carried his bag. Zuri focused on his upper arms. The weight of his bag caused the muscle to expand, the resistance moving against his shirt's material. His arms moved in unison with his stride, his stride long and purposeful. There was something almost hypnotic about the way his shoulders moved—steady, precise as he tackled the uneven path.

Zuri didn't mean to stare, but her thoughts betrayed her logic, uninvited and intrusive. But that didn't stop her. She continued shamelessly tracing the shape of his back with her thoughts, the line of his shoulders, the way his shirt clung to his skin with each drop of sweat. Her gaze traced the sweat's path as if it had every right to engage, lingering where it pooled at the base of his neck. Her mind was already halfway down a path that had nothing to do with the trail in front of her—curious, bold, and far more intimate than she'd ever admit aloud.

Her thoughts were drifting far from the trail beneath her feet—and it showed. She didn't even notice she was veering slightly off course, until Zoe's voice cut through her daze.

"What do you think, Zuri?"

She blinked, snapping back to reality. "I'm with you," responding automatically. She had no idea what she'd just agreed to.

Nick looked back, recognizing her response was one of compliance. He slowed his pace until he was walking beside her. Without missing a beat, he started talking—granted, it was small talk. Zuri responded without thinking, her voice organic, and unguarded. It surprised even her how easily the conversation flowed. Connection wasn't something that came naturally to her—at least, not often. But with Nick, it felt... effortless.

They shared a rhythm in their banter, their wit cutting quick and sharp. Sarcasm passed between them like a language only they spoke— often too dry, too blunt for most people to get, but not for each other. They laughed quietly, and when silence came, it felt intimate, not awkward. Even in the stillness, there was comfort.

As they walked, Zoe joined in the conversation, shifting it back to the task at hand. She and Zuri had outlined the plan to install signal boosters along the perimeter—devices that would reinforce the antenna feed and support the surveillance system. The terrain had been causing trouble for weeks. Zoe's attempts to keep a stable connection had been hit-or-miss, blocked by the dense rock and metal deposits beneath the surface. The enclosed nature of the area made it nearly impossible to get a clean signal to the satellites orbiting above.

Zuri listened, nodded, and offered her ideas about the details—half of her in the conversation, the other half acutely aware of the man walking beside her, and the strange, unexpected sense of ease he brought with him.

"We've made it to the first spot." Nick grabbed a few things from his bag, while Zuri took a rope, gloves, and climbing materials from her sack. Just as Nick was about to position himself to start climbing the rocks to the area for the booster, he noticed Zuri putting on her gloves.

Nick blurted out, "What are you doing? I don't need you to come with me." It was said as his way of protecting her. The climb was dangerous—the rocks cold and damp.

Zuri gave an annoyed look. "It's not your call. I don't even know why you're here in the first place. This was supposed to be Zoe and me—like we couldn't handle it without you."

Nick looked as if his ego had been deflated in front of the others. The words stung, deeply. He thought they had a connection. Realizing what she had done, Zuri tried to minimize the impact of her words, but it was too late, Nick had already turned away. Without a word, he started climbing. By the time Zuri found her verbal footing, Nick was already halfway up the wall, out of reach.

Nick installed the booster.

Zoe and Tim worked on testing the booster while Zuri unhooked her climbing gear, placing each piece back into her sack. Tim called up to Nick.

"Everything is working, you can climb down."

Her instinct to retreat, to disappear, was front and center. She hadn't taken more than a few steps when an unusually shaped tree caught her eye—nestled in a place where it seemed almost impossible to be able to grow. Its position was strange, yet the tree itself was beautiful, with a unique design that seemed to belong—grown in that spot since the beginning of time.

It reminded her of a tree she had seen during the ceremony in Africa—sacred, powerful. The trunk curved, shaped over time, though the rugged terrain around its base seemed to have fought against it. The roots dug deep into the mountain, clinging desperately to the rocky face as if they were unwilling to let go. *It should not be here, in such an unlikely place, and yet... here it stands, as though it was always meant to be.*

Zuri had often heard Jack's stories about the special nature of the land. Standing before the tree, she could feel there was truth in them. If this was any indication, the land was more than just beautiful, it seemed to hold a mystery—an added charm expanding time itself. The tree's branches arched outward, reaching across the fading light of the evening, weaving patterns in the sky that seemed to touch the very edge of heaven.

A small path separated the tree from the mountain, with about ten feet of space beneath its sprawling branches. Zuri moved beneath them, standing quietly in the stillness. As she did, she felt an unspoken connection, as though the tree was speaking to her in the language of her ancestors; one she couldn't fully understand, but familiar, felt deep within her. The conversation wasn't in words, but in something older, more primitive. And, somehow, she was at peace with it.

"Zuri lets' go." Nick said as he picked up her sack and threw it over her shoulder. He stood there and waited for her to rejoin.

Zuri was startled. She had been lost in the atmosphere of the tree.

Nick liked her, though he rarely knew how to show his emotions. Both he and Zuri struggled with personal interactions. What had been a comfortable encounter with each other earlier, now once again became awkward. No one mentioned what had happened, letting the silence hang between them with a quiet understanding.

By the time they reached the next stop, Nick was already preparing himself for the climb. Zuri stood back, watching quietly, her gaze distant. It was only when they reached the last spot for the booster that the tension between them seemed to lift, the team finding their rhythm once more.

Nick hesitated for a moment, then reached out, his hand lingering in the space between them. "Come, climb this one with me?" he asked, the words softer than he intended, but filled with something more than he knew how to express.

Zuri instinctively agreed, as her heart smiled with a chance to undo the damage she knew she had caused earlier.

It was getting late.

"We should camp out tonight. There is no way we can make it back home before nightfall." Zoe said. She was always in charge, or so she thought. But after a brief discussion, just to let her know she was not, they decided to spend the night outside the compound. Zoe sent a message to Paul to let everyone know they were safe and would be camping out.

As the guys headed off to gather sticks for a fire, Zoe, and Zuri set about making a campsite. The chill of the evening air began to settle in, and Zuri could feel the cold creeping into her bones. It was colder than they had expected for this time of year, and they hadn't packed for staying outside overnight. Though Zuri had thought ahead and brought a few emergency items, she hadn't considered shelter. They'd have to rely on each other for that.

Despite the lack of proper gear, Zuri had packed something perfect for the situation. She dug into her bag, pulling out a small flask of tequila, a container of fresh limes, and two sandwiches wrapped carefully in paper. As she laid everything out on the ground, a quiet chuckle escaped Zoe.

"Zuri, you are always prepared," she said, shaking her head with a grin.

The guys returned shortly after, their arms full of sticks for the fire, and the mood lightened. Laughter bubbled up between them as they gathered around the makeshift campsite, the warmth from the fire mingling with the warmth of their growing closeness.

"Never leave home without it!" Tim said while pulling out a joint from his bag.

"Of course, you would have that. What are you going to do when you run out." Gerard said in a jokingly condescending tone.

Tim responded, "Under control, I'm going to grow it!" They all laughed.

The four of them sat huddled around the fire, the warmth from the flames landing across their faces, as they shared secrets. With each confession, each story, the bonds between them deepened. There was something honest in the air, a sense of freedom in releasing their most intimate truths, the things that had been locked away for far too long. Laughter more easily expressed than it had in months, the genuine, uncontrollable laughter that comes from a shared moment of vulnerability and understanding. For a while, it felt as though they were untouchable, free from the weight of the world, sitting high about everything.

But then, just after midnight, the air shifted.

A loud, deafening *boom* shattered the peace, so sudden and forceful that it rattled their bones. It was distant, had to be hundreds of miles away, with an undeniable force. The sky seemed to tremble in response, as if the explosion had cracked the very air open. The moment was surreal. The universe had just jolted them back into reality.

Before they could process the first blast, another explosion followed, this time even more powerful than the first. The ground beneath them seemed to quiver with the impact. There was no mistaking it now. Whatever had caused those explosions, the damage had to be immense.

They had heard the crack in the ground—earthquake.

The laughter stopped, replaced by an unsettling silence. The cheerful banter they had shared moments ago felt distant, almost irrelevant now. As the seconds ticked by, the weight of what they had just heard settled in. The reality of their existence, the very reason they had come to this place, the constant tension that lingered on the edges of their lives, came rushing back.

No one moved. No one spoke.

The world they had escaped, even if it had been for just for a little while — the danger, the fear, the uncertainty — had returned, louder and more undisputable than ever before. The fire, which had once felt like their only refuge, now felt small, insignificant against the vast, unspoken threat that had just made itself known.

"We should get some sleep."

Zuri woke to the warmth of the sun gently caressing her face, the soft light filtering through the trees in the distance. Her mind was still fuzzy from sleep, but the clarity came quickly as she realized where she was. She had fallen asleep in Nick's arms. Shifting slightly, trying to compose herself, hands fidgeting with the edge of her jacket.

"Sorry, I didn't mean to…" The words failing to connect to complete the thought.

Nick interrupted, simply smiled, and replied, "Anytime."

His nonchalant response made her feel more at ease. She quickly pulled herself together, collected her things, and made her way to the path where the others were waiting.

The morning air was crisp, the remnants of the night's chill still lingering in the shadows of each of their minds. They had all packed up their gear in silence, the awkwardness still hanging in the air between them, but it wasn't uncomfortable. Just a curiosity of what the explosion had been—yet too afraid of the answer.

Once they had their supplies, they began making their way toward the opening. Zuri kept her gaze focused ahead, trying to clear her head, but the quiet between them felt more. There was something unspoken that lingered—though none of them could quite put into words.

When they reached the cliff outside the entrance into the compound, Zuri took a deep breath, feeling the weight as it settled in. Reaching into the side of the mountain, she grasped at coldness of the lever. Then pulled it with ease, releasing the massive stone door.

Once inside, the narrow, winding staircase was a welcome sight. At the bottom, the passage opened into the vast area Stephen had discovered during excavation. It was a hidden part of the mountain.

The perimeter's entrance had been designed as a precautionary measure, with a series of traps and paths that only those who knew the way could navigate safely. If you didn't know the precise steps to take, you could easily teeter off the edge or get lost in the maze of the mountain. They had made sure that no one would stumble upon this place by accident — it was a stronghold, meant to keep the wrong things out.

As they continued descending the stairs, Zuri's mind wandered back to the previous night, her thoughts still tangled in the aftermath of the shared moment with Nick. She wondered if he too was processing it all. But for now, the mission had to take priority. The mountain had a way of demanding focus, its silent presence forcing one to stay alert.

The air grew colder as they descended deeper into the mountain, and Zuri's pulse quickened. Time running out. Whatever they were about to face with the asteroid, she knew it wouldn't be easy. The explosions had solidified it for all of them.

Zoe, Gerard, Tim, and Nick went directly to the security room. It had been days since they were able to get any information about the status of the asteroid. Zuri found her dad working in the weapons room. She had been the reason Paul left special forces. But Jazzette, Lizzie, and the twins were the reason he left active duty.

"Howdy Captain," Zuri said as she approached Paul. "Hi Dad, we just got back."

"How was the install? It took longer than expected, did anything happen?"

"No, not really." Zuri tried to minimize the events of the evening, but Paul knew her. He could tell when she was being evasive. He had learned the key to getting inside her head. Although most of the time it took some maneuvering.

"So was it just Zoe and you. How did the two of you get along?"

"Nick, Gerard, and Tim came with us. At first it was annoying having them with us, but it turned out good. So, Dad what are you doing, let's go shoot something. I need to practice with my bow. It's been a while."

And just like that, the conversation about the trip was over, for now.

Choice

It had been several days since the explosions were heard. The constant reminders from various news reports had gradually quieted, and the public broadcasts had become fewer and far between. Most people were settling into what had become their new normal, adjusting to the quiet aftermath, as if the world was slowly trying to move on.

Those who had lost loved ones or seen their homes shattered, reduced to rubble by the destruction of the space center and pieces of the asteroid were scattered across relief centers nationwide. But no matter how well-meaning the efforts, the centers were little more than holding pens for grief — places where hope could only flicker under the weight of reality. They could never offer safety. Nor could they shield any of them from the looming catastrophe on the horizon.

Time was a luxury, and in the fullness of time, what is willed, shall be done—and its outcome will be that which was willed—equally justified for everyone.

Jazzette, forever the optimist, often reminded everyone, "At least it gives them hope."

But Zuri and Zoe could never bring themselves to share that sentiment. To them, hope when misguided was dangerous. A mere distraction, a false sense of security that dulled the urgency and kept people from confronting the truth. The relief centers weren't salvation. They were just a brief reprieve—a mere pause button on despair. Yet under such crushing circumstances, how could anyone accept anything else, what could they do.

The group was glued to their communication devices, desperate for any new information. There had to be more out there. Updates from other countries had been sparse, and the silence from global leaders was suffocating. Germany's action had triggered a crisis, but even that seemed insignificant now compared to the devastation still looming on the horizon. Honestly, no one could blame them. They had acted out of a sense of duty, doing what they believed would be best for their people. In many ways, it felt more honorable than the secrecy and manipulation coming from those who had buried the truth for so long.

Still, even with the end drawing near, humanity still stumbled into the same patterns of mistakes. In the name of self-preservation, people continued to do the wrong thing, clinging to power and control when they should have focused on survival. It was a bitter irony — the world wobbling on the edge of collapse, yet man still unable to get pass his own self-interests.

Zuri and Zoe, especially, couldn't escape the fact, man had created this mess, sown seeds of its own destruction. Secretly, Zuri wondered if God was using man's self-inflicted catastrophic outcome to bring about the end of time.

She never voiced how she felt—not to Zoe, not even to Paul. Although she knew she could go to him with anything, this felt all too strange. It would more likely end up with them all thinking she was unraveling under the pressure.

No one understood the prophecy like she did. Since her baptism, she had carried a quiet knowing—an unshakeable awareness of things before they occurred. But now, when she needed someone to hear her the most, there was no one. Over the years, she had tried to test the waters with others, and all fell short, leaving her with her own set of doubts. They would misunderstand her, see her as someone who thought she was more than everyone else. That had never been her intent—but with a lack of words to clarify what was in her heart, she would always shy away. Perhaps that was the main reason she withheld herself from others.

She had never heard the story the elders had told Paul nor the recurring dreams of Clarice.

Zoe's team had been working relentlessly, sifting through data streams in search of a connection, any clue that could give them an edge. With the newly installed boosters, they now had the ability to tap into each country's security systems with little effort, a strategic advantage they couldn't afford to waste. Time was running out, and their window of opportunity was narrow.

"We should each take a region." Realizing the urgency, Tim suggested.

They all agreed and decided to divide and conquer—each member assigned to pull as much information as possible from their respective regions before the satellite went out of range. The clock was ticking, and with the space station damaged, they knew it would be another eight hours before the next satellite would be in position to aid them.

Every second mattered.

Each member of the compound had their own list of things to carry out before they were all sequestered. They all worked in pairs, regardless of how easy or difficult the task. It was a way of ensuring if anything happened to one person, another could step in seamlessly. The pairing system wasn't just practical—it was a safeguard as well. It created a network of trust, where each person knew their partner's strengths, weaknesses, and how to adapt when necessary. In an environment where danger felt like it was always just a breath away, the bonds formed through the partnerships gave them a measure of stability.

Lizzie and Clarice had been paired together. One of their primary responsibilities was the food supply. While preparing dinner, Clarice told Lizzie everything about the food supply. She knew they wouldn't be able to grow enough to sustain them.

"Early on," She told her, "I knew we would need another source of food. I love your granddad, but I was not going to depend on him to feed all of us for an extended period of time—but don't tell him I said that." They both laughed.

"I promise." Lizzie said, still grinning as she continued to chop the vegetables.

"Sarah and I did some surveillance on several food warehouses. We managed to, well... *redirect* several food trucks. One's parked in the warehouse now, and we have a few others stashed across the country, close to all the safehouses.

"G-Mom, you and Ms. Sarah, I don't believe it. You guys are always coming up with some scheme. How? Stealing food trucks. Really." Lizzie laughed teasing Clarice.

Clarice had to admit it seemed a little far-fetched. Carrying the bowl with the rest of the vegetables, "OK, you caught me. I asked for Zoe's help, again—but don't tell Stephen."

Giving Lizzie a slight hug. Laughing, Clarice went on to say, "Zoe ordered nonperishable foods and had the delivery truck sent to the addresses of the safe houses, nicely parked in the garages. Like I said for us, one truck was delivered for immediate use, and several others are at an underground storage facility. The facility is locked with a combination that only we will have. It's about twenty miles northwest of the compound. Far enough away so that if the compound is destroyed, we would still have a chance to survive. All we would have to do is get to it."

"I think we should send the address and combination to everyone's com-cards." Lizzie said enthusiastically. "That way if we get separated, we know what to do for food."

"That's a perfect idea! We can also make a plastic card too, so if the com-cards get broken, they will still have a physical copy. Brilliant Lizzie. I knew we would be good together." Clarice said proudly.

Clarice and Lizzie were still discussing their assignments while they prepared dinner when Zoe rushed in.

"Is everyone going to be at dinner tonight?" She said with such a flair.

Clarice looked perplexed.

"We need to make some decisions, and everyone should have an input."

As quickly as she had entered the room, she left the room. Lizzie smiled while looking at her grandmother. "So dramatic!" They both laughed and continued the dinner preparations, engaging in small, lighthearted conversations.

Clarice had been showing Lizzie how to navigate the kitchen, hoping to take her mind off what was happening around them. The upcoming months were going to be devastating, especially for her and the twins. She was a lovable kid. And even at a young age, a teenager, Clarice knew Lizzie loved God. It would help her when the time came.

Lizzie stopped chopping the vegetables, the knife still in her hand, frozen midair. Her tone shifted, becoming more intense.

"G-Mom," she said. She was the first one to call her that. Clarice loved it. It made her feel special, reminding her of the deep bond they shared.

Clarice immediately felt the change and braced herself. "Ask me anything," she said softly, setting down her own work. "I'll be as honest as I can."

Lizzie's eyes were steady. "I saw this movie about how giants were created—that when the angels were cast out of heaven, they had children with humans." She made a face of discomfort. "Is that true? That's... awful."

Clarice felt a heavy weight settle over her. She didn't have easy answers for this. She took a slow breath, praying inwardly for the right words. "I've heard of that," she said carefully, letting Lizzie know she was listening.

Lizzie continued, her voice steady. "They taught people how to make weapons... how to do evil things. But I thought only God could create. So how could the angels show humans how to make those things?"

Clarice placed her hands flat on the table, grounding herself. "Lizzie, you're right. Only God can create life from nothing. God speaks, and so it is. What the fallen did was different. They couldn't create—but they could corrupt."

She watched Lizzie's face, saw how closely she was listening, and continued.

"They took what God had already made. Things like metals, minerals, other natural raw materials, and taught men how to twist it. How to reshape things for purposes for which it was never meant. They manipulated what was good and turned it toward man's own destruction."

Clarice paused, then spoke with even more care.

"It's the same with us. Each of us is made for a purpose, wonderfully and intentionally designed. But life can pull us away from that purpose. Fear, pride, anger, envy, hatred... they can all distort what we were meant to be. But the original design remains. No matter how far we stray, the design of who we are meant to be is still there, waiting to be accepted, and used for the Glory of God, our creator."

"But, G-Mom, how do we prevent ourselves from straying away from our purpose? How can we not feel bad when we do all those things?" Lizzie asked with a sincere, puzzled look, voice sounding defeated.

The kitchen was quiet. The air thick with obvious inner thoughts. Clarice nodded slowly, the weight of the questions settling over her.

"Lizzie, you know the crucifixion of Jesus— His blood shed?" Clarice asked. "You've heard how He took on our sins when He died and rose from the grave. Correct?"

"Yes."

"We will never be able to do the right thing—consistently—Adam and Eve saw to that. No one ever has. But the good news is simple. When the Romans went to retrieve Jesus at the garden, from that moment on, everything they did to Him was a representation of some type of sin. Sins carried out on Him—betrayal, greed, unbelief, pride, a brutal shedding of blood, abuse of the body, blasphemy—all sin. All those things that were done to Him in some form. Even the people with Him took part in it."

"How?"

"They denied Him, they abandoned Him—ran away and hid—betrayal. He took it, for people like you and me. So, he died with the burden of sin—inflicted, undeserved."

"G-Mom, that's so sad."

"But necessary. He had to conquer sin to death." Clarice changed the tone. "When I was a little girl, the preachers would always use the next part to stir up the people. He would say, 'Then on the third day, He got up!'" Clarice mimicked the preacher.

"The church would go wild. Then the choir would bring it home with a hymn *'He rosed in His glorified body, sinless.'* Lizzie I joke but we are thankful—grateful."

"I know G-Mom."

Lizzie broke the silence, "I think I understand." Retreating to her lightheartedness. "So, it is like someone created an AI to override systems to gain access to buildings for emergency purposes, *but* then *'somebody,'*" holding her hands up creating air quotes, "manipulates that AI so they could break into *'someone else's'* home and *'borrow'* their helocraft."

Both laughed uncontrollably. "See all men fall short of the Glory of God! Thank you Jesus, for the blood."

Everyone was scattered about doing their own thing to help them deal with the disaster lurking, overshadowing each of them. They were in a busy state, the time quickly approaching. Zuri was practicing with the sword under a tree outside of Jack's cabin. She was lost in technique and didn't hear Zoe as she approached.

With a frantic tone, she started talking before she reached Zuri.

"…We have some new information; everyone should be at dinner to discuss it."

Zuri wanted to ask what type of intel, but she knew Zoe well enough to know, it would be a futile exercise—ending up following a rabbit down the hole. Once Zoe's back was against the wall, she was like her mother. You wanted them on your side. Both very emotional, yet brave, intelligent, and undeniably loyal. Once a crisis had been avoided or dealt with, they would retreat back to their place of vulnerability.

Zuri watched in silence as Zoe turned and disappeared into the distance. The interruption had unsettled her more deeply than she cared to realize. Her focus broken, she knew she couldn't continue practicing. With deliberate care, she slid the sword back into its scabbard and let the silence consume her.

Leaning against the tree, her head bowed, Zuri let the tears come. She made no effort to hold them back. Paul had always told her that tears were God's way of cleansing the heart, that each tear made room for a new measure of joy.

But in that moment, joy seemed so far away.

The harsh reality of her beginnings, the weight of a future that felt both fragile and finite, a limited number of tomorrows pressed down on her. The grief that rose in her chest was not misplaced. It was the accumulation of too much uncertainty carved by the brutal events of the past few years.

She wept for what was—and for what might never be—for the small, stubborn sliver of hope that still refused to die within her.

Zuri remained under the tree for what felt like hours, letting the silence devour her. When she finally lifted her head, tears still trailing down her cheeks, she caught sight of the evening sky. The clouds, touched by the setting sun, had shifted into deep, solemn colors—hues that mirrored the ache and quiet hope inside her. Gold, crimson, and violet. A sky mourning the end of day.

A familiar peace washed over her, the same steadying calm she had felt when they were setting up the boosters. It carried with it a deeper understanding of a past that was over. There was no changing that. The riots, the explosions, the frantic scrambling for solutions—all of it faded into a distant memory, with no regrets, no approvals. It meant nothing against the reality of what was to come.

The future was delicate, hanging on by a thread. The looming threat of the asteroid and the brutal uncertainty of human survival was undeniable. Each passing moment would force a choice.

She knew, without question, moving forward would require a readiness—a willingness to adapt to whatever new challenge that might come up, no matter how unexpected. She also understood, with absolute clarity, that if she was given even the slimmest chance, she had a responsibility to use every skill, every ounce of knowledge she possessed, not just for herself or her family, but for the survival of all who still had breath to fight for another day. Even if no one understood, she wanted to fight for God, in whatever capacity He might want her too.

***

The table was full, even Jack and his wife were there. Clarice and Lizzie were busy bringing out the food, serving drinks. Intense side conversations were going on. Everyone was trying to figure out the purpose of Zoe's summons. Even the members of her team didn't know exactly why they had been *requested* to be at dinner.

There was an empty seat next to Nick. As Zuri walked toward the seat, Nick looked up at her, smiled and motioned her with the chair to sit. Zuri smiled, hoping the butterflies she was feeling did not show, to him or anyone else, how much she really did like him.

Stephen stood up and tapped his glass. "Shall we hold hands and give thanks." Everyone quieted.

"Our heavenly Father, to you be the glory!"

"Father, I am reminded of the Last Supper. The last meal you had with your disciples as a unit, together. I listen to the side conversations at our table, just the way it must have been so long ago. We thank you, Father, for an opportunity, knowing what is in store for this world, that all of us have one more chance to join hands in love for each other, with family, friends, old and new."

Nick locked eyes with Zuri, affectionately squeezing her hand.

Stephen continued. "Lord, we thank you for this food. We do not know everything that lies ahead, but we do know you are with us. We just ask for Grace to see us through, Mercy when we pivot from your direction, and recognizable Favor to help us with any fear as we walk through this valley of death. Amen."

The twins in sync, "Let's eat!"

They were about twenty minutes into the meal when Zoe stood, tapping her glass. Little comments, sly remarks bounced across the table, laughter filled the room. For a few moments, they had forgotten about what lurked around the bend.

"The communication team," Zoe started. Clarice and Lizzie looked at each other, almost laughing as if they had an inside joke. Lizzie lip syncing, '*Drama queen.*'

"The team split the world into five global regions. We each took a group to see if we could find chatter in their assigned regions. We now have a better picture of what is happening. Each global region is doing their own thing. The one thing that is creating an even bigger disaster is the secrecy that has plagued the world. Everyone has a piece of information, but none has everything.

"In each region we have found people who are basically in the same position as us. They have been provided with information about the dooming crisis. They have been discovering information, working behind the scenes just as we have. Each group has been given a name— Jade 1, Jade 2, Jade 3, Jade 4, and Jade 5. We will be known as *Jade 3.*

Just like us, their governments also played games with each of the other governments. Now, it's too late."

As Zoe spoke, her voice trembled. She was trying to be brave, in command. With each word spoken, she could hear them echoing back as they ricocheted off the facial expressions of each person sitting at the table. The heartbreak, sadness, empathy, and yes, even failure was all on display.

Zoe continued, "We've done nearly everything we can to prepare ourselves. At this point, our part in the larger plan is small but could be vital for some. Tonight, we're putting a question before you. We're not here to convince anyone to see things our way—that's not the point. Instead, we have a set of voting chips."

Lizzie burst out laughing, loud enough for everyone at the table to turn   and   look. She quickly apologized, catching Clarice's eye; Clarice winked and gave her a knowing smile.

Zoe gave her a disappointed glance and pressed on. "We're considering sending a global announcement. If we choose to move forward, Nick and Zuri will drive to a specific set of coordinates tomorrow morning. Zuri needs to be within one hundred yards of the target to attach a device."

"What target? What device?" Zuri asked, sounding genuinely confused, hearing about it for the first time.

Zoe smiled at her. "I'll get to that in a moment. First, let's talk about the package. We've built a device that can deliver a message across multiple platforms, in multiple languages, anywhere there's a communication network. It doesn't matter who controls the network— our message will be displayed." As she was about to tell Zuri about their roles, people started mumbling.

Paul was the first to jump in, sounding slightly irritated. "Shouldn't we be talking this through a bit more?"

"I knew this could turn into a long, messy debate," Zoe said, her tone calm but firm. "Everyone defending their beliefs, arguing over moral compasses, and dragging the whole thing out. But none of us has the right to sway someone else's choice. That's why we designed a voting system to make sure the decision is made fairly, by majority rule."

With that, Zoe finished speaking and took her seat.

Nick and Tim passed the chips out, one of each color.

'Red for yes, tell everyone everything—facts only OR—black for no, why panic the world if there is nothing that can be done.'

As they got their chips, everyone retreated to their own space. They had until midnight to make their individual decision, placing their color chip in the canister. No one would ever know how they voted unless they chose to tell.

For most, it was a moral decision. Others questioned why they should throw the world into chaos when so much of it was about to be destroyed anyway.

Would this be the moment when people gave in to their strongest fears and weakest impulses?

What about those who would simply want one last supper with their families? Who were they to deny them that?

There would be riots, people stealing food and water for their survival. But what about stealing helicopters and food trucks? Still stealing, just a little more sophisticated. Yes, for some it was a moral decision, yet, at the end of the day, survival of self.

Midnight.

No one could sleep. Somehow, everyone had made it to the kitchen, eating leftovers, carrying on conversations from earlier. Paul picked up the canister, while taking the top off, commenting on no matter what the decision is, he said, "We will all support the outcome."

Paul flipped the canister over so all the chips would fall out at the same time, clapping down on the island to try and prevent them from rolling on the floor. In the mist of the slapping down, it was obvious that the communication would be carried out as planned. Red was the obvious choice for everyone.

The world will know what is ahead. What the people decided to do with their last few potential hours would be in their hands.

Drop It

The sword was still in Nathaniel hands when he woke the next morning. He could feel the nervous energy radiating throughout his body—tremors just beneath his skin. He was on alert, body tense on the outside but small constant flutters inside. He laid there for a few minutes, making sure the events of the previous day had actually occurred, reviewing with himself.

Germany kicked all Americans out—because of our government. The harbor was destroyed—by some unknown object from space, and now I'm here lying on a strange floor with a sword in my hand—from where? Just more questions.

Nathaniel knew none of his answers would be based on intel or any type of facts. He only knew he needed to get to Nebraska.

He rose with a determination. As he gathered his things, he decided to take the sword. It hadn't felt like stealing, but more like they had found each other. There was no sheath to contain it, so he needed a scabbard. He knew he couldn't just carry it around exposed, not without killing himself—or someone else. So, he searched the house. There had to be something there to protect the sword. It was in perfect shape. He checked everywhere—closets, trunks, looking for anything that might serve as a makeshift cover.

Nate was just about to give up when he opened an old cedar chest tucked beneath the stairs. Inside, wrapped in layers of dust signifying time, was a strip of thick, weathered cloth—faded, but intact. It looked ancient, older than anything else in the house.

He didn't know why, but something about it felt… right. Carefully, he wrapped the blade, the cloth molding around the steel like it remembered the shape.

Nathaniel grabbed the rest of his findings and tucked the sword between the straps of his backpack. He stopped in the doorway. Just as he was about to walk out, he turned looking around to make sure he was not leaving anything of use. That's when he felt it.

A subtle shift stirred the air. A wavy haze shimmered briefly across the room. Nathaniel blinked. Assured that his eyes had misled him, he dismissed the shift, pulled the door shut and he left the safety of the only standing building. It had been his refuge through the night. Now the ruined harbor was at his back, the compass was spinning, settling with a guiding force of certainty—an unyielding pull in a direction he would now follow.

Nathaniel began searching for a car. He tried several before he gave up.

"Damn-it!" Yelling out of frustration.

The only pair of dry shoes he had found, and now they too were wet. All the cars had been submerged in water, just waiting for someone to come and release the valve. Nate considered the intensity of the storm surges to reach so far inland. He was lucky to be alive.

Nate gave up looking for a car and focused on walking towards higher ground. He was halfway out of the city, when he came upon a group of people escaping the city as well.

"Howdy." Nate called out, waving his hand, "Where you guys headed?" He said, feeling lucky he had come across anyone still alive in the area.

One of them shouted, "We have nothing! Leave us alone."

"Sorry," holding up both hands. "I meant no harm. After all the things I saw in the city, I thought companionship would be good, helping each other when we can. I am headed to Nebraska."

The group exchanged guarded glances. Finally, one of them spoke. "Thank you. We are not sure where we are going. The city is not safe."

Another, "We can't be too careful. Forgive us, we don't want any trouble."

"Understood," Nate chimed in.

Nate joined the group. They continued walking together, making small talk. Trying to get a better handle on his new companions, Nathaniel asked a few non-provoking questions. He wanted them to be comfortable with him. He wanted to help, knowing what was going to happen in just a few days.

Most were willing to share their stories, but one member of the group remained evasive. His answers were clipped, gaps that didn't quite add up. Nate's familiarity with interrogation, caused an immediate sense of something being off.

He pressed him gently but firmly.

Reaching his hand out for the stranger to shake it, Nate introduced himself.

"How rude of me, name is Nathaniel, Nate" hand gripping, lingering, waiting for a response.

"Nathaniel - Nate, Raphael - Ralph."

"I was in the harbor when something fell from the sky. Lucky to be alive!" Nate was continuing the conversation when Ralph interrupted.

"Sounds more like divine intervention."

"Miracle - luck, whatever it was, I thought I was a goner for real."

Eventually, Ralph began to open up, and some semblance of truth began to emerge. He explained how he had recently been at a hospital—and when everything was over, he searched for the people he was assigned to escort to their destination.

Something about the story still didn't sit right with Nathaniel. Raphael was too perfect to be true. His choice of words seemed deliberate, his every moment was ordered from deep within. Nate knew before they reached Nebraska, he would have to make a decision about this stranger—whether he could trust him enough to bring him to Paul's door. The others, at least, had appeared to be honest about how they had come together. He felt he could trust them.

Nathaniel glanced at him now, walking a few paces ahead of the others. Raphael was relaxed as if the weight of the world didn't touch him. And that, more than anything, unsettled Nate. They had been walking most of what was day three now when Ralph noticed everyone was exhausted.

"Evening is upon us, we should probably find a place to sleep for the night." Ralph said, directing his gaze towards Nathaniel for his agreement. He didn't want Nate to feel like there was a power struggle between them.

"Agreed." Nathaniel replied in turn. "Let's camp in the foothills near Mount Rainier. It looks like it's just a few miles ahead."

It had been several days on the road, and the group had stayed off the main highways. The journey had proven to be hazardous with too many disruptions to have to fight through. They had seen a lot on their journey—vehicles overturned, shops ransacked, barely making it out without any serious altercations. Chaos had been everywhere. People were desperate, trying to grab whatever they could—regardless of the technique they used.

By the time they found a sheltered spot in the mountain's foothills to make camp, the ground itself felt uneasy beneath their feet. Subtle tremors rippled under the soil—brief, unsettling pulses that left them glancing, questioning each other. They had heard of geothermal activity from other travelers trying to make it further inland to Wyoming. It had been rumored that Yellowstone had been struck, with the blast being felt hundreds of miles away.

Looking around, Raphael said to Nathaniel, "I'll go look for wood. We need to make a fire. It gets pretty cold up here in the mountains at night."

Before Nate could respond, Ralph was already gone, disappearing into the fading light.

They had been at the campsite for only a few minutes when a woman appeared from the tree line. She appeared to be suffering from some type of distress. One of the team members immediately took off their jacket and draped it over her shoulders. She told them how she lived on the mountain, and how her family had been killed during an explosion a few days earlier. She went on to tell them she had barely escaped and hadn't eaten or drunk anything for days.

Almost an hour had past, Ralph was still not back.

The other three members had been huddled around a small fire, involved in what seemed like a heavy conversation with the woman. Nathaniel was fidgeting with the uneasiness that had tiptoed to the back of his neck. He knew something was amiss with the state of the woman's attire. He no longer trusted his internal sensor. He had been mistaken about Ralph's intentions. But now, to see this woman, and listening to her story, he couldn't shake his assessment. His gut was screaming at him now. She reeked with evil.

Nathaniel shifted his weight, the fire crackling six feet away. The woman's voice was calm, too calm, considering what she claimed to have endured. Her tone didn't falter when she spoke of her family's deaths. In fact, there was a strange precision to her words, as if she were making them up as she dug deeper into the conversation—adding details that were a bit too convenient.

Nate lingered in the background, not fully engaged in the conversation. He allowed the others to be drawn in, so he could watch from the sidelines. The air around her was stagnant, not like someone needing a bath, but rather someone who was entering a dimension for the first time and hadn't yet adapted to its world. *Am I being paranoid?*

Nate noticed a stray ember floating from the fire in her direction. He was about to shout look out when the ember landed on her hand. Nate had to shake his head to focus. The woman didn't flinch. It was as if it had never touched her.

The woman looked up suddenly, locking eyes with Nate. For just a heartbeat, he froze—it couldn't have been what he thought. She smiled, slow and knowing. Sitting there by the fire, Nathaniel could have sworn he saw something else—*a demon?* But then in a flash the image was gone. She turned to continue the conversation with the others.

"I am going to go look for Ralph." Nate turned, looking at one of the men in the group, "Might be best if you come with me. No reason for someone else to need help out there and find themselves alone."

Nate grabbed his backpack, threw his makeshift scabbard across his shoulder. Just as they were about to leave, Ralph entered the camp, eyes locked on the woman who had entered after he was gone. He moved with purpose, walking with a stick. At first, they thought he was hurt. The stick—staff at first glance was unassuming, old, worn by the elements of weather over the age of time. Then after a closer look, Nathaniel saw an unintended glow.

It was mesmerizing. Nate stood there, motionless, quiet. He needed to explain to himself how. Each time Ralph took a step, he would hit the ground with the staff. At each strike, the staff colliding with the dry ground would quietly stir the dirt causing a haze of dust to rise. The backdrop from the sun caused a light to pass through the dust particles, thus the glow.

Yet, with each step the exact same thing would happen, a pattern—precise, unwavering. The staff hit the ground—dirt turn to dust—light pierced the dust, forming a luminous train behind Ralph.

Technically explained. So, why did it seem like so much more?

Ralph interrupted Nate's quiet examination of the strange vision—the glow, the dust, the rhythm that still pulsed faintly in his mind.

"I found a place for us to sleep," Ralph said, eyes never wavering from the woman's—his voice warm yet mysteriously piercing into a knowledge no one knew about, except him and the woman.

"Debris hit the home, but everything appears to be mostly intact. I had a chance to look around, it seems to be empty. We might be able to gather supplies and there's a couple of cars—for tomorrow's journey."

A soft voice broke the silence that followed. "Let's go. I could use a shower," came the weary echo from the wife of one of the men, her tone a mixture of fatigue and hope.

No one objected.

The walk to the house was short, the light from the day fading into the darkness overtaking the sky. Hues of early dusk seeping in.

They followed a cracked, winding driveway that curved gently through the fallen trees, with stones blocking the path. They came to an open gate, ripped from its hinges. Beyond it, an abandoned house revealed itself. Broken glass, bricks piled on one side of the house. As if the power of whatever hit it pushed everything in its path to an abrupt stop. Running water from the fountain—spilling over the top.

Even in its damaged state, one could tell the property had once been beautiful. Large windows glinted faintly in the fading light. Vegetation still clung to the far side of the fallen stone. The darker it got outside, the more the house became a bad choice. Their steps began to slow, more cautious.

"Are we sure we want to stay here?" someone murmured.

"It will be fine. Probably better than being out in the open. This time of year, there is no telling what animals are lurking about for food."

"But to be on the safe side, let's stay together."

Just as they entered the house, they heard something scrambling to exit. They all looked at each other. Too afraid to move, breathe heavy. The air was stuffy—thick.

Nathaniel broke the ice. "Ralph, let's see if we can find a flashlight. They might have a generator."

The two started their journey through the kitchen, looking through drawers. It didn't take long before Ralph turned one on, shining the beam around to get a better view of their surroundings. He located the exit to the back exterior of the house, hoping to find a generator.

"This way."

Ralph led them out of the kitchen, down a hallway with a slight turn, through the glass doors leading to the back of the house.

Generator located. Pushing the start button a few times, floods of light covered the house. Ralph and Nathaniel lingered, making casual conversation. Nathaniel took the opportunity to get a closer look at the staff. He could already see the craftsmanship. It wasn't crafted by human hands that was for sure. It was carved by nature itself.

Nathaniel reached for the staff but stopped as if an invisible force field prevented his touch. He quickly pulled his hand back in reconsideration. "You didn't have that when we first met up, where did you find it?"

Raphael responded looking at the staff. "It's remarkable, don't you think?" Deflecting Nathaniel's attention. "I feel like we have a connection. Like I should be the one entrusted with it until it finds its assigned master."

Nathaniel understood, it was the same with him and the sword. He wanted to mention the encounter he had with the woman, but in the end, he didn't say anything. Simply turned and started walking back to the others. He didn't care to engage with Ralph about it and hear his carefully chosen, almost condescending words.

"Nice job!" One of the others said as they entered the room.

"Looks like a war zone in here."

"You can tell it must have only been a few days since this happened. Whatever hit the harbor or Yellowstone, must have hit here as well."

"Or an earthquake." Ralph said as an afterthought—or was it a correction.

Nathaniel had gone from one crisis to another, flown across the Atlantic, catapulted into the Seattle harbor, and now, he had no idea what to do next. He needed to talk to Paul. Having been on the road for the past few days, he had no idea what had actually happened. Communications had been down—at the least, questionable—since he left Germany.

Looking around, trying to find some type of comm device, Nathaniel could see why they said the area looked as if it had been in a war zone. Furniture, tossed about like a pet's toy, left just as they had dropped it, pictures with broken frames lay on the floor.

The group continued to venture about the house. The three stayed together with the woman, whispering among themselves. They didn't realize Ralph had been observing them throughout their short time together. So, when one of them offered to stand the first watch, neither Nate nor Ralph objected.

"Hey, why don't you guys get some sleep? I'll light the fireplace and stand the first watch."

Nathaniel replied, "Sounds good. Wake me in four hours. I'll take over."

A Lifetime

Clarice was walking towards their bedroom, carrying coffee and pastries on a tray.

"Good morning, Mom." Jazzette said passing her on her way to the kitchen. "I see you and Stephen are planning on a late morning. Breakfast in bed?" Teasing her mom.

Clarice made a slight movement in her walk, swaying her hips from side to side, giving as much as she received. "We are not dead yet!" Jokingly, as her voice raised an octave as she moved further down the hallway.

"MOM!" both giggling.

Clarice and Stephen loved their early morning time. They didn't get to do it very often, especially now with a full house. It had indeed been a while. In the early years, this was their most intimate time of the day. The moments were quiet—peaceful. It was during this time they felt God was giving them a jump start on the day, accentuating potential pitfalls, those seen and unseen.

"Did I hear you talking to someone?" Stephen said, smiling at Clarice as she used her legs to close the door behind her.

"Jazz, she was teasing us about having breakfast in bed. No worries..." placing the tray in the middle of the bed. "We always give more than we take."

Stephen made a slight chuckle, "I'm not sure that's how that goes." Pausing for a moment as Clarice climbed back into bed.

"Um, maybe that should be our saying."

"I love you too." Clarice playfully ended the conversation before it got too heavy.

Sipping his coffee, "I think I will take the boys with me. Keep them out of your hair while everyone else is off doing last-minute tasks."

"You know that's not necessary. They love spending time with Jack, and Lizzie and I have minimal plans for the day. We'll just be making strawberry preserves—your favorite."

"They have been asking a lot of questions about the water system. Rain has been constant for the past few days, and still in the forecast for part of today. It'll be a good day to show them everything, and while we're at it, we can have a little fun playing in it."

Pausing, "I forgot, Nick is bringing back some materials for the water system. I should probably prepare the site for that as well, so by the time they get back we can just store it in the right place." Stephen said as a confirmation of his plans for the day. His mind, already made up.

"As long as, you are sure. Speaking of Nick and Zuri, what do you think of Nick, I mean his character."

"Nick is a good guy. He seems to be honest—trustworthy, with a kind heart. He spoke with me about Zuri." Chuckling, "He really is smitten with her."

"You didn't tell me." Clarice looked excited but disappointed. "I can't believe you didn't tell me."

"Forgive me, my Love. It was not intentional. The day after their booster trip, he asked me if it would be wrong to pursue something with her, with all the uncertainty."

"What did you tell him?" asking with an inner curiosity about how Stephen actually felt about it.

"Honestly, when I started talking, I didn't know what I was going to say." Stephen said with a sigh and broken smile.

"I prayed."

"And?"

'None of us knows the amount of time allotted to one's life. It is not measured by the number of years, but by what you do with that allotted time.'

Looking in Clarice eyes, welcoming her gaze, he began with all sincerity, "What if, when we met, we walked away because we were in the last moments of our life? Too afraid of the remaining length of time perceived…and yes, I know you considered walking. But faith overcame fear."

Clarice was sitting on top of the bedding, legs tucked beneath her, listening. Stephen's tone had changed. He was purposeful. Leaning closer to reposition herself, Clarice freely gave all of herself to him in the moment.

He continued, his voice filled with years of wisdom. "We," aged hands moving with a slight tremor, gesturing between them, "You and me, we've had a lifetime together. Oh, I know most will say we have not been together long enough for it to be considered a lifetime."

Clarice nodded.

"By man's measure, it may seem brief…But God's time is something entirely different. We have chosen to live by the guidelines of His time, the time God set aside for us. Time is His, held in His hands. And in His mercy, and by His favor, He gave us a lifetime, full of redemptive moments—time redeemed—His word. For that I am eternally grateful."

She loved him. He loved her.

Gratefulness— often becoming overwhelmed by it all. Her eyes filled with tears, pooling at the corners, searching for an escape. With nowhere else to go, they finally surrendered, spilling quietly down her cheeks.

Clarice's voice cracking, "Stephen."

He interrupted her before she could complete the thought, His voice in a whisper, "We've known other couples married for over seventy years, and it felt like seventy years of misery, for each of them—a prison sentence." His gaze softened as he continued. "And I've known others bound in a marriage for mere months, each day a reminder of regret."

Drawing her near to him, wrapping his arms around her, with resolve, he whispered, "I would not exchange any of us. I found my other half—the answer, the void. God has been so generous to us, giving us far more than Grace and Mercy. He's shown us so much favor over the years." Pausing, "Look around. This, us—all Him! Clarice, look what He's done."

Wiping the tears from her cheeks, she began to look around. "My Love, I am thankful. My life was missing a piece. I knew it! I felt it! There were times when I felt guilty. I knew how much I had been given—and yet, I always felt incomplete."

Clarice hesitated for a second, searching for a particular memory. "But the moment I saw you leaning against the column at the university, I knew the missing piece had been found. I love who we are, our life together. Our end!"

Tears flowing freely, raising her face up to look him in the face. "Stephen, I'm afraid. How are we going to do this? How can we protect the kids?"

Pulling her hands up to kiss them, "Even now when the world is at risk. Favor—protection. I don't know what is going to happen today or tomorrow. I don't know if Nick and Zuri will truly find each other. But what I do know is, God has a hand in it. He is in control."

"You're right."

"He has given us the pieces to prepare us for whatever happens. Think about it. Jack was placed in the right place at the right time, our refuge. God has provided for us here." Clarice smiled, nodding in agreement.

"Paul at the State Department, our captain. He will keep us safe, fight for us.

"Zoe—Timepiece. She will make sure we are always informed.

"Paul finding Zuri all those years ago. That cannot be a coincidence. I wonder if this had been orchestrated—long ago."

Clarice spoke with assurance. "Without insight into the future. I'm not sure how, but I think Nick and Zuri have yet to play a role in the aftermath."

"I think you're right." With a small level of sarcasm, Stephen joked. "Oh yeah, you and Sarah at a cocktail party planning a helocraft heist." Both laughed, settling into a quiet zone. "I am not sure that was part of the intended plan."

A couple of hours later, they decided to join the others.

"You want me to make you breakfast?" Clarice asked through the bathroom door while Stephen dressed.

"No, had enough for breakfast!" Winking as he walked out of the room.

Calling out the boys' names as he walked down the hallway, Stephen shouted, "Boys, let's go. We are working on the water treatment equipment today."

Coming from downstairs, "Granddad, we are down here."

Everyone was outside, in the courtyard. Each preparing for their own duties of the day. Nick and Zuri loaded the SUV with the necessary gear. Zuri stepped carefully off the porch, but before she could reach the ground, Paul took her hand.

Looking her in the eye, "Be safe. Don't forget to always assess your surroundings."

"Dad, I know. I'll be fine," she replied with a soft smile. "I'll be back before you know it."

Paul hesitated, then added, "I know you've been trying to hide how you feel about Nick. Just…be careful. The last thing I want to do is dig a grave for him in the middle of everything we're about to face."

Zuri gave a mischievous grin. While hugging Paul, she teased! "I will help you dig the grave if he does anything out of order."

Paul smiled, shaking his head, and kissed her on the forehead.

Once Nick and Zuri drove off, Stephen tapped the boys on the head, "Follow me."

Cody took off, grabbing Stephen's hand. "Granddad, are we really going to work on the water treatment?" Looking up at the rain trailing down the side of the mountain. "I want to know why we don't float away like Noah's ark."

Stephen smiled. He knew he was in for a long day, full of questionable curiosity. "Today's lesson, water!" He didn't mind. "Look there, there, and there." Pointing to the three different areas of the compound. "The ledges, can you see them? There is a long flat plate that's slightly tilted inward toward the walls of the mountain."

"I see them." Paul Jr said with such enthusiasm.

"When it rains, the water is caught on those ledges and redirected to inside crevices of the mountain." Stephen said, trying to remember words to describe everything as simple as possible. Even though the boys are actually advanced for their age, they were only ten. Living in the house with all the brain power, of course they would outpace others in their age bracket.

"But Granddad, all the water doesn't flow against the wall."

"True, look down. What are you standing on?"

"Looks like things on the streets at home."

"Exactly, they are part of the drainage system. We have these all over the property. So, when it rains, the water goes through the holes, filtered so the big stuff doesn't get through."

The boys were quiet, really interested. "Come, let me show you what happens once it flows inside the wall or go through the drainage tunnels in the ground."

As they were running towards the warehouse, they passed Paul. "Hi Dad, Granddad is going to show us the water system."

Paul reached out to slow them down, "Be good, stay together, AND stop running." Water and mud splattering about as they deliberately ran through the puddles.

Paul was headed to the security room. He had not heard from Nathaniel, and worry was rising within him. *Why hadn't Nate made it?* He had contacted him with the latest days ago. It wasn't like him not to check in.

Zoe and the rest of her team were in the security room, monitoring the global networks searching for other information.

"Zoe, have we heard anything from Nate." Paul started talking before he fully entered the room.

"No, not yet." Zoe, trying to ease his worry, "Communication is shaky, maybe he just hasn't been able to find a signal."

"Let me know if you hear anything."

Paul left as abruptly as he had entered. Zoe watched him go, her eyes widening slightly, looking to the others for affirmation. There had been something off in the way he spoke to her. There was nothing said or tone to insinuate an unkind nor harsh thought. But there was an undeniable distance. His interaction with her was felt. Not in the normal positive way, but out of obligation. He was treating her carefully. It was subtle, but noticeable. It hung in the air.

Is he still mad about me being Timepiece? Maybe Germany? At this point, she could only hope no one else had caught the tension—his obvious tone.

"Hey, what's up with your dad?" Tim asked partly out of curiosity, never considering how the question might disturb Zoe.

Zoe just stood there, not able to find the words. Gerard wanting to protect her—spare her feelings stepped in before she had a chance to respond.

"That's just Paul," he said. "Probably got something on his mind. Everyone is out and about. He just feels it's his responsibility to take care of all of us—so of course he is worried." His tone was light, but his eyes staring at Tim with such intensity—sharp and deliberate, sent a direct signal for him to *let it go*.

Gerard understood exactly what that kind of encounter would have meant to Zoe. Over the course of their relationship, she had confided in him—more often than not. Paul preference for Zuri over her was undeniable. No one doubted it. In Paul's eyes, Zuri could do no wrong. But it was also understood, Zuri never really had parents, Paul was her world. He had raised her as his own since she was a toddler.

Yet, understanding didn't make it hurt any less. His efforts were always centered more for Zuri. Zoe had been young, thirteen when her dad died, and fourteen when her mom married Paul. Even though her parents had been divorced for a few years, and she lived with Jazzette, her dad had always made her the center of his world, just like Paul did for Zuri. Only now her world broke her when it ended.

Zoe secretly ached for her father—the loss had left scars that were still quite visible—if you took the time to look. It had laid the foundation for a wealth of irrational emotions and a persona she couldn't believe was a part of her. So, to see Paul and Zuri together was always a reminder of what she had lost.

Zoe's thoughts spiraled, slipping out of her control. "I need to grab my bag," she mumbled, voice barely above a whisper, words incomplete, cracking as she rushed out of the room. Everyone knew it wasn't a good moment for her. Zoe felt the split, she was losing control. The symptoms of her shattered mind were letting her know someone or something else was about to take over.

"Look what you did!" All eyes on Tim.

"What? I was just making an observation." Tim said with that *special* expression that screamed *unrealistic expectations*—his signature look.

The others just turned around, shaking their heads, and continued with whatever they were doing. The discussion they were having before Paul's entrance had been effectively derailed.

Zoe barely made it out of the door.

'You know what his problem is, why are you upset? He is jealous of you and the way people follow you.'

"Stop it. I don't want to hear it!" Zoe said aloud, trying to keep herself from pursuing the negative conversation.

'Running won't make it go away. You need to take control of the situation. Paul doesn't know what he is doing. He wouldn't know as much as he does if it wasn't for you. Pretending won't save the world. Your skills are the reason survival is even possible.'

Zoe started to relax and allow the conversation to take over. She started to shift the way she was seeing thing. *Maybe Paul was jealous because of the way she was handling things. His way of doing things is outdated.*

"Maybe I need to ignore Paul and just do things the way I know they should be. I've got all the skills, and the network." Zoe continued talking aloud.

Just then, she was on her way to her room when she spotted Paul coming out of his and Jazz's room. She did a complete about-face. She didn't want anyone to see her that way, especially him. After all he was the problem.

"Zoe, could you be any more obvious?" Paul called out to her, looking a little confused.

"Oh, Paul," covering, pretending to be herself and in control, while forcing a fake smile she said, "I forgot to grab my bag and was going back to get it. Nate or Zuri might be calling." She knew he would drop it, cause anything to do with them always took priority.

But he didn't—drop it.

"Zoe." Paul called her name. His tone softening, loving, as he walked towards her. "Wait a minute, please." He reached out to put his hand on her shoulder. "I need to apologize for my behavior earlier. I'm just really worried about Nate. It's not like him."

The Huntress had almost gained control, but felt herself diminish. And in that moment, Zoe felt herself getting stronger. Paul's touch had been enough to stabilize her and bring peace.

Yes, her feelings were justified, but this was not the time. Hitting her like a ton of bricks, she realized, with everything going on, this was not the way to spend what little time they had left—wasted on such trivial issues, like ego.

Trying to put Paul at ease, "Have you tried any of the old communication techniques you guys would use in case of satellite issues? You know, when you were out in the middle of nowhere, doing whatever it is you guys, do!" Zoe said giving it the *'top secret'* respect it warranted, of course with a hint of sarcasm.

Zoe was indeed brilliant, but she lived in her own world. She enjoyed displaying her bossy side—that *I got it together* persona. However, she could only dabble in it for short spurts of time. Like her mother, it was not her natural state. At her core—even before the split, Zoe had hero syndrome—swoop in, save the moment, but no accountability, nor sustainability. In her impulsive state, she would create situations without thought, leaving everyone else to pick up the pieces.

And yet, for all her contradictions, Zoe loved just as fiercely as she demanded. Her loyalty might be reckless at times, but you knew she would fight for you, even drive the get-away car for you.

Paul's eyes lit up. "There is this old military program that used to be operational when we had to communicate long distances without the satellite. If he remembered, and couldn't get a message out any other way, perhaps he tried it. It just might be the one way."

Paul reached out and hugged her. "I love you! You are remarkable!" Kissed her on the head and left, leaving her standing there in awe.

Step Back

One of the men-was still on watch. Hours had passed since he'd volunteered for the first shift. The fire's glow was fading fast. Nathaniel was stretched out in front of the hearth, he turned over, pulling the blanket tighter around him. The chill had taken over the room. Ralph had pulled the couch into the far corner. He'd chosen the spot deliberately. Out of the way to have a strategic advantage to everything happening in the room. He didn't trust the others. His loyalty was to Nathaniel. His task was to ensure he reached his destination.

"What are you doing?"

Ralph asked, catching the three-off guard. His voice clear, sharp, undeniable.

The woman who had been with them, knew Raphael had seen her true self, and was afraid of him. So, she poisoned the others against him and Nate and slipped off during the night. Her exit was as mysterious as her arrival.

The three thought Nate and Ralph were still asleep. The larger man was standing over Nathaniel, his hand wrapped around the handle of the sword, freeing it out of its cover. Before he could unwrap it completely, he felt movement on the other side of the room. Startled, a shadow bounced off him causing him to take a step back as a reaction.

"Uh, we…" quickly pushing the sword back in its cover, searching for a lie to appear out of thin air. "We uh…uh, we were just going to load up the car so we could get a fresh start."

"I see." Ralph interrupted, striking the staff against the floor. A hollow ring, echoing from the contact. They could *see* the sound growing from the base of the staff. They trembled instantaneously.

"Take what you've gathered." Ralph said, voice low but commanding, taking care not to wake Nathaniel. "Put the sword and backpack exactly where you found them." He paused, eyes hard and piercing. He continued, tone, final and judgmental, yet with laced with mercy. "You may leave, go through the front door. Leave everything else."

The one carrying the sword and backpack ran to where they had found it. Quickly dropped it and ran out of the front door. The other two had already made it halfway down the driveway.

Ralph retreated to the couch.

Early morning sunlight washed the room in the gentle warmth of a new day. Looking around, engaging in a well-deserved stretch, arms in the air, Nathaniel commented. "I don't ever recall sleeping like that, not since I left bootcamp. I didn't hear a thing last night." The light penetrating through the broken windows, spilled across his face.

"Where are the others?" Blinded by the light, he turned his head and directed his question towards Raphael.

"They must have left in the middle of the night. There aren't any signs of them in the house. Some of the provisions are gone as well."

Nathaniel looked surprise. He knew there was more to the story. Never would he have pegged them as people who could be capable of just leaving, not like that, in the middle of the night. Since he'd been back to the States, he was quickly becoming an adaptive person. Even though he had been out of the country for the past decade, he had heard talks about how American *exceptionalism* was diminishing. Not just financial, but character—the American moral compass was all but gone.

Nate had to remember, nothing like this had ever happened on US soil. Nate didn't remember America's history. The tragedies of the past few days had left people in survival mode. Things they normally would not do suddenly became all they did do. But who knows how one will react when put in a drastic situation?

His guard was officially up. Nathaniel understood he had to find a new normal. His trust would be earned moving forward.

Nebraska, getting to Nebraska was the only thing on his agenda.

"I found a security room last night. We can possibly put enough equipment together to get a signal out."

They were both looking around the security room for a way to contact Paul. Nate knew a little about radios from the military. He found an old school messaging device and keyed in the message...

"Lost all communications. Outside of Seattle. Meet in 24 hours @ 06:00 @ old hotel."

Runza

Zuri's sniper skills were needed. Zoe had finally explained the mission.

'Shoot a digital gadget on a communication satellite receiver.'

Only Zoe would have thought of buying this type of military technology. In lots of ways, Zuri envied her. She was always five steps ahead of everyone else, strategizing. If not for the emotional roller coaster ride you would find yourself on, she would make an excellent military officer.

They understood it would not be safe once the word got out. Travelling would be risky. So, their goal was to get to the site, plant the device and make it back to the compound before Zoe sent out the message.

"I did surveillance around the area, thinking maybe we might do some sightseeing before everything is possibly destroyed. The world would want to have documentation of what it was like before the upcoming cosmic collision." Nick said, trying to convince Zuri without admitting how much it would mean to him to spend more time with her.

In a squeaky, high pitch tone, "So, what did you find?" She too, failing to disguise the excitement.

"Nothing!" They both laughed. "This is Nebraska."

Recovering, Zuri commented. "Cosmic collision. That's the first time I heard it described that way. It's a perfect way to define it."

That seemed to break the ice. Both relaxed and allowed the flow between them to grow organically.

"Let's see…we do have to make a couple of stops on the way back to pick up a few supplies, bags of Zeolite and other stuff. Stephen needs it for the water system."

"I dared not ask what he is going to do with it. I am sure he has always been ahead of his time in this kind of stuff."

The two continue their conversation, listening to music, playing silly road games.

Nick checked the GPS, "Twenty minutes to go. Let's stop for gas, and lunch. We are a little early."

Zuri checked the time on her watch—confirming. "Sounds good!"

Nick pulled up to a charging station. "We can eat over there while we tap off the charge." Grabbing their things, they made their way over to a quaint café across the street. Each making sure they had a direct view of the truck.

"What can I get for you today?" the waitress asked as she set up drinks on the table.

"Do you guys have a special?" Zuri asked playfully, adding, "What do you eat and love from here?" Zuri speaking to the waitress but secretly smiling at Nick. She was an absolute delight—radiant, effortlessly captivating. With Nick, she'd found her rhythm, and now she was in full bloom. Every word, every glance, every small gesture became part of a quiet, magnetic dance, a melody meant for him alone.

The waitress gave them her preferences with the same level of lightheartedness. She didn't see many out-of-town customers, so she welcomed the distractions from her daily routine.

"Runza, we make the best runza on this side of the Yellowstone."

"Perfect, we'll have that."

While the waitress was gone, Nick asked, "What's runza?"

"You'll see—and love it! I discovered it last year…trust me." Zuri continued weaving her web. Inside, she smiled. Flirting came naturally, and she enjoyed the control felt when leading the dance. She was having an awakening inside that she had never truly known. She was almost giddy. Yet, it was all quite innocent, which made it—special.

They stood on equal footing now. Zuri opened up about how Paul came into her life and had become her dad. In turn, Nick shared the story of his parents—how their friendship began back in the Philippines, how their families lived next door. His parents had gone to middle school together, and when her family was transferred to another base, they made a promise they'd go to the same college someday. And they did.

"The rest," as Nick said with a smile, "was history!"

Zuri loved hearing the stories. Nick had heard a lot about her from Zoe, but she knew very little about him. She wanted to know everything. His eyes would light up when talking about his parents.

Nick continued, eyes soft with the reflection of memories. "Dad would say, '*she was the prettiest girl I had ever seen.*' Mom would just smile. She had these slight dimples, with rosy cheeks surrounding them, that would glow whenever something embarrassed her."

Zuri could tell how much he loved his parents.

"Where are they? Your parents, now." Zuri asked wondering why he would choose to be here instead of with them.

"They died several years ago." Nick responded and before Zuri could say anything else, he said, "I will tell you about it someday." Sending a signal he did not want to talk about it.

Zuri respected his signal.

"Oh, this looks good! Thank you." Zuri said as the waitress sat their food in front of them. Nick took his first bite and paused, savoring the flavor.

"This reminds me of something my mom used to make. Good choice," he said with a nod of approval.

Zuri and Nick allowed the world to fade for the rest of the afternoon.

In the meantime, Nathaniel and Raphael had managed to find a mode of transportation and had set out to arrive in North Platte, Nebraska. The location and time had been sent to Paul. All they could do at the time was trust he received the message and would be there.

The waitress returned sometime later, refilling their glasses. "Can I get you guys anything else?"

They both looked up, shook their heads to acknowledge, still caught in the easy rhythm of their conversation. Neither of them had realized how much time had passed. Zuri had been completely drawn in by Nick's stories—some lighthearted while others more reflective. The connection between them had only deepened.

When they finally finished their meal, they left a generous tip, exchanged a quick thank-you with the waitress, and stepped out into the soft light of the late afternoon. Having retrieved the SUV, they continued toward their destination.

By the time they arrived, the sky was already shifting. Daylight melting into dusk, stretching long shadows across the rugged terrain. The air had cooled, and the wind moved in low, whispering through the scrub and rock.

They had only a few minutes to get everything in place. Nick unloaded the gear while Zuri moved ahead, scanning the area for the right vantage point.

The area was remote—too remote. Wide open.

"This won't work," she muttered, half to herself. "Too exposed."

"I need to walk ahead. This will not do," she called back to Nick without breaking stride.

Just then she spotted up ahead, an opening between two oversized boulders, partially hidden by an overgrown brush. It offered just enough cover and a clear line of sight—perfect for what they needed.

She turned, raising her voice. "There! Let's set up over there!"

Nick hauled the rest of the gear toward her. Zuri kneeled and began unpacking the projectile launcher.

Nick stood to the side, watching her as her fingers moved with a calm precision. She snapped the components together. She was checking the balance, adjusting the scope when she sensed his eyes on her.

Zuri turned slightly toward Nick, embarrassed, yet with the touch of a flirt, "Are you, looking at me?"

Nick didn't look away. The words slipped out before he could stop them.

"You're incredible."

It hung in the air, raw and unfiltered—honest in a way that neither of them expected. He handed her the digital device. "You've got five minutes."

"Almost set," Zuri replied, her voice low and focused.

She inserted the device, keyed in the coordinates, and positioned the launcher just as Nick confirmed the target through his viewfinder.

Zuri exhaled slowly, steadied her grip, and pulled the trigger.

The projectile cut clean through the air.

Impact.

"Bullseye!" he grinned, eyes lighting up—proud. "Perfect!"

Zuri let out a short, triumphant sigh of relief. They slapped a high five, the sound crisp in the still air.

"Mission accomplished." He said, still grinning.

Zuri nodded, already powering down the launcher. "Textbook." Thinking about how she would tell her dad about the moment she pulled the trigger.

As they gathered the equipment, Zuri had Zoe on speaker. "The device is in place."

"Hold on a minute. Let me make sure we have a connection." Zoe left for a few minutes and came back. "Got-it! See you when you get back. I should have everything set up to broadcast in.." Zuri cut her off, took the com-device off speaker.

"How long do we have?" Zuri asked.

"I can get everything up and running in less than eight hours. That will give you plenty of time to get back."

"What if you waited until tomorrow to broadcast? I know it is selfish, but before everything is…" She paused, not knowing how to not sound insensitive to the world on the brink of such devastation. "I want to stay the night with Nick, at least once before."

Zoe chuckled, "You got it. But I can't wait past noon. Make sure you guys are off the road by then. The country will be in disarray once we broadcast."

"Thank you. You're the best. We'll be back in time. See you tomorrow morning."

Zuri and Nick were still loading the car, and just as Zuri had mustered up enough courage to suggest they spend the night, her communication device went off.

Zoe called back. "Hi Zoe, what's up?"

"I was telling dad you would be back tomorrow." She whispered, "Sorry!" Then she continued, "Dad needs to talk to you?"

"Hi Dad." Zuri was eager and a little scared why he would need to talk to her, now.

"Hi Sweetheart, I got a message from Nate." Zuri eyes lit up, while at the same time, holding her breath waiting for whatever news. Paul continued. "He and another person are on their way here. From what I could gather from the short message, they are coming from Seattle and will be at a place I previously told him about in North Platte."

"Okay, great!"

"Not sure of the circumstances, but he gave us instructions to meet him at 06:00 in Platte River. You guys are only a couple of hours away. I will send you Nate's message."

"Got it, we'll wait for the message to come through."

As the call ended, disappointment had formed on Zuri's face, visible to Nick. "I'm sorry, that was Dad. He wants us to pick up Uncle Nate in Platte River."

Nick saw the disappointment in her eyes, though she was trying to hide it. He hadn't known about the plans she had for the night.

"So, the adventure continues." Speaking with a playful grin, which seemed to relax Zuri somewhat.

In return, she responded with a softer feel, her demeanor returning. "I guess so! I've missed Uncle Nate. It'll be good to see him. You're going to love him."

"I have a list of things we need to get for Stephen." Nick's eyes sparkled with a hint of mischief. "Let's spin a couple of hours gathering everything along the way."

"I like how you are thinking. A road trip and a scavenger hunt. Who would come up with that?" They both laughed. "Now it's an adventure!"

Zuri was fully invested in the next leg of their adventure. Platte River no longer felt like a detour, but more like the adventure they had started together. She was with Nick. Everything else was a backdrop to their story.

The couple remained at the site, camped out beneath the vastness of the sky, while they mapped out a plan for the hunt. Nick pulled off his jacket and spread it across the ground. Dusk was upon them like a whisper. It was a setting created with ambience, above and below, patiently waiting for them to engage.

Even the sounds of the day's participants—insects buzzing in the overgrown weeds, birds singing as they gathered food for the evening feed—were all settling into their own under the cover of darkness. The world had stopped for them.

Sitting next to Zuri, Nick read off the list of materials they needed to get for Stephen, as they plotted their route. They had a couple of hours before all the stores would be closed. Nick didn't care about any of it at the time.

Without warning, before he even knew what was happening—before he could second guess himself, Nick leaned in and kissed Zuri. It had not been planned nor pondered—just pure instinct. It was right.

Zuri didn't pull away, instead she responded—embraced the touch with an obvious approval.

A big downpour interrupted the moment causing them to pull away, ending the kiss, flickered with surprise of himself, heart in full cadence, and a touch of embarrassment, Nick apologized. "I'm sorry. I didn't— I mean I did but, I'm sorry." Coming to his senses, his voice—softer, intentional. "I didn't realize how much I wanted to kiss you, until I felt you."

Zuri replied politely, "I'm glad you did." As quickly as she said it, she stood up, grateful for the rain as it soaked them.

Nick grabbed her hand as they ran to the truck. It gave her an excuse—a moment to retreat within herself. She didn't know what to say or feel. She was officially in new territory. Her mind spiraled, colliding thoughts before they could find focus. Each louder than the last, drowning out any hope for clarity.

'What have I done? What am I supposed to do now? This is too fast!'

Zuri's thoughts now in full overload. 'Does it mean he thinks I want us to sleep together.' Her inexperience was torturing her. I don't want that, not yet, do I?

She heard Clarice's voice, 'In the fullness of time, there will be no doubt.'

It settled her.

"We will find a place to stay for the night in Platte River. We can search for Uncle Nate once we get there. In the meantime, first stop, Grand Island."

Nick was just as excited as Zuri. He let down his guard when around her—except, however minuscule, he still felt the sting from the booster trip. But the awkwardness from the anticipation of the first kiss was over. They could move forward without apprehension.

The rain had been unrelenting in the area all day. The sky never made it to its full brightness, hidden by thick, dark clouds. At least the rain had finally stopped.

***

Stephen walked up to Clarice, leaning in to kiss her from behind, softy speaking, "What's for dinner?"

"Your favorite on a day like today, beef stew."

"Nice, I'm starved."

"Where are the boys?" She asked, engaged with him in conversation about the activities of the day. "How did they do with the water treatment? Did they drive you totally mad?"

"We couldn't do much. The rain coming in through the ducts was too much and unsafe for them to be around. We will get started first thing tomorrow."

"Two days in a row, the boys are a handful. Are you sure you want to do this again?" Clarice asked out of concern. She knew how taxing the boys could be. Stephen was too polite to say anything.

"They keep me young," smiling, "I'm going to take a shower before dinner."

Mudslide

It was well into the night when the GPS announced their approaching arrival at their destination. The break in silence caused a sudden intrusion on her thoughts, startling her.

"Crap!" Zuri gasped as she jumped.

Nick reached over, placing his hand gently on her thigh, "You okay?" he asked her with a slight chuckle.

Smiling, Zuri responded, "Yes, sorry. I was deep in thought." Placing her hand on top of his, she quietly continued staring out the window. Engrossed in the outside shadows that stretched along the empty road. The smell of fresh rain still in the air.

"We have about ten miles to go."

"Just look at the world Nick." Turning to him, her voice soft and distant. "It saddens me. After tonight, nothing will ever be the same."

Nick could see her tears reflecting the ambient light in the car. He started to look beyond the road—past the surface of things, as if watching the world. The headlights of distant cars projected rays of light bouncing off the highway, small communities nestled in patches of landscape—from valleys to mountaintops, miles from other communities, with spotlights from the occasional refilling station.

"Tomorrow the world will have to react to an unforeseen crisis. If we fail to get the message out in time, I'm afraid the weight of guilt will be unbearable. It will feel as though we stripped away their choice—their hope—their faith. There will be no place we could hide."

She went on. "Just look at all the homes with their lights glowing between the darkness. Fragile webs of hope being played out in preparation for another day. Imagine the innocent lives that will be destroyed, all under the deception of a tomorrow that will be swept away in the impending obscurity of a disaster—a cosmic collision."

A twinge of sadness began to creep up in Nick's throat as well. The detour had indeed created an unexpected adventure. It had been a good for both. But now, on the eve before the big awakening for the world, the distraction from the inevitable was quickly fading. It could no longer be a reprieve from what was waiting for them ahead.

Nick glanced at Zuri. She seemed to be staring at things beyond what one could see with physical eyes. He knew no matter how close they had become—how much he loved her, it would have to take a back seat to reality. The situation they had been cast into would be fluid. They knew they had to be prepared. Falling in love was not preventable, but what they did with it had become a choice that neither was free to make. The only thing of importance now was to find Nate and make it back before the warning broadcast hit the airways.

"You have arrived at your destination on the left."

"This can't be the place," Nick muttered, easing off the accelerator as the SUV slowed, expecting to see the hotel lights nestled up against the mountainside.

Before he could finish registering the emptiness that was in the place where the hotel was expected to be, the SUV hit a pocket of mud. Nick slammed his foot down on the brake, but the momentum carried them forward violently. The tires screeched against the slick road, spewing mud in all directions, spraying the windows with sludge, leaving only thin slits for visibility.

"What the hell was that?" Nick shouted, his hands locked on the steering wheel, frantically fighting against the pull, trying to gain control of the vehicle. But his desperate actions only made it worse. The back end of the SUV went into a tailspin. The more he struggled with the wheel, the more it spun around.

Zuri was screaming, "Let go of the wheel," voice echoing as the SUV continued to spin out of control.

Nick released the wheel, throwing his hands up in surrender without hesitation. The SUV continued its wild spin, inertia dragging it sideways, fighting for traction. Breathless moments filled the space, suspended— then the mud-covered vehicle made contact with something solid— pebbles, gravel. The momentum slowing—stopped, under the increasing traction, landing against a tree.

"What the hell was that?" Nick said, freaking out while looking at Zuri, voice cracking.

"Looks like there was a mudslide, at least a couple of days ago. All the rain in the area lately must have caused it. Strange though, usually you don't see slides until the spring when the snow melts." Zuri said, trying to make sense of what happened.

"But we're okay."

"We were lucky." Nick added. By now they had both exited the car. Walking around making an assessment, "We'll have to walk the rest of the way. We won't be able to see the extent of the damage until first light."

Nick's demeanor had shifted. His voice was steady. The panic that had gripped him only moments ago now caused him to be overly self-confident—almost cocky. Zuri smiled within, not saying anything to shake his newfound confidence.

Nick grabbed a couple of bags, and two flashlights out of the SUV, handing Zuri one and her scabbard. She threw it over her shoulder and turned the light on without saying a word. Each understood they might find anything up ahead. They needed to be prepared.

The duo came upon the parking lot of what was once a hotel. A beacon of hope in the middle of nowhere, perched gracefully along the mountainside, was now a half-buried lump of broken brick, covered in fresh mud. Where the central area of the hotel had once connected the two wings, with seamless elegance, was now only a pile of wet, sludge-filled ruble.

The mudslide had torn through the heart of the building with a vengeance. Zuri walked towards it, looking for past glory, but found splintered timber, uprooted shrubs, and collapsing walls. The closer she got, the disbelief of what her eyes were witnessing intensified. Standing before her was the fractured remnants of what once represented a safe haven for weary travelers. The jagged roof with dangling shingles, intensified the wave of shock. Reality set in, the air clutched at her chest, choking out anything coherent. The resemblance of a hotel remained—windows, doors, balconies, and shattered rooms—all exposed to the elements.

The sorrow followed, heavy and unrelenting—the apparent loss. Then, finally, fear took hold.

Nick was holding Zuri's hand, escorting her as they walked around taking in all the devastation. They were tethered to each other—a quiet surrender. They both felt like they were part of a rescue team, with no survivors. Zuri's steps slowed to almost a crawl, but the thought of Nathaniel being caught up in all of this was more than she could bear. Zuri felt the fear that comes with hopelessness. She pulled away from Nick and ran towards the lobby, screaming, calling out Nathaniel's name.

"Uncle Nate…Nathaniel Jenkins…Senior Chief…Uncle Nate!" Zuri's voice rung out, clinging to the edge of sanity. Desperation entered the lobby, well before she crossed the broken doorway. Her flashlight beam flickered over the shallow graves of the lobby's remains. Sheets of mud cascaded across the marble floors. Zuri was one level below hysteria. Running into the lobby was a catalyst for hope. Instead of a sign of life, all she found was more evidence of the destruction.

All of it, buried—consumed. Zuri fell to her knees.

There was nothing, only silence. Zuri screamed Nate's name again, and again. Each time louder than the last. The flashlight slipped from her hand, rolling across the floor, casting a line of light as it made its way towards the entrance. The light suddenly stopped as if it had hit an invisible barrier.

"Zuri!"

Her name cut through the haze of grief like a lifeline tugging at her heart. Zuri turned her head, eyes blurred with tears, frozen, searching for the origin of the familiar voice, *impossible*. She wiped her cheeks with the back of her mud-stained hands. Then she heard it again. This time it was clearer, stronger.

"Zuri!"

"Uncle Nate!" Zuri responded with a whisper in disbelief. Too afraid it would disappear if she called out too loud. Before he could respond, she saw Nate's familiar silhouette. She jumped to her feet, the sounds of mud cracking beneath her. She leaped into his outstretched arms, welcoming her.

Zuri had been in a full-blown crisis. She allowed her mind to wander back to promises whispered beneath the tree in the middle of the compound. She had made a vow to herself. One of strength and resilience. She would be there to protect and support her loved ones. But the first test had come, and she had failed. She had allowed grief to drown out all logic. She knew she would have to re-evaluate. But for now, she would accept that her emotions had overruled all logic. She didn't care. She was just overjoyed with knowing Nate was alive.

Zuri hadn't noticed Nick and Raphael standing in the doorway. She was relieved, yet too afraid to let go of Nate. Nick had felt helpless. There was nothing he could say or do for Zuri to settle her. He had been a witness to grief unraveling before him for someone he cared about deeply. It was like standing on the edge of a cliff, watching someone fall to an uncertain landing beneath a fog. He hadn't known what to do, so he prayed.

It was then the headlights from Nate and Ralph pulled into the parking lot.

Stay Here

The rain had been relentless throughout most of the Northwest. Nebraska had been under a flash flood for several days, so broadcast of mudslides was not letting up. Even at the compound, the ground was over saturated. But the rain was gone now. Today's forecast was for clear skies, and everyone was grateful. They had only a few hours left to complete their preparations before the global broadcast would be released.

The communication device was in place on the satellite receiver. Zoe and her team had aligned the signal and were now waiting for the countdown of the satellite's position. Zoe was asking about Zuri's return every ten minutes.

"Zoe, they will make it!" Tim said with an awkward, caring voice.

Smiling at Tim, Zoe spoke in her usual controlling tone. "I know, thanks." Falling flatter than she intended.

Zoe was feeling somewhat guilty. She knew she should not have agreed with Zuri to extend the time of the broadcast. She wasn't considering Nate in the equation. If Zuri had not made it back on time, she would have to tell Paul and the rest about Nick and Zuri's connection. Paul had finally shown some caring motions toward her since she told him she was *Timepiece*. Looking at her watch constantly, she knew she would feel better if she at least knew if they had made contact with Nathaniel.

"Give it some gas!" Nathaniel yelled out to Zuri. The three men were trying to push the SUV out of the ditch. Every time Zuri would push on the gas, the tires would spin, kicking up mud over the three of them.

Zuri would laugh at them secretly. She knew the tires would spin without any traction. Finally, after about thirty minutes of this, she got out, snickering.

"What if we put the car in neutral, grab some debris to put under the tires, and then try to push." Ralph had a smirk look on his face, almost like he was impressed with the way she handled the situation. He had seen her shaking her head and snickering in the truck.

"Great idea," Nick said, more because Zuri had made the suggestion.

Once they had the SUV out on solid ground, they explained how they only had a few hours to make it back before the message would be broadcasted.

Raphael asked Nathaniel if he could take the vehicle they had been driving to make another stop. He needed to be somewhere to make sure some special people made their journey safely. His request had been strange, but Nate was grateful to Ralph, so he didn't question him. He simply gave him the keys and told him to be safe.

Zuri gave Ralph the location of the compound, as if he needed it, the car or the address.

Before he left, Ralph pulled Nick to the side. "I believe this belongs with you." Ralph handed Nick the staff. "Use it wisely. In the fullness of time, you will know its power."

Nick stood next to the truck, holding the staff, confused—but honored. He was admiring the staff when Ralph drove off, leaving him wondering, *why does everyone keep saying 'in the fullness of time?'*

***

Stephen had started the day early. The boys were excited to complete the lesson about the water system. Stephen was working against time and really didn't have the time he wanted to devote to the boys. He had already made the promise, so after they ate breakfast, he included the boys in the plans for the day.

Jazzette solicited the boys' help. She needed them to take a few items to Jack and Logan. Although their help was valid, she did this mostly to give Stephen a chance to complete his major tasks before the twins joined him as distractions.

"Cody, you, and your brother take these supplies to Jack. If they are not there, just leave it at the door on the porch." Jazzette said handing them the handle of the cart. "When you are done, please find Logan and ask him to meet me at the apartment building. You can meet granddad in the warehouse once you're done."

It had been several days since the last of the workers had been dismissed. Quietly, and outside of the influence of the others, Stephen and Clarice made a personal decision. One rooted in their own personal beliefs. The construction crew had been with them since the very beginning. They felt more like family now. In the face of the pending catastrophic event, possibly wiping out most of the country, it would have been quite hypocritical of them not to provide some type of solution for their safety.

So, they created a plan to help provide for their families. When the final phase of the project ended, each of the core workers received a substantial bonus. It was meant to give them a lifeline.

They framed it as an investment in their future.

"With the path this world is heading," Clarice told them, "Please use the money to help secure a future—a chance of surviving whenever things go wrong."

On that last day, Paul and Logan met privately with the five individuals that had managed each area of the construction. They presented them with a choice. They laid out every detail, according to the way they understood things. Nothing about the crisis was withheld from them.

"You have one chance to accept," Paul told them. "We'll take you home. Pack everything you might need—gather your essentials, keepsakes, and other personal items you cherish. Gather your family members—only the ones previously listed as your immediate family. We will bring you back to the compound to stay here with us."

After Paul and Logan laid out the guidelines for each to make their decision, three of the five decided to stay while the others wanted to travel across country to be with their families. Knowing what was about to happen, they owed it to them. To try to protect them.

"There is one condition—no exceptions he told them. You cannot tell anyone—not your neighbor, not extended family, nor your closest friends about this place. Not even when the threat is over."

It had been simple—and non-negotiable. There was no room for debate, and Paul needed them to understand the weight of it all. Their specialties were needed to sustain the compound in the interim but even more so once the crisis was over, the rebuild would be just as challenging.

Over the past year, the construction crew had designed and built an apartment complex on the compound grounds. Each apartment featured two bedrooms, mirrored on the other side, connected by a common area—kitchen and bathrooms. It allowed two separate families to live in technically a four-bedroom apartment. It mimicked the practicality of military barracks.

The crew had always been told the complex would be used for the Taylor's extended family vacations. The construction crew, until the end, had no idea they were building it with their own families' survival at stake. It would become their refuge. They had all been working together for several years, and now they too, had become a part of each other's family.

Even before any threat had been known, Stephen had secretly wanted Logan to move onto the compound. There were many decisions to be made during the early design, and Stephen was under no illusion about the amount of work that would be required. His age no longer allowed for the hard labor. But everyone knew the compound was his vision.

Logan had lived back on the farm with him after his father died. To Stephen, Logan was as close to him as his own son, and over the years Logan grew to love and respect him as a father. So, it was only natural he would offer Logan the job of running the compound, overseeing the day-to-day operations.

When Stephen was a small boy, his grandfather had been the guiding inspiration to him. His presence seemed to carry the weight and history of the family and the faith of a mustard seed. He had the kind of wisdom that didn't come from books but from years of working the land and listening to God in the stillness of his soul. It was he who taught him how to conduct his life with integrity, grounded in the Lord, and enough wisdom to know we all have to establish and live by your own personal code.

"With responsibility comes accountability," he would say in the middle of a task. Always engaged in some activity, while appearing unengaged in conversations.

Stephen's grandfather would often spurt out sayings that sounded ridiculous at first glance, but in time, he learned the level of wisdom behind each of them.

Years later, after Logan lost his father, Stephen passed on that same torch. He found himself walking in his grandfather's shoes. His footsteps ordered by the same guiding principles as he mentored Logan.

"Use your head for more than a hat rack." He would tell the boy. As soon as he spoke the words, he recognized he had turned into his grandfather—carrying that same sense of pride and wisdom to the next generation.

While everyone else was thinking about which bedroom would be theirs, all Logan wanted was a small corner to call his own. He found the perfect spot, neatly tucked away in the back of the warehouse. To him, it would be a place that he could retreat to, away from everyone. And with the vertical farming in full bloom, right outside his room, it reminded him of home.

***

A few hours later, Nick pulled up at the house. Zuri and Nate got out grabbing their bags. Zuri threw her scabbard over her shoulder and was about to hand Nate his wrapped sword, but with it half uncovered, she saw an opportunity to really look at it.

"Uncle Nate, this is really nice. Where'd you get it?" Zuri said examining—admiring the sword.

"It's a long story. I'm sure we will have some time to catch up." Nate responding.

Nick got back in the SUV. "I'm going to offload the supplies for Stephen." Looking at Zuri as he drove off, headed to the warehouse, "Let's meet up later."

Responding with a quick nod, Zuri and Nate walked into the house. Dropping the bags, she took him into the kitchen. Paul and Clarice were sitting at the table. They hadn't heard them when they came in.

"Hi Dad, look who I found on the side of the road."

Nate and Paul were already embracing.

I'm Ready

Nick grabbed one of the supply bags and threw it over his shoulder with ease. The staff Raphael had given him rested against the side of the SUV; its surface etched with whispers of long-forgotten history. It seemed almost alive, quickly becoming his companion, feeling like an old friend. It radiated a kind of quiet power, as if it belonged more to mythology than reality. He still didn't understand why Raphael would say it belonged to him.

With a flicker of something stirring within—confidence laced with a touch of hidden arrogance, Nick kicked the bottom edge of the staff upright, with the side of his foot, causing it to flip up in the air, end over end, gracefully cutting through the air. He caught it with his free hand, mid-stride, his pace unbroken. Actions that he would have secretly watched from the sidelines, too afraid to even try it. Now, the action felt effortless, instinctive.

Since Zuri had stepped into his life, something inside him had shifted, shedding layers of hesitation, self-doubt, and fear. He was finally stepping into himself—fully. It was though she had unlocked a door within him. He had started to feel—right.

Yet, lurking beneath the surface was a shadow of something he had not known existed —pride. When she looked at him with that quiet intensity, it was as if she saw the man he was capable of being, and in that reflection, he could see it too. She amplified him. Her presence was like a mirror place before him to show his potential.

He didn't want to be arrogant, nor to become the kind of person he'd always despised. But with every step toward confidence, he edged closer to that line, flirting with the danger of it all.

"Stephen, we're back! Where do you want the supplies?" His voice echoed off the dense walls of the warehouse. *That's strange*, thinking out loud. Logan had mentioned he was in the warehouse with the boys when they drove up.

Nick dropped the supply bag against the wall, his voice ringing out in the empty space. "Stephen!" Calling his name again. This time the echo was not alone. He heard what sounded like a groan, broken. Nick stood still, listening, head pivoting from side to side, trying to pinpoint traces of the sound. He started to walk again—slowly, intentionally. Staff in hand, prepared for anything—cockiness returning.

There it was again. The faint sound, hidden just beneath the whispers of trickling water. The tiny droplets performing a serene melody, each drop playing with its own symphony, building to the crescendo of what he would find.

Nick moved around the narrow wall separating the open area of the warehouse from the water treatment area, tucked away neatly in its own secure section. The floor in the treatment area was natural, left over rocks and sand used to make the concrete floor on the main side. The water ducts for the water system around the compound all led here. Nick concentrated on each sound—separating the sounds—the forced pressure of water in the ducts overhead, the trickling water from the overflow in the distance, the sound of the hydraulic pump used to extract water from the underground well. There in the midst of it all, a quiet voice—wounded.

Just as he turned the corner, near the water's edge, his eyes locked—first, to Stephen's shoes, lying haphazardly—several feet from each other. Nick quickened his pace.

Next—there sprawled across a jagged rock was Stephen's body—bloody. Dark streaks of old blood smeared against the stone beneath him. Splatters of fresh blood, thinning from the water's dilution. His face was pale, eyes half opened, obviously in pain.

"Stephen!" Nick's heart pounding as he went into action. He rushed to the intercom, slamming his hand against the button.

"Get Jazzette to the warehouse! It's Stephen!"

Before anyone had a chance to say anything in response, Nick diverted his attention back to the lifeless body lying before him. He didn't hesitate for a second, his hands went to his shoes, fingers fumbling at the laces. He was about to dive into the water when Stephen stopped him.

"No," Stephen's voice strained, barely more than a whisper. With his blood covered hand and forced strength, Stephen motioned—stop.

His arm quickly fell back to holding the stone, "NO," he repeated the word drowning in blood from his lips, eyes barely open but full of desperation.

Nick froze, confusion setting in. "What are you talking about? I have to get you out of there."

Before Nick could move another inch, the water around Stephen began to ripple, like a giant walking, shaking the ground with each step. Without warning, the overflow cylinder released its hold on its gallons of water collected from all the ducts. Water burst forth from the overflow into the spring.

Nick watched in horror as the waves surged forward, slamming Stephen's broken body against the stone. A sickening crack echoed off the walls, with Stephen's body holding firm against the rock, no choice but to be tossed about from the pressure of the gushing water. His hand slipping into the water, no more power to hold on.

Nick's hesitation shattered. He lunged forward, diving into the spring without thought. The cold water gnawing at his lungs. But it didn't matter, he grabbed Stephen by the shoulders and pulled him from the water. His breath—uneven, faint.

"I called Jazzette and Clarice. They'll be here soon, hold on!" Nick breathing hard, his hands ripping his shirt off to use to apply pressure on the wounds, trying to stop the bleeding.

"Dr. Jazz will fix you right up." His voice trembling, trying to instill confidence—hope. Nick knew it was bad.

Stephen's eyes fluttered, the dim light catching the glassy sheen over them. His lips moved, barely forming the word, "No…" He swallowed, choking back the blood filling his stomach. "No.." he repeated, his voice cracking under the weight of knowing.

Nick looked down on Stephen. He had never viewed him as old or frail. He was the epitome of strength—a quiet strength. But in that moment with Stephen, now, lying there before him, vulnerability in full bloom, Nick saw him. He saw his own immortality. He looked at the lines, etched with a lifetime of stories—laughter and tears. The puffiness under his eyes, what this man must have seen, lived through. Nick felt ashamed of what he had been thinking earlier—arrogance, pride. Just the opposite of the man lying before him.

In that moment Nick recognized the power of humility.

Holding Stephen's hand, trying to give him his strength. Nick began to pray.

"Lord, this man loves you, I know I am not worthy to ask but let me take some of his pain. Whatever you ask of me…" Nick's heart was full of despair. He didn't know what to do or how to help. He was failing again, just as he had done with Zuri at the hotel. The compassion that he had was unwavering. But he didn't have the wisdom to understand how to use it.

God had already shown Stephen grace—mercy, no one knew it—except for Stephen.

Nick heard the door to the warehouse swing open. Jazzette's voice calling his name.

"Over here, we're by the spring!" he shouted, his voice bouncing off the walls. The echo of footsteps rushed across the empty floors. Nick felt a sense of relief. Help had arrived, thinking...

Everything will be okay now.

The weight of Stephen's body in Nick's arms was getting heavier. His body seemed denser. His breathing, shallower. Nick's begging for him to hang on a little longer became more hopeful. Jazzette appeared around the wall, her expression quickly shifted from determination to bleak. She had worked in enough emergency rooms and trauma centers to know it was too late.

Jazzette knelt beside Stephen, hands moving swiftly, fingers trembling as she assessed the bleeding, eyes wide and frantic, scanning the wounds. Nick gazed upon her face, searching for hope, for some flicker of life she could latch onto. But Stephen's breaths came ragged and thin, each one a labor that seemed to scrape at the edge of his being. Jazzette could hear the amount of lost energy being expelled. His chest rattled like an old gate opening to the next level. Tears streaming as acceptance crept in.

Stephen searched for a tether to life for her, just for her in that moment. He wanted her to feel what was in his heart. "Jazz, it's okay." His voice scratched, eyes showing the window into his soul. "It's my time!" He wanted her to know he was ready. He was just waiting for his wife.

"Clarice." He murmured. "I'm waiting for her."

Jazzette pressed her hand against her mouth to trap the scream within her. But there was no stopping the wave of grief that crashed through her. "No...no, this can't be!" Shaking her head and with a broken voice in a whisper, Jazzette cried.

Nick kept looking in the direction of the entrance. He could hear Clarice's footsteps, light and hurried, gaining speed as she got closer.

"Clarice, wait," Nick called out in desperation, stepping forward to intercept her. But she would have no part of it. Her pace quickened, shoulders tense and unyielding.

Nick's hand reached out for her, grabbing only air as she broke past him, stumbling forward. Clarice fell to her knees beside Stephen's torn body. Clarice's hands hovered over his wounds, trembling, too afraid to land a touch, in fear of inflicting more pain. Her eyes wide and glistening, crowned in a sea of disbelief as she cradled his face, fingertips tracing the familiar lines of his face, trying to anchor him to herself, whispering his name.

"Stephen." She whispered, voice cracking, shattering, "My love, what is this foolery? What have you done to yourself?"

Clarice was having an out-of-body experience. Her words were frantic, framed with hysteria, as if speaking to them would give clarity of truth. "We will just have to get you better."

Stephen's gaze softened, a flicker of light in the storm of pain. His breath grew steadier, stretching across the years of their life together, weaving through memories and promises kept. His voice became stronger, deepened—supernaturally.

"I'm sorry," he whispered, eyes fixed on hers. "Not this time. I was granted only enough time to see you once more."

Clarice shook her head, her hands still trembling as she wiped the blood from around his eyes. "No...Stephen, don't say that. You're going to be fine." Knowing in her heart she was wrong.

A smile touched his lips, fragile but true. He knew she knew better. "I saw the boys." Tears falling. "I'm going to meet them now. Just needed to tell you...you were right. I love you!" His eyes locked with hers, smiling. In the fullness of time, the truth of love fulfilled—until death do us part.

Stephen closed his eyes—he was gone!

Silence—emptiness felt across time. To her gaping wound...a void had been created in the world.

Clarice felt his life leave. She didn't need to debate or reject the possibilities. There was no space for denial. She knew—she *felt* it.

"Mom, are you alright?" Jazzette tried to comfort Clarice, but there was no need.

Clarice did not flinch, she did not blink. Her gaze never wavered from Stephen's face. There was no shock, no disbelief, only a resounding understanding. There was no hesitation in her voice. She had already resolved the matter. She understood death—his death was final.

Her voice, when it came, was steady. "I'll be fine." She murmured, her hands moving gently, taking care to place Stephen's hand on top of the other. She bent over to meet them, she gently kissed them. She pulled her shirt from where it was tucked into her pants and used her shirt tail to gently wipe his blood-stained face. Her hands were careful, her movement delicate, washing all traces of pain away. Her voice dropped to a whisper, relaying words only meant for him.

"Thank you, my love." Her voice loving, "You saved my life in more ways than I could ever list. Our latter years were indeed our best years. You go on now, I'll see you soon. Don't you worry about me."

With a calm steadiness, Clarice rose to her feet, the epitome of grace. With her spine straight, eyes forward fixed on *hope*. "I need to take a walk," she said while adjusting her clothes, her voice unwavering. Her footsteps were quiet as she ascended the stairs, her hands tightly gripping the railing—she was in control, resolute—steadfast. She stepped out the side entrance of the compound, she stood for a moment taking in the air, disappearing into the light of the sun's glow.

As Clarice vanished, Stephen's spirit stood on the water spring's ledge next to the stone that had been the backdrop for his battered body. His voice no longer strained by his blood-soaked body. He turned!

"I'm ready!"

***

Just as Clarice disappeared through the platform door, her footsteps fading in the distance, the warehouse fell silent. Everyone, stunned, stood there in disbelief, not knowing how to comprehend the sight of Stephen's body—cold, wet, lifeless, lying on the ground. The silence shattered with the sudden crash of footsteps racing towards them.

Paul and Nathaniel turned the corner. Paul locked eyes with Jazzette as soon as he saw her. It had only been a second, but it felt like an eternity. Paul slowly turned his gaze to what appeared to be a body in front of Jazzette. His breathing, halted. Jazzette was kneeling in a pool of blood over to the side.

Jazzette didn't look away. "I tried…" she kept repeating. "I…I tried. Paul, I couldn't save him. It was too late." Her voice cracked with guilt. She had lost hospital patients before, but this was Stephen.

Paul knelt beside her, the warmth of the blood seeping through his jeans. He pulled her into himself, squeezing her just enough to ground her. Tears freely flowing.

"I'm sure you did everything possible." His voice cracking in disbelief.

Nick and Nathaniel were standing over to the side. Neither knowing what to do or say. They didn't notice when Zoe walked in.

"Mom!"

While the three of them were in the moment, Nathaniel asked Nick, "Where are the boys?"

That's when he spotted two sets of kids' clothes and shoes, next to one of Stephen's shoes. The boys were nowhere to be found.

Holistic Christianity

It hadn't taken long to find the boys. Their bodies lay side by side, tucked into a narrow crevice behind the spring, alongside the mountain wall. They had drowned—both of them. The ledge was scarcely wide enough for anyone to crawl onto. And yet, there they were, lying side by side, barely an inch between them, as though someone—something, had taken care to lay their bodies at rest within the mountain's divine embrace—sacred ground.

They were as they began when they entered this world, as they lived their brief life, and now, how they left—together.

When Clarice left Stephen's side, she was in a state of shock—no longer tethered to this world. The finality of it—the idea of everything between them—all of it had ended. Stephen had been the heartbeat that steadied her. Without him, she could not connect to the rhythm of her life. Her world had been upended—collapsed inward, there was nothing left, all she knew was emptiness—a void where her very soul had once lived.

Heartbroken—literally.

Clarice felt herself standing at the edge of reality.

Without intention or awareness, her steps carried her farther away from the estate. She was trying to put as much distance as possible between her life and this life. The veil was no longer torn. A life that had been created in an instant had now cast her into a sea of uncertainty.

She hadn't recalled the walk—having put one foot in front of the other was unfamiliar. Yet somehow she had wandered along the same path as Zuri had the day she came upon a tree that she described as *a gateway to heaven*.

Though Clarice had no memory of how she got there—nor how she would have known which tree out of the many trees. But somewhere beyond the veil of her grief, she saw it—she knew it was the one. The tree Zuri had spoken of with such reverence was in full view, in front of her. Amidst the fog of her grief, blinding—damping her senses, Clarice heard Zuri's words blaring through, as if she was standing next to her.

'After I had displayed such horrible behavior, I felt so alone. Then I felt this invisible pull. Like a tractor beam drawing—guiding me forward, beyond the existence of the reality I had manifested.'

Clarice understood the phase Zuri had said, pondering the correct order of words. She could feel Zuri's hand entwined in hers.

'The tree felt like…if there really is a heaven, it would feel like that—a refuge from a storm. But not just any storm, my storm.'

As Clarice got closer, her movement slowed. She felt it too, the tug—subtle, quietly leading her to what must be the refuge from *this* storm. She wasn't sure what she'd expected to find, how anything could help her, but she knew enough to know that without some divine intervention, her body could not sustain another breath, without Stephen.

Just as she reached the outer limbs of the tree, Clarice's fragile heart released its physical hold on her. The chemicals released in her body that had once protected her—prevented the magnitude of what had been lost, stabilized and a rush of reality hit her like an invisible barrier—a crumbling dam. It knocked her to her knees, there beneath the heavens. The pain was no longer kept at bay. It had taken its toll—claiming every part of her—consuming all completely.

The grief. The finality. All encompassing.

On her knees, Clarice felt every emotion of loss—raw, vulnerable. Her tears, rushing back in torrents. Grief's release from every cell—each one recognizing its loss, mourning—overshadowed by brokenness. Her body trembled beneath the weight of it all, as if her entire essence was being unraveled thread by thread.

The momentary seconds of relief—the fragile hope she'd felt when she first saw the tree had vanished. Instead, in its place the pure, unrelenting ache of loss settled. She hurt all over. It wasn't a sharp pain as if an enemy was wielding a dagger. Instead, it was the breakdown of her internal organs. It was a sickness that had invaded her body from within, quickly replacing happiness with sorrow, life with death. She could feel it weaving itself, blocking out the light of life.

Clarice felt the force of gravity covering her like a blanket, soft— even grounding at first. But quickly shifting to a thick awareness— suffocating, smothering. It clung to her skin, her lungs, her soul—a weight she could neither shake nor survive.

She cried.

She mourned.

She grieved.

And just when Clarice had reached her limit, at the end of herself— when there was no more room inside her for anything else—grief shifted. It changed shape. It became something colder, quieter. It had manifested itself as *doubt.*

At first, through the shroud of tears and pain, her grief had felt almost sacred—like communion with something eternal—holy even. Death, after all, in some enigmatic way, was a necessity in the divine order, and God, in spite of her flaws, had kept a hedge around her.

She believed!

Even in this final hour, with everything that happened, she believed.

So still, even now, her spirit prayed—groaning through the weight of loss. Her mind—her spirit—her heart hadn't stopped reaching, pleading.

But her flesh…her body…her broken humanity had begun to fall silent.

There on her knees, drained and undone, Clarice felt something else begin to take root. A hollow stillness. A bitter knowing.

Crying out to God no longer felt necessary—because the one thing she needed, the one thing her soul screamed for, would not return. It was impossible. And though she feared God too deeply to be angry with Him, she couldn't deny the emptiness rising in the cracks where faith had once occupied.

And yet—she was angry.

The spirit in her not only acknowledged it—but understood it. It was not rebellion, nor a rejection of God. There had already been given enough grace and mercy for such a time as this. But her flesh—fragile, wounded—flesh with its secrets—in hidden places, was mad.

Deeply mad.

It was a dangerous anger—the kind that didn't scream or lash out, but sat heavy. Nevertheless, it was still, festering in the shadows of silence. It was the kind of rage never given a name and rarely allowed a voice. It had been tucked away beneath duty, beneath faith, beneath the fear of divine punishment. She had never dared to examine it too closely, nor address it. She had never dared to even look at it too long, in fear of just acknowledging it might bring down the wrath of God Himself, or at the least, He would be disappointed in her—irrational belief.

Clarice had always believed that faith meant the absence of such emotions—that if she truly trusted God, there would be no room for this type of doubt, no room for all the confusion, and certainly no room for the ache that now made her chest feel like it was collapsing.

What she didn't know—what she had never fully grasped despite all the scriptures, all the prayers, all the years—was 'where there is fear, faith cannot abide.' They are not enemies, but they cannot coexist on the same ground. Not in the same breath. Not in the same heart. Not in the same moment.

If only she had known that to feel fear was not failure, but a warning—a sign. If she had known that even in the trembling of her existence, it could lead to *trust*.

If she had understood that it was never in the absence of anger, but in the choice to bring it—raw, authentic—before a God big enough to hold it.

But fully in the moment, she just knelt there, torn between the spirit that whispered peace, and the flesh that wanted to burn the world down.

Clarice made every effort to mask the emotional storm brewing within. The world would not see her in her brokenness, not like this—this was between her and God. Her pain, her doubt, were not for public display. She stood up, brushed the dirt from her clothes, straightened her back, and stood proud—just as she had so many times in her past. She tucked all of her emotions away, forced them into submission—locking them behind the walls she had built over the years for her survival.

She had reasoned with herself, and now, everything was under control. This was her version of manifested faith.

Control first. Composure next. Finally resolve.

But somewhere, in the quiet corners of her heart, pride had taken root—fed not by arrogance but forged by the sheer necessity to survive.

Her unchecked—unresolved grief had allowed pride to creep in, subtle and sure, now it was standing at the helm—steering her to self-preservation.

She retreated into the woman she had been before Stephen—the one who didn't need help, who didn't unravel, who didn't fall apart. But that woman was a shell, and she was already cracking inside.

Now, her neat little facade was about to come tumbling down. Pride was showing its mature head. It was revealing its age, a maturity, a quiet dominance. It had been years in the making—being nurtured in the shadows, biding its time for destruction.

But now…pride was entering holy ground.

Clarice allowed herself to question her spiritual beliefs. She just couldn't come to grips with God allowing her to experience such a loss. How could she reconcile a God who had given her Stephen with a God who had allowed him to be taken. *Had it not been God who had placed him in her life? Had she not thanked Him enough for such a gift?*

Her thoughts overtook her, childlike in her protest—pouting as if the world was hers to will as she wished. The tears began to flow again. But this time it was out of anger, as if her entire life she had believed something that could not be true.

She let the anger steadily rise—unchecked. It felt dangerous, even blasphemous, but it was real—raw. The kind of anger she had spent a lifetime suppressing. Her chest heaved, and her fists clenched into the dirt as if to brace herself against the unraveling of her soul.

There was no way forward for her, not without Stephen. He had been her rock, her greatest love, her shield, her best friend. Her defiance was unprecedented. To have had an unrealistic expectation about life had distorted her every belief. As she cried and yelled into the wind. Her voice breaking, her words confused in their landing—prayer or accusations.

And then, in that moment—out of nothingness—came a voice.

"Stop! I have had enough."

The voice was not harsh with anger. It did, however, carry the weight of finality—the end—no discussion—the last word. Clarice froze. Every part of her, stilled—her limbs, her heartbeat—stopped. She was motionless. Even her breath had paused.

The voice continued, solid and undeniable.

"You speak as though you are here for your own glory. This world was never meant to serve at your convenience. There has always been Grace set aside for you. There has always been Mercy shown to you— in spite of your behavior because your heart has been seen. Favor has always been your refuge. But you have forgotten."

The voice did not give her time to respond.

"Let Me show you what this world would be without that which you wrestle against."

In an instant, her eyes were opened—lifted beyond time and space to—truth.

The valley outside the mountain they called home laid spread out before her, covered with a sea of burnt, decaying bones, dead trees, smothering dust protruding from cracked earth—a dry and desolate land. What had once been green meadows, vibrant with vegetation—was now nothing but a blanket of death, stripped bare of life itself.

The vision faded as quickly as it came—less than ten seconds, but it was more than Clarice could bear, hollowing her to her very core.

Yet, the voice continued, moving through her, not in volume but in weight.

"He, the One whom you fear, is the logic that governs the system.

The sacred and the strategic—one and the same, threads of the same divine tapestry.

This is holistic Christianity.

Integrated thinking…woven together into the very fabric of your being.

All of it belong to Him…every part of your life.

Reality unfolding from the inside out.

Beyond time lies the truth—the point of origin for all reality.

You were known before you were visible.

Grace has always known where you were.

And in the fullness of time, truth is revealed!"

She lifted both hands to her face. She didn't need any more evidence than what had been presented before her. She wiped her tears. The case she had built before herself—the accusations, the doubt, the pride—had been incinerated in the presence of the truth.

There was nothing more.

She knew. Completely. To believe otherwise would be to willfully choose a lie.

Humbled and shaken, Clarice gathered herself. With quiet reverence, she was ready to step away from the safety of the tree, ready to return to the compound, to whatever waited on the other side of the wall. Her voice had become irrelevant—not even worth a soft note in the vastness.

But then, the voice came again, gentler now, yet carrying the weight of revelation.

'Grace has always known where you are. In the fullness of time, all will be revealed.'

Clarice felt so ashamed—unworthy. Her behavior was disappointing, not because of the voice's reprimand, but because of herself—the woman she had believed herself to be. She now realized she had always lived a secret lie. Suddenly exposed.

At some point—unaware, she had stretched out on the ground—castrated before the voice echoing around her, but yet, somehow it also rose from within her.

"Stand. Look to the east."

Clarice stood and turned her head, just slightly, obeying as instructed.

There perched atop a distant mountain peak stood two figures—a man and a woman. At first glance, Clarice knew, instinctively, they were of divine origin. She bowed in reverence. They radiated goodness—something eternal—holiness with the One. Their features were unmarked by time. Not flawlessness as defined by the world standards, but completion as defined in an original blueprint of man's design.

They stood side by side, hands gently clasped, their posture both serene and purposeful. Facing west, with their backs turned toward the rising sun in the east, the couple stood in front of something greater, as if in waiting. But Clarice could not see anything beyond them.

"Look to the west."

Her gaze followed the command.

In the vast valley below them, stretching from the base of the mountain outward like a sea of life, stood a multitude. More people than she could count—more than stars scattered above, across a midnight sky. Generations of faces multiplied over and over, all emerging from the couple's origin—expanding across all races and nations. Their backs faced west.

Although they were all facing east, toward the couple, their purposes were clearly different. Some stood still, waiting with a focused anticipation. Others were busy, distracted by the cares of the world around them, more concerned with their environment—were unaware of the moment at hand. And yet, others waited, but their faces betrayed uncertainty, as though they were not sure of what—or for whom—they were waiting.

Clarice felt the magnitude of the scene, the power it held. She knew this was not just a vision, but a glimpse of a truth, one outside of consciousness.

The sky shifted, reflecting the quickening of the day. The sun rose in the east behind the couple. It spread across the sky and began to set behind the vast sea of humanity. Just as the sun touched the horizon—to set in the west, behind the multitude, a greater light began to rise behind the couple. Just then, the couple seemed to glide down the side of the mountain, turning to face the approaching light—something, someone with a brilliance unlike any earthly source—not of sun nor moon, but pure energy, spectrums of light which before now, human eyes could not see.

Clarice gasped.

The people who had been waiting steadfast, attentively, began to be transformed into a flash of light. One by one, slow at first, then all at once. The sea of those waiting—had suddenly turned into millions of fireflies dancing across the night sky. There was a strange sound of ethereal music, reminding her of her dream when she saw Stephen and the boys on the staircase. She heard Stephen's last words.

'I am going to meet the boys. You were right.'

The voice began again, "In the fullness of time, you were allowed to be yanked from your home like a thief in the night. But the blood line of your ancestors was made strong. Though over time the blood was diluted, it did not lose its power—for even a drop is more than sufficient. Outward appearance has never mattered. It has always been about the blood. That which was created in the beginning and that which was sacrificed.

"Your lineage has been set aside for the glory of God Himself. You have suffered in the flesh, but your reward has never been of this world. This world will pass away, and yet you are blessed according to your faith."

Clarice had fallen to her knees. She rose slowly with an understanding. She wiped the tears from her eyes and allowed her steps to guide her back to the compound. She knew—deep within—others would be lost before this crisis was over. She was not quite sure about what had happened or what she had seen, but she knew beyond all doubt—He whom she had always searched for was in control of everything.

3:33

As Clarice walked back towards the compound, her steps had become steady. The air around her that had once been suffocating was now clear. The vision still lingering, gave her faint glimmers of what was to come. She understood the fireflies were the inheritance for the bloodline promised. All were connected—bound across time and nations—just as she was—part of the same tapestry, bound by sacrificial blood.

As she neared the compound's door, she saw Jack sitting on a large stone. He stood up to greet her. Just as he started to say something, she cut him off.

"I know. The boys and Stephen are together."

Caught off guard, Jack simply opened his arms and gave her a hug. Clarice took a step back and asked, "Have Zoe sent out the broadcast?"

"Not yet. She was waiting for you."

"Then let's get the information out as soon as possible." With that, they went inside.

***

Everyone had retreated to their own space. Zuri was sitting under the tree in the courtyard—too broken to talk to anyone. Zoe and the others in her group were in the security room, debating how much time was left before they would miss their window to use the satellite. Paul and Jazzette were in the living room. Paul had lit a fire, and Jazzette was lying in his arms, shattered. Lizzie's heart was consumed with grief. Not understanding how Clarice was going to get through it. She more than anyone knew how much he meant to her. So, she did what she thought Clarice would do, she started to prepare dinner for everyone.

As Clarice and Jack descended the warehouse stairs, Clarice glanced at the last spot she would ever get to share with Stephen. The place where their last words had been spoken—the last place she had held his torn, blood-soaked body in her arms. His body now gone. The stains scrubbed away, leaving no trace of the man that once lived—died. Removed, rewinding every one of his footprints as time started its process of memory—slowly fading.

Jack noticed her lingering gaze to the area, and quietly whispered, "We moved his body, and the boys…we moved them to the medical facility."

"Ah." She murmured. "Good idea. You'll need to have a service." Jack noticed she did not include herself in the comment, but he dared not question her.

By the time they had made it to outside, and reached the main house, Zuri spotted them and started back towards the main house as well.

"I am going upstairs to take a shower." Clarice said, her voice steady, measured—trying to reassure everyone she was okay. Directing her comment to Lizzie, with a balanced smile. "I'll be back to help with dinner."

As she walked away, with no one in mind. "Ask Zoe to release the announcement—before it's too late for the satellite."

As she entered their bedroom, she felt the emptiness. The air was without all of its elements. A substance missing. She closed the door behind her, then asked aloud, "Time?"

The ibot responded with a resounding, 3:33.

Clarice stood for a moment and then headed towards the bathroom.

'The Father, the Son, and the Holy Spirit. In the fullness of time, all three will be revealed as the One.'

She heard Stephen's voice—Clear. Distinctive. Close.

Unaware of its origin—and yet she didn't question it, she just accepted it. She then showered, threw on one of Stephen shirts—taking care with each button fastened. Smiles beaming through the heartbreak. She knew he was at peace. He was with the boys, and they were in heaven, together.

She returned to the kitchen.

By then Lizzie had finished preparing dinner. It was simple but it made a big impression on Clarice. She was another layer of assurance. She knew they would be taken care of.

Everyone was already sitting around the table—including the construction crew who had agreed to stay. Paul had reached out to Sarah to let her know what had happened, and she'd made it to the compound.

When Clarice walked into the room, clothed in Stephen's oversized shirt, her eyes glanced around the table, with a grateful heart. Her eyes stopped when they met Sarah's. Her friend, face already covered in smudged eye makeup, and tear stain sleeves from where she had tried to wipe them away before Clarice could notice them.

Clarice began to speak. Her voice temperate, arms folded, body wrapped.

"Before we get started, I would like to say a couple of things. Paul, Jazzette…I am so sorry for the loss of the twins. I know in my heart—there is no doubt Stephen did everything he could to save them. I want you to know that the three of them are together. You can be assured of that! There is no greater loss than that of a child.

"Logan…" She paused, making eye contact with him. "Stephen loved you as if you were his own grandson. He often talked about how proud he was of you. You so reminded him of himself. He trusted you to do the right thing in life, just as his grandfather trusted him."

Clarice made eye contact with each member sitting around the oversized table…perfectly seated for the number of people that had come together.

"Stephen loved you all…You can be assured of that, too! When we were married, we dreamed of this place not just as our sanctuary—but also as a place where family and friends could come together. Always surrounded by love, peace, and the safety of belonging to something greater than oneself. That vision has not changed. See to it, that it never does."

She bowed her head. "Let us pray."

Her voice did not waver in tone or strength. It carried the weight of the world, but it was not by her own strength. Wearing Stephen's shirt helped her to be anchored with just enough strength. It was his arms wrapped around her. She felt him, smelled him.

"Lord, we come before you on the brink of a cosmic collision, tangled in the destructive nature of man. We do not know if this is the end—one bathe in a prophecy yet to be fulfilled. But what we do know is, regardless—You are in control of all that is and all that will be!

"We—I, ask You now, that these around this table be protected. Help each of them find strength in one another to become whatever role they have been called to play. They have been divinely positioned, given supernatural skills, and provided with divine weapons. May the choices they make each day carry them—sustain them through the trials of tomorrow, for I know they will surely come.

"The impending obscurity of the disaster coming, is not just the obstacle that's lurking in the sky, but the blindness of You, that has settled in our human hearts.

"This place is now their refuge—built on sacred ground. You are the guiding star in the storm that is upon them. Protect them. Even if they don't believe in You, I do. So let my words—my spirit stand in the gap until, in the fullness of time, they come into their power through You.

"Tomorrow will be different, this we can be assured. But You will forever be the same.

"Bless this food. It was prepared out of love, that I am assured. Amen!"

Clarice quietly filled her plate with food she knew she would not eat. She offered faint smiles to those around the table. She spent a moment with Sarah, gave her a heartfelt hug, thanked her for everything, and then slipped away, retreating to their room. She sat the plate on the table next to the bed, said a quiet prayer, and took the small, framed picture of their wedding day in her arms. She laid on Stephen's side of the bed—looking up through the glass ceiling as the evening gave way to the nighttime heavens.

It was there that Clarice surrendered her life—in the fullness of time, a life complete—a life fulfilled.

It Begins

"Quick, the world is reacting to the announcement." Zoe said as she clicked the power button on the main screen. "The governments are trying to deny it, but it is too late. The group out of Egypt tapped into the East Satellite and is live streaming parts of the asteroid as it enters into Earth's atmosphere."

Nick chimed in, "No one can now predict where it will hit—not even the amount of damage it will cause."

"It's not quite in the West Satellite range for the astronomers in Victoria to calculate. There is too much debris from the initial contact, can't get a clean reading to make a prediction." Tim said.

"But they don't believe there will be a direct hit." Zoe said looking at Jazzette and Lizzie's expression. Trying to remove some of the fear they were obviously experiencing. "We were able to connect with other rogue technicians, monitoring the laser to recalculated what the governments had programed. The best they could do was provide a bump to the larger piece of the asteroid at the last minute and hope it was enough to veer it off course, even if only slightly."

Gerard noticed the horrific look on everyone's face, jumped in to support Zoe. "Looks like it did." Turning to the others, "We decided not to say anything just in case it didn't work. We didn't want to cause any more stress after everything that had happened. So, we made the decision."

Nick had not been a part of the discussion, but Tim had filled him in. "I agree with what they did. They were in an impossible position. The morning before we lost Stephen, they found out the Space Station were developing weapons—mostly nuclear. When Germany fired on the asteroid, and it hit the station, a leak of the nuclear material made a ring around the station. The bump sent pieces of the asteroid through that ring, coating them in highly radioactive material. When the pieces of the asteroid breaks through our atmosphere, they will be carrying high levels of radiation."

Paul brokenly said, "This just keeps getting better, the pebbles that are burning when they hit the ground, will emit hazard amounts of radiation."

"Paul that's true, but theoretically, most of the pebbles will burn out before they hit the ground." Gerard sounding hopeful, said before Nick could respond.

"Got it." Paul had no fight left.

By now, while all the others were glued to the live broadcast, Paul, Zuri, and Nathaniel slipped out the side door. Engaged in their own silent conversations, they managed to find themselves standing in front of the main house.

Finally, Zuri whispered, "The past twenty-eight hours have been more than horrific," as she laid her head on her father's chest. "I'm so sad. I'm not sure how we will be able to survive without Clarice and Stephen...G-Mom and Granddad."

Zuri looked up at Paul and saw the pain in his face. "Dad...oh, Dad, the twins!" Tears, flowing trails of shimmering water, reflecting in the moon's glow against her skin. "I am so sorry. As much as I'll miss my brothers, know I can only imagine a fraction of the pain you and Jazzette must be feeling, even in the midst of..." Looking around to every corner of their environment, that which had happen and could happen, she continued, "I need you to know...I will gladly take some of your pain, while you take care of everyone else."

Paul leaned and kissed her head, "I know."

Nathaniel was standing in the background, quietly feeling the pain of helplessness. He stepped up next to Zuri, and wrapped his arms around her, connecting his hand to Paul's back. It was a warm embrace of a heart filled with sorrow for his friend, his captain, his family.

"Look." Nick said in an urgent but controlled manner. They had not heard him approaching them. He too had quietly slipped away from the others inside. They were still discussing the technicality of sadness, sucking the very light out of the room, allowing nothing but darkness to creep in. He couldn't hear the despair any longer.

In the distance they could see, it had begun—a world unraveling. Speckles of glowing light were dancing across the sky, sliding between light and darkness, gaining in size and speed. Then, just as they broke through the nighttime clouds, rocks of blazing tendrils burst forth like rockets searching for their targets. Some of the fragmented projectiles fizzled out, breaking up into dense pockets of smokey gas layering the air.

While other fragments grew into blazing circles, with trailing lights of fire. The closer they got, the more they could see the flamed edges of the rocks as they hurled to the ground.

The air shifted, the burning rocks made a layer of heat overhead as they were extinguished. The fog started to choke out all outside noise. They moved to the top of the steps, under the cover of the reinforced porch, looking at the beginning of what felt like the end of all things.

"We better get inside, the radiation will start to emit into the air." Paul said as they rushed inside, closing the world out behind them.

***

The night was long.

Everyone sat in silence, scattered around the living room. They didn't even have the background noise of the fireplace. Everything had been sealed off—windows and doors.

They just waited.

Paul was leaning against the wall separated from the others. His focus on the sky on fire outside his window. It reminded him of that first day standing at the window in his office, staring at the vision of today—three years ago. He imagined what the city must look like now, and could only hope most found safety.

As he looked out the window, each time one of the blazing rocks seemed to be headed directly towards the compound, he'd flinch, startled...afraid.

His mind drifted from the window at the State Department, to the burning of the sky in the middle of Nebraska, surrounded by a mountain built on holy ground. Sacred. He had gone through the full cycle—from discovery of possibility to reality.

Paul started looking around, watching each member of the group, remembering Clarice's prayer. The words had seemed strange at the time, and no one else had made note. She was in distress, grieving after all. He had been thinking about it in more detail ever since they found her lying in bed. Dead.

How could she have known? What did she mean by divine weapons? As soon as the thought entered, he looked at everyone—in detail, focusing on *weapons...skills.*

His sword was leaning up against the fireplace. Zuri and Zoe's bows were hanging on the opposite wall. Nick had the staff given to him lying across his lap, rolling it back and forth. Everyone had mentioned the uniqueness of the staff, describing it as being carved out of wood from an ancient time.

He remembered the story of how Nathaniel had found his sword—ancient, with impeccable craftsmanship, hanging in the only abandoned building left standing in the aftermath of Seattle's harbor. Zoe's team meeting a doctor who just so happens to have a bow and a sword that he left in their van.

"This cannot be a coincidence." Paul said.

"What can't be a coincidence?" Jazzette asked Paul, overhearing him.

Paul was unaware of himself saying it out loud. "Your mother made references to 'divine weapons.' I look around and we each have or have come into some type of weapon or skill."

Everyone started to look around and take note of the other's gift—weapon—skill. Sarah spoke up, jokingly, "Well I guess that leaves me out!"

But as quickly as she said it as a joke, Logan chimed in. "Who do you supposed is going to keep us environmentally safe. Did you not forget, we don't know what the radiation will do to the ground or water supply. We will need you to keep us alive."

"Who's going to make the wine? That's what G-mom always said." Lizzie said, jokingly.

A few minutes later, Logan spoke with an insight that none of the others had been privy too.

"A year ago, we uncovered something unusual in one of the sections of the warehouse. At first, it looked like ordinary rock, part of the mountain. But one day, the light hit it at just the right angle and Stephen noticed it was not just rock, but more. He took a sample to the university for identification. It turned out that it was silver and gold, both living together. Large chunks of it in large quantities. It was such a find that Stephen wanted to keep it a secret. The only people who knew about it were Jack, Clarice, and me.

"Then, about three months ago, I came into the warehouse and Stephen had set up a forging station out back. He had cut cedar stacked up against the wall. He had made several dozen arrows. Some were coated in silver, while others were coated in gold. I asked him about it, and he simply said I would know when the time was right and asked me not to mention it."

"Are you saying, Clarice and Stephen had already discussed the weapons. How would they know they were divine weapons?"

"Do you think they will be used to kill demons?" Lizzie innocently asked.

Everyone looked at her thinking how could she say something so ridiculous. Jazzette spoke up. "Let's not get ahead of ourselves. We don't know what tomorrow will look like."

"Tomorrow will take care of itself. Let's just make it through the night." Jack interrupted the direction the conversation was going. He knew that Clare's prayer had been about more than dinner. She had changed when she came from the tree. Had she seen tomorrow? One thing was for certain, she had known she would not be a part of it. That the team would have to fight a battle with an enemy they did not yet recognize.

Paul agreed with Jack.

"Tim, tomorrow morning, when things have subsided, let's see if we can't fly the drone around to get a look at the damage." Paul said, taking command of all that was left of them. He knew, with Stephen and Clarice gone, he had to step up in all things.

"Will do." Tim said, not acknowledging Zoe.

Just before dawn, the rain returned, washing the air, burying the evidence of the cosmic collision the night before.

But what had been left in its place?

Shortly after sunrise, the rain stopped as quickly as it had started. Lizzie had started breakfast, but no one could eat. Instead, they huddle around the monitor to watch the first take on the outside world. Paul and Tim had set up the drone.

"Tim, let's see if all those gaming skills can be translated with flying the drone." Paul told him with an attaboy slap on the back.

Tim gave a half chuckle, but you could tell it was laced with a certain level of arrogance. "I got this!" He said as he powered on the controller and the drone. He paused with a level of confidence rarely seen by him. He was in his element.

"Ready." Tim pushed the takeoff button and watched the drone as it lifted off the plane. As it hovered a few feet off the ground, all eyes were on the display monitor. As he used the throttle to control the altitude, he flew the drone beyond the mountain peaks around the compound.

Watching the first images, Paul said Jazzette, "I gave your mom a hard time when she planned the heist to get the plane, but it was brilliant."

It gave Jazzette a comfort. "She would be thrilled to hear you say that. She was probably the only one who would have predicted such a need." She said as she smiled with the memory of her mom. It had been the first smile since she was gone.

The speed of the rocks had made indentations in the wet ground. The ground itself had been forced to receive the rocks from the invasive attack of the asteroid. Invaders into the soil quickly caused the ground to implode upon itself, caters drowning out the fire, leaving seeps of smoke as it escaped through the quickly dried mud. Beneath the harden surface, atmospheric rocks embedded into the ground. The early morning rain caused the mud to bury the rocks even deeper, neutralizing any radiation that may have escaped.

"The compound seems to be in tack. Let's move farther out."

Tim guided the drone to the immediate area around the compound. There were burnt patches of vegetation scattered in all directions. Tim drove the drone around the entire perimeter. The immediate area around the compound was virtually untouched.

Tim continued the surveillance, moving a mile or two out. They stood around the monitor with mouths open and in shock as the devastation took shape. There were burnt bodies in burnt fields, animals running around erratically. He increased the distance.

The world was on fire.

The End.

Epilogue

Zuri was desperate. As she ran, the forest around her blurred. She tried to dodge the limbs, and overgrown bushes, as her feet skimmed over the ground. She kept looking back, trying to see what this thing was that was chasing her. It wasn't like the others she had faced in the spirit realm. She had crossed though the portals before, but this was the first time she had seen an entity like this. It was different from the others. This one seemed to have some type of control over the others. There was an aura that surrounded it—with an appeal, seductive. But there was a warning written within—screaming, "Run, flee."

In this realm, Earth was as it was in the beginning. There were no buildings or technological advancements. It was there that the divine weapons that Clarice spoke of came into play.

She had thought that crossing into the spirit world this time would be quick—get in, get out. She hadn't considered the repercussions. All she had wanted to do was save her friend from a fate worse than death. She had forgotten one of the main lesson they had learned—just because you know, it doesn't mean your choices are simple.

Now she was fighting for her life. She knew if she lost her life here, in this realm, this way, she would be lost for good. No one would be able to find her body. The more she ran, the more she wished she had made another choice. It was reckless of her.

Meanwhile, Lizzie was busy in the kitchen preparing dinner. It had been almost a year since Clarice and Stephen had been laid to rest. Paul and Jazzette had moved back to the East coast. The country—world was in disarray. The bulk of the asteroid may have missed Earth's atmosphere, but the radiation it had left behind had played havoc on the environment. Millions of lives had been lost globally. No one country came out ahead of another. There was destruction on almost all continents. The only regions that were not hit with the projectiles were the Middle East and Africa; with Europe, Canada, and Northern America sustaining the bulk of the damage.

Nick and Tim had been working on the water filtration system in the warehouse when a strange light glowed from the portal. Nick also felt the strange sensation coming from his staff.

"What's happening?" Tim said once he saw the expression on Nick's face.

"I'm not sure. Something is wrong, I can feel it." Nick said as he grabbed his staff and hurried out of the warehouse, heading towards the main house.

"Nick?" Tim called out with a raised voice, "Where are you going?" Nick ignoring as the doors shut behind him.

Entering the kitchen, and with a panicky voice, Nick yelled Lizzie's name, asking, "Where is everyone?"

"Not quite sure." She started naming everyone before Nick could interrupt, she said, "Oh yeah, Zuri said something about a quick trip through the portal."

"How long ago?"

"Maybe half an hour ago."

Nick turned and ran back to the warehouse. His heart was in distress, pounding in his chest, visible under his shirt. *I can't lose her.* A glow, beaming from the staff warmed his hand as he hurried to the portal's entrance. Without hesitation, he passed through the stone wall.

It was Jack who had discovered the hidden door—portal. It was a common story amongst his people about a place, deep in the mountain where you could enter the spirit world. These portals were hidden gateways to the spirit realm scattered all over the world, hidden behind some of the most amazing waterfalls. Where supernatural beings—good and evil, could enter. Each with their own set of doors. One could not cross over the other's threshold.

Once Nick had made it through the portal, he stepped from behind the waterfall. Looking around, searching for Zuri. His staff in full glow in his hand. He knew he was close to her, he just had to find her.

It had only been a few minutes when he saw Zuri defending a large rock. She was wielding her sword, fighting images of various forms, covered in a shadow until most of its form was dim. But you could tell beneath the layer of darkness was a light of enormous brilliance.

Each time the sword would come in contact with the entities, a spark of light would break through. When the blow was deep enough, fatal, the light would burst through the darkness, separating light from darkness. The light would rise, and the darkness would return to the ground, and the entity would vanish.

"Zuri!" He shouted.

Just as Nick reached the edge of the rock, he thrust himself between her and swarm in front of her. He took position, a practiced stand welding the power of the staff. He slammed it onto the ground, hard.

An invisible force erupted outward, sending a shockwave, knocking back all the shadowy entities that were there. The ground reacted sending wind and dust as a barrier. But then that's when he saw another.

Larger. Darker.

It was about to take a deliberate step towards them when a radiant figure appeared behind Zuri.

Raphael.

Acknowledgment

I am deeply grateful for all who sat quietly with me as I worked through the process of writing this book. What began as a simple idea quickly grew into a passion, and with the help of a few gifted and generous professionals, I discovered myself within the written words on each page.

To my family and friends, thank you for your patience and encouragement while I bounced off my imaginative ideas your way after long hours of writing. To those who offered their wisdom, insight, and technical expertise, your guidance made the journey not only possible but meaningful.

Most of all, I give thanks to God, whose Grace, Mercy, and Favor carried me from the first spark of inspiration to the last word written.

Author's Note

A Cosmic Collision with Faith was born from my fascination with the space between faith and science, the seen and the unseen. It explores how humanity responds when the impossible collides with the inevitable—when cosmic forces and spiritual truths meet. While it tells a story of asteroids, and survival, it is also about legacy, family, and the unseen hand of God guiding ordinary people through extraordinary circumstances. My hope is that as you read, you'll recognize reflections of your own journey—the quiet struggles, the small victories, and the moments of grace—remembering always that in every collision—cosmic or personal, there lies the possibility of faith, renewal, and purpose.

Thank you...